The Rules of Chivalry

Tim Jerrome

Published in Great Britain by
L.R. Price Publications Ltd, 2021
27 Old Gloucester Street,
London, WC1N 3AX
www.lrpricepublications.com

Original Edition:
ISBN: - 9781838061074

Amazon Edition:
ISBN: - 9798713493196

For Mum and Dad

The Rules of Chivalry

Tim Jerrome

Prologue

I have never really bought into the concept of chivalry.

Of course, I do not mean that in a literal sense. The French word for horse is *cheval*, and so really, that's all that chivalry is: a man with a horse. And I have always loved horses.

But ask a churchman, ask a poet, and he will provide a different definition. He will speak of honour, of loyalty, of fairness and of courage, and it seems this is how chivalry will be remembered. He will not speak of the realities of battle, of the exhaustion, the blood, and above all, the terror. He will not mention deception in war, of the subtle manoeuvre that takes the foe unawares, of the power of fear. Yet without these, any mention of war is a fabrication. All that matters, in war, in life, is winning. If you win battles, take land, gather power, ensure loyalty, then you will have "chivalrous" values attributed to your name, regardless of your true personality.

This is why I have decided to write this tale of my life – I wish to be remembered as I am, not as some foolish "chivalric" ideal. When my descendants read this, they will know the truth of my exploits, and my legacy of victory at any cost. That is the code I have lived my life by, not an idealised concept of honour and virtue.

Across all the lands I have travelled, across all the cultures and religions I have encountered, I have learnt that those who hold honour above all else are the first casualties in any conflict, be it political or military. Ironically, then, those who are "unchivalrous" are far more likely to survive and have histories written of them, which will depict them to be the honourable people that they could not afford to be. Of course, those who fail as rulers or soldiers are instantly condemned as cowardly, fearful and dastardly.

I have forged my own chivalry. I have written my own rules of war.

I served two kings, one who loved me and gave me purpose, and another who despised me and sought to bring me down. Ultimately, the men of chronicles will treat them as opposites, and certainly I am tempted to do so, but in many ways, they were not so different. Both resorted to devious means to keep power. One succeeded, one failed. That is their difference. Thus, chivalry is a lie. For I am Alistair Fitzwalter, soldier of thirty years, brother of a traitor, servant of Richard and John, and this is my tale.

Chapter 1

I shall never forget the sound of my sister's laughter on that fateful day, early in the warm spring of the year 1188. Perhaps it is all I have to cling on to, given that it was the day my privileged life, one almost absent of responsibility, was abruptly ripped away by the cowardice of one close to me.

How happy she was, how infectious her joy as she excitedly explained every nuance of her betrothed, a noble named Gilbert Peche who held the title of Baron of Bourn. The announcement of their engagement had brought mixed emotions at the time; Alice was one of the few people I could truly name as friend and unburden myself to. Yet her imminent departure to the district of Bourn in Cambridgeshire was at least a five-hour ride away, and so our time spent together in the future would be limited. Of course, as the heir to the barony of Little Dunmow, I could not spend time on unimportant travelling. According to my father, his heir was not permitted to be emotional over something as trivial as the departure of a sibling, a mere woman at that.

He never did like me much.

Fortunately for him, he had sired a second son, Robert, who boasted every trait deemed valuable in his eyes. Robert was boisterous whilst I chose my words carefully, he was stocky where I was skinny, he loved mock combat where I excelled at horse-riding. At sixteen he was already one of the strongest men in the settlement of Little Dunmow, whereas I, at eighteen, struggled to swing my father's sword properly. My father always blamed my mother for her refusal to force me into strenuous combat exercises – she seemed to believe in the idea that her children could explore whichever pastimes they enjoyed, and not just be moulded in their parents' image. Shocking indeed.

As per normal, my brother had curtly refused my offer to ride with myself and Alice; he seemed intent on spending his free time in fist-fights with the other boys his age in the village, knocking what few wits they possessed out of each other's thick skulls. And so we rode through the sun-streaked forest that bordered the village, the light filtering through the vibrant leaves to reflect my sister's glorious mood.

"The age difference doesn't mean anything to me," she declared. "I have friends who have married men thirty, even forty years their senior. With only a twenty-year age gap, I feel I've been quite fortunate!"

"Twenty-three years," I corrected.

"Oh Alistair, you can be so wretchedly pedantic sometimes," she said. "He's perfect for me. You'll love him too when you meet him. His singing voice is simply divine, and I have never seen a finer moustache upon a man!"

"I'm sure I'll find his moustache absolutely captivating," I replied with a smile. She laughed and spurred her horse forwards, forcing me to give chase, the wind ruffling the mane of my chestnut gelding, Raymond. We galloped a winding path through the towering trees, a route more familiar to me than any other, until we drew up at the edge of Little Dunmow, whooping with exhilaration at the ride.

"I believe Baron Gilbert will be getting rather more than he bargained for," I grinned. "You're probably handier with a pair of reins than he is!"

"I should rather hope not – if I embarrass him too much, he might replace my reins with a set of needles and force me to sew!" she replied in mock horror as we walked our horses into the meandering streets.

"He'll regret that – I've seen how straight your stitches are," I said. "Anyway," my smile faded, "it's time for my tuition with Father Geoffrey. You'd think that after eighteen years of my life he'd have run out of Bible text to drawl at me. I honestly think that he makes up new passages as he goes along. Last week he harangued me about the evil of wives and how their complaining is a curse sent by the devil!"

"How absurd! If I were his wife, I would have nothing to complain about," Alice responded in an acerbic tone. Her sarcasm was easy to understand. Father Geoffrey was a most unpleasant creature, a balding man in his forties, who enforced the word of God with the sharp edge of a vine stick. Both myself and Robert had suffered blows from him during our childhood, and a hatred of the priest was one of the few things we had in common. The priest was also infamous for his tendency to take bribes in return for absolution of sins, exacting payment either in silver, or through sexual favours from young women who could not afford to pay. I often feel that had our priest been of a higher calibre, then Robert might have been encouraged to become a man of God, as was customary for second sons. Instead, he turned his eye to other ambitions.

Just another reason to hate Father Geoffrey, I suppose.

As I bade my farewells to Alice and picked my way through the bustling marketplace of Little Dunmow, the snatches of news concerning the outside world reached my ears. Whilst the vast majority of the townsfolk never travelled more than three or four miles from the village itself, foreign merchants occasionally passed through, and no news had caused a greater stir than that of the fall of Jerusalem to heathens in the east. Indeed, a papal emissary, despatched by the Archbishop of Tyre, had arrived in the midst of winter to harangue my father about the new Crusade. Although he was forced into acquiescence by the fact that our King Henry had taken the cross, it was evident that he had no intention of riding to the Holy Land, because of his total lack of preparation. Consequently, I had anticipated that I would have no part in this wild campaign to the mysterious eastern realms. For the moment, my only concern was avoiding the lash of my viperous priest.

Robert was waiting at the entrance of the church, yawning languidly. "Enjoy our dainty little ride, did we?" he said as I approached.

"Just trying to spend some time with Alice before she leaves," I replied lightly, refusing to rise to his provocation. "And besides, if you ever intend to receive your knighthood, you really must give your horsemanship some attention. You boast of the tournaments that you'll win – obviously, you intend to joust on foot. That ought to make an entertaining spectacle."

Robert scowled. "At least I'd stand some chance in a melee. You'd be more at home with the ladies viewing the tilts. If we fought, right here and now, I'd have you hoisting up your skirt and running to mother within seconds."

"As much as I would love to take up that challenge," I said, rolling my eyes, "our beloved Father Geoffrey is waiting. Shall we?" With that, I made my way into the church, with Robert reluctantly following. Not for the first time, I observed the barren nature of the interior of Little Dunmow's house of God. The walls were plain and unadorned, with little evidence of the elaborate golden decorations evident in the few other churches I had witnessed at that age. The ancient benches viciously delivered needle-like splinters to anyone unfortunate enough to sit through one of Father Geoffrey's services, and the altar and font were crumbling and in desperate need of repair. I quietly suspected that the money saved on maintaining the church funded Father Geoffrey's rich lifestyle, yet it was unfathomable to voice such thoughts about a man of God. Instead, we meekly approached the priest, hoping that he was not in one of his fearsome black moods.

As usual, however, our hopes were swiftly dashed. "You're both late, you wretched, stupid boys," he snarled, showering both myself and Robert with spittle.

"I am no boy," Robert declared sullenly.

"To a man anointed by God, all other men are boys," Father Geoffrey snapped, fingering his vine stick. "One more word of impudence out of you and you shall feel the wrath of the Lord."

Having grown accustomed to such exchanges, I ignored them both and began to gather some vellum sheets from Father Geoffrey's table, but froze as the priest swivelled towards me. "Not yet, boy. First I must hear your sordid brother's confession." I could hear the gleeful menace in his voice, and despite our differences, I felt a pang of concern for my brother.

"Confession?" Robert asked, clearly bemused. "What exactly must I confess?"

"The most abhorrent of sins," the priest hissed, turning and stalking away. "I have... evidence!" he roared, swivelling back and glowering at Robert, his pugnacious face inches from my brother's. "Evidence that you used the name of your father to ensure the silence of a girl; a girl who you violated in order to satiate your satanic lusts. You are a disgrace to God's church!"

Usually, I was not inclined to interrupt Father Geoffrey's tirades, but I was too stunned at what I'd heard to not intervene. "Is this true, Robert?" I asked him, gaping. "Did you... did you rape a girl?"

"So what if I did?" Robert answered, shrugging almost nonchalantly. "I felt it was about time to prove I was a true man, unlike you. And it's not as if she complained about it afterward. She should feel privileged to receive the seed of one of such noble blood. You always have been too gentle with women, Alistair. Another reason why I should inherit Father's lands – I doubt you'll ever beget an heir to continue our line. Perhaps you should wear skirts yourself."

Shocked as I was by the revelation of my brother's actions, I was unsurprised by its cause. Robert was ever envious of my position as firstborn, and although I did not flaunt it, he imagined slights where none had been made. That is the problem with most of the nobles in this land – they guard their prickly pride so zealously that oftentimes they launch pre-emptive strikes against those they feel would sully their prestige, when no insult was ever intended initially. Such is the problem of failing to properly limit the power of such ambitious people.

I made to respond to Robert's scathing words, but Father Geoffrey spoke first, his face turning a crimson that was mottled by rage. "You have some nerve to even step into this holy place!" he thundered, his strident voice echoing throughout the church. Christ surveyed the scene with consternation from within his majestic window of stained glass, as if the noise was disturbing him. "And do not speak to me of a man's lusts," Father Geoffrey continued, "for I have nobly refrained from such base desires in the name of the Lord for many, many years. As such I banish you from my church – unless you grovel and beg forgiveness from God, in which case a beating will suffice as punishment."

Robert rounded on him. "Only if you grovel first," he sneered. "We all know that you've taken more girls to your bed than you have hairs on your head. This isn't a church, it's a third-rate brothel. When I come into power in this village, your head will be the first to roll!"

I didn't even notice the implications behind my brother's words, so caught up was I in the confrontation. "Can we all just try to..." I attempted to intervene.

It was no use. "Devil-spawn!" Father Geoffrey screeched. "I shall flay your blasphemous skin off your bones!" He moved forward to strike Robert with his cane.

Whether my brother acted instinctively or deliberately, I shall never know. Swinging with all the strength of his powerful shoulder muscles, his fist connected solidly with Father Geoffrey's scrawny head. The priest's face barely registered surprise as he was flung backwards, his head colliding with the marble altar with a sickening crunch, and he slid to the ground, limp as a sack of oats. "What have you *done?*" I said to Robert, aghast. Even the most dim-witted of peasants knew that it was a truly unforgiveable sin to strike a priest. Robert, his face acquiring a deathly pale pallor, did not respond – he seemed enraptured by the priest's prone form. When I turned to examine the extent of Father Geoffrey's injuries, the reason for his panic became apparent.

Chapter 2

Father Geoffrey was dead.

To me, at least, that was obvious. Living a sheltered life as a baron's son did not engender many situations in which I had experienced death, but I found the ghastly bend in the priest's neck to be fairly conclusive evidence. My revulsion was replaced by an icy wave of apprehension as I realised just what my brother had done. Damnation and exile would be his – in this life. What he would face in the afterlife would be much, much worse.

Robert seemed to recover from his paralysis before I did. Tearing his eyes away from the soulless gaze of Father Geoffrey, he turned to me, eyes as wide as a cow in an abattoir, and stuttered, "I'll go and get help. You stay with him. He can't be dead!"

"Robert, no! It's no good!" I shouted after him as he fled, in an attempt to talk some reason into his panicked mind. But there was no point; the church door was closing after him even as I finished speaking. Growling in frustration, I turned back to the corpse sprawled upon the altar, determined not to avert my eyes. Father would no doubt be at the head of the group that came to investigate, and the firstborn son of a baron did not flinch from death. Or so I was told.

The priest's gaze was somehow not as intimidating in death as it had been in life. His permanent snarl had softened into a slack-jawed expression of peaceful serenity, which made me wonder whether he was greeting St Paul at that very moment. Could a man reach heaven simply for the title he had, or the robes he wore, regardless of whether his deeds in life were good or evil? It occurred to me that the same applied to Robert; would he be condemned to hell for this ungodly act, even if the rest of his life were filled with holiness and repentance? It puzzled me greatly. There is no doubt that I myself had wished for Father Geoffrey's demise several times in my life, but the fear of damnation had always stopped me from acting rashly. But I was only a naïve boy then – if an abomination like Father Geoffrey ever accosts me now, I may well kill him myself.

My gaze flickered to Christ, wondering if his expression had changed to one of horror and disgust at witnessing the murder of a holy man. Yet it had not. He simply did not seem to care. I wished I had his apathy.

The church door banged open and my father, the Baron of Little Dunmow, strode in, accompanied by his physician and several members of his council – evidently, they had been in session before being disturbed. Robert trailed behind them, sweat beading on his forehead. I wondered whether he had told Father the true story of what had occurred here. I would soon find out.

Father regarded me with an icy stare, his brow furrowed in a frown. It struck me as peculiar that all his attention seemed focused on me, rather than the corpse of his priest of twenty years. I had always thought of him as a cold man, with a distant and unforgiving attitude to all his children. Accustomed to his frosty demeanour, I had long ago learnt not to look to him for affection or warmth. Yet now his gaze was not merely indifferent, but sinister, and I felt apprehension boiling up inside me. In spite of my instinct to shrink away, I resolutely returned his gaze, determined to show no weakness or squeamishness. Despite the way he had treated me for eighteen years, I desperately wanted to impress him.

If I'd known what his next words were to be, I probably would have spat in his face.

"Alistair Fitzwalter," he growled, his stare burrowing into my eyes, "you are hereby banished from the Barony of Little Dunmow, as well as any holdings that come under the control of myself or my heir. For the murder of Father Geoffrey, an act of heinous sacrilege, you now forfeit the name Fitzwalter and the protection of my holdfast."

I could physically feel the blood draining from my face as my father spoke these two sentences which had obliterated my life in an instant. This was the most shameful sanction that could be imposed upon a baron's son. What made it truly appalling was that the crime was not mine. "But... Robert..." I stammered.

"Robert," my father seethed, his cold mask slipping into a welter of fury, "just had to witness an unprovoked murder of a man of God! In his own church! I should have you strung up like a common criminal and throw your corpse into the river so that you do not befoul us with your presence any longer. But for your mother's sake, I have agreed to an exile. If I ever see your wretched face again, and if you have not left my land within the hour, I will have you killed." His councillors stood uneasily behind him. Some, if not most, must have known of the injustice being done, but none spoke. At the time I thought them spineless. Now I see how sensible they were being.

Despite the charges that had just been levelled at me, and despite my father's certainty of my guilt, I should have said something. I should have met anger with anger, or else with reason. Even if I could not have changed my father's mind, I should have left them with defiant words and a measure of pride, so that they would know I was not broken. Instead, like a craven rabbit fleeing his prey, I brushed past my father and fled, a single tear stinging at my eye.

Hindsight is both a cruel and wonderful thing, and now, of course, I realise that I should have anticipated Robert's usurpation of what was rightfully mine. Throughout his childhood, he was constantly bringing my father tales of great lords and kings who were not first-borns, his favourite being Godfrey of Bouillon, who rose from being a French count's second son to become ruler of Jerusalem a hundred years ago. My father should have steered Robert away from these childish dreams, but being a second-born himself, he gently encouraged them by teaching my brother a baron's duties. Robert was even known to be present in a council meeting from time to time and became unbearably smug whenever this happened. My mother refrained from discussing the issue, and Alice drily remarked from time to time that if the firstborn was to be envied by Robert, then it should have been her who was targeted, not me.

I should have seen it coming.

As I shouldered my way through the curious crowd gathered outside the church, these thoughts were not on my mind. In fact, I would not say that I had any thoughts at all – rather, in the light of the destruction of my entire future, my mind latched onto the animal instinct to escape, and clung to it like a drowning man. My father had given me an hour. I could have gone to my mother and begged her to change Father's mind, or at least to say my farewells. I dare say that the man I am now would have gathered what supporters I had and taken my sword against those who opposed my birth right. Yet instead, I ran for the stables and frantically saddled Raymond, oblivious to the baffled stableboys who had only just tethered the horse from my morning ride. Hurriedly placing my feet into the stirrups, I touched my knees to Raymond's flanks, and we hurtled through Little Dunmow's placid streets, leaving the village, which had been my home, through the southern exit.

It was only when I was half a mile down the road to Waltham and London in the south that I realised that I had no plan. In truth, at the age of eighteen I was a fully grown man, yet I certainly did not feel like one. When I look back on myself, I see nothing but a mewling child. Perhaps I cannot be too critical of my father, for he surely saw me in exactly the same light. I had no weapons, and no skill at arms with which to use them. What friends I'd had were now my enemies, and my name – once my greatest asset – was now a deadly burden. As such, I had no refuge to go to which was safe from the wrath of my father and brother.

Having slowed Raymond to a walk, considering my options, I suddenly became aware of the sound of horse hooves behind me. Wary of being tailed by opportunistic townsfolk who favoured my brother, I rapidly spun in the saddle and spied a cloaked figure atop a black charger, who was two hundred yards to my rear and approaching swiftly. Frightened into a blind terror, I spurred Raymond into a gallop and tore down the road, careless of rocks and bumps which impeded my progress. Risking a glance behind, I saw to my consternation that the cloaked rider had also increased his pace and was now in full pursuit. Desperate to escape, I leaned low over Raymond's neck and gasped, "Come on, boy! Faster! Please!", my voice hoarse with panic. Seeming to sense my urgency, the horse discovered a new burst of speed and sprinted with renewed energy, the wind whipping through his chestnut mane as I clung to his neck. Yet still we had not put any significant distance between ourselves and our pursuer, whose mount looked as strong and well fed as my own. Putting faith in my equestrian skills, I turned off the main road and plunged into the parallel forest, following an overgrown and spindly path.

Weaving in and out of the densely packed trees, I smiled inwardly, knowing that I was safe. No man in the village of Little Dunmow could match my horsemanship, especially in the tight confines of a forest. Trampling ferns and a carpet of virgin bluebells, Raymond expertly navigated the foliage for at least a mile before I felt safe enough to slow down and allow the horse to rest in a small clearing with a pond. As Raymond drank, I nervously checked the treeline, wishing I was armed with my short-sword which could at least deter my assailant.

My wishing was in vain, and I soon paid for my arrogance.

Bursting from the trees a mere hundred feet away, the cloaked rider hurtled towards me, his horse sweating profusely. Savagely sawing at my reins, I kicked Raymond into a frantic run, wincing at the thought of an arrow, crossbow bolt or sword penetrating my back. My pursuer shouted something in a curiously high-pitched voice which was lost to the wind, but I paid it no heed. I was now not following any discernible path, but rather crashing blindly through the undergrowth, oblivious of anything but the need to escape. I did not see the ditch until it was almost underneath me. Well-trained as he was, Raymond soared across the ditch without any guidance, but lost his footing as he landed amongst the roots of a towering, ancient oak tree. As I was not braced for the landing, I tumbled roughly from the saddle and sprawled in a large patch of nettles at the base of the ditch. Wincing from the pain, I scrambled into a sitting position, as the rider on the huge black horse drew up in front of me, blotting out the brightness of the sun.

"Oh, Alistair," the mysterious figure said in a voice that was ever so familiar. "You never could keep your balance whilst jumping. I swear it'll be the death of you one day."

The rider drew back her hood, and for the second time that day, I felt like an utter fool.

Alice gave me a resigned smile as she dismounted from her borrowed horse, and firmly grasped my hand to pull me from the ditch. The pain I had felt from the fall, and the fear gnawing at my heart since I had left

Little Dunmow, were washed away instantly by a wave of relief at the sight of my sister. If anyone were to believe me innocent of the murder of Father Geoffrey, it would be her.

"I'm… I'm sorry," I said as we embraced. "I didn't recognise you. Your horse, and… I've never seen you dressed that way."

"It's true, I usually dress even less fashionably than this," she joked, though her bright blue eyes were creased with concern. "But I had no choice. Father forbade me from leaving the house for the rest of the day, but I'd heard what had happened from Mother, so one of the hunters, um, lent this to me so I could sneak out. As for the horse, my own mount was being kept under guard, so I decided to take Father's new stallion for a bit of exercise. I don't think he'll mind, will he?"

I imagined the scowl on Father's face when he found out. "He'll be furious," I said, grinning despite myself. "What does Mother think, though?" I asked, my expression becoming serious. "She surely doesn't believe I'm capable of murdering a churchman? Even one as vile as Father Geoffrey?" As I spoke, I retrieved Raymond's reins and we led our horses into the clearing, where we sat beside the sparkling pond.

"She doesn't know what to believe," Alice sighed. "I couldn't get much sense out of her through the tears. Regardless of what she really thinks, she can't be seen to contradict Father. Not in her position."

I nodded, fighting back my own tears, which were threatening to well at the corners of my eyes.

"So was it Robert who killed that bastard priest?" Alice asked. "Or was it the pox that finally got him?"

"It was Robert," I confirmed, grateful for the change of subject. "Though I don't think he meant to kill Father Geoffrey. He just attacked him with such force... Alice, I've never seen him that angry. I know he can be a snide git sometimes, but I had no idea he was capable of such a thing. If I didn't hate him so much right now, I'd probably be concerned for him."

"Honestly, I believe that whoever rid us of Father Geoffrey's foul presence is deserving of a knighthood," my sister commented dryly. "But, in truth, I've always known there's a vicious side to Robert." She paused, gazing sombrely into the sky, her expression distant.

"He wouldn't... he's never hit you, has he?" I asked, outrage creeping into my voice.

Alice gave a wan smile. "No, nothing like that. But I've had friends who've worked alongside the physician. Each of them has a story of a boy, often much younger than Robert, who had come in for treatment covered in bruises. One such boy, who was no more than ten or eleven years old, had broken ribs. Each of these boys was told," Alice looked me directly in the eyes, "not to mention the lord's son, or the lord himself would mete out punishment."

"And now," I said wearily, "that lord's son, that coward and bully, is the heir to the baronage of Little Dunmow. But there isn't a great deal we can do about that, is there?"

"I'm afraid not," she replied. "But Robert isn't our main concern at the moment. Nor is he the reason I followed you out here. We need to find you someplace safe, away from the reaches of Father and his friends across the country. I will not have my little brother hunted down for a crime he didn't commit. Even if you had committed it, I would still defend you to my last breath."

I felt a surge of affection for my sister, but it was marred by a tinge of despair. "Where can I go, though?" I asked, despondent. "I don't have the skill at arms to become a mercenary soldier, I don't have the resources to become a trader, and I don't know anyone outside Little Dunmow who will give me refuge!"

"But I think I do," Alice asserted, "or at least, Gilbert does."

"Gilbert?" I said, frowning at the mention of her betrothed. "But he doesn't even know me. How could he help me? He doesn't know I've been exiled!"

"Slow down, slow down," she said, raising a hand to calm me. "Not long ago, Gilbert mentioned in passing that his butcher, a man named Henry Fox, had emigrated to the town of Châteauroux in the Berry region of France. It's a long shot, I know, but there's a good chance that this Henry Fox will require an assistant, an assistant who speaks English. And Châteauroux is well beyond the reach of Father. It's contested land in the middle of the conflict between the King, his son, and the King of France, but I hear the war doesn't touch civilians, so you'll be safe. Much safer than here, anyhow."

Struggling to understand the implications of Alice's suggestion, I managed to grasp at one of the many questions which swirled in my head. "How do you know this butcher will accept me? He may not need help, and I have no proof that I'm connected to Gilbert in any way. If he turns me away, I'll have wasted a terribly long journey."

"Oh, I'm certain he could use a new servant to clean out his chamber pot," she said with a hint of her usual mischievousness. "You do make a good point about your lack of connection to Gilbert, though." Alice furrowed her brow in thought for a moment. "Here," she said, removing a small locket from around her neck, "take this. Henry Fox will be sure to take you in when he sees it."

Curious as to what I was receiving, I flipped the locket's lid open. Inside was a miniature portrait of an elderly lady, who stared back at me with an impervious gaze. "She's Gilbert's late mother," Alice explained, "and that locket is precious to him. Don't worry, he'll be pleased that I gave it to you. Anyone who carries it will be recognised as a friend of his."

"Tell him I'm grateful," I said. "And that I'll return it to him someday."

Alice stared at the ground for a long time, as if reluctant to speak. Eventually, she exhaled deeply and turned back to face me. "I need to go back now," she said in a voice that was wavering slightly, as she rose to her feet. "Father will send men out to search for me soon, and they might encounter you. I don't care how angry he is – if needs be, I'll go to Bourn and stay with Gilbert. Father can't touch me if I'm there. You'll need this," she handed me a large bag of silver shillings, "for the journey. I know you can do this, Alistair. You're stronger than you think you are."

"I don't know how to thank you," I said, hugging her fiercely. "You're the greatest friend a man could ask for. If there was any justice in this world, it would be you ruling Little Dunmow, not Father or Robert." I stepped back and took a deep breath. "Look after yourself, Alice. Look after yourself and Mother."

She gave me a sad smile as she mounted her horse. "I will, little brother. I promise you we will see each other again someday. And you will take Little Dunmow back. I know it." With that, she pressed her knees to the flanks of her horse, and my most trusted friend left me alone, with both sorrow in my heart, and a determination to make her proud.

Chapter 3

In the months following my departure from Little Dunmow, I learned a great deal about myself. I found my place in the world, I discovered my limitations, I met lifelong friends, and I became a warrior.

On my journey between Dover and Calais, I learnt that I hated ships.

It was not just the food, the sleeping conditions or the temperament of the captain – all of which were terrible. The worst part was the nauseous movement underfoot. It was as if I lived on a child's wooden toy boat which was constantly being picked up and thrust in different directions. The whims of the sea seemed almost sadistic; as soon as I had recovered from one bout of vomiting from the aft deck, the cruel waves would roll in with a mocking serenity and set my stomach to churning once more. Some start to my grand adventure into the unknown, I remember thinking – I didn't recall many chivalrous tales in which the knight spends most of his coin for passage on a rickety trading vessel, and then heaves his noble guts into the sea for the next few hours.

I consoled myself with the thought that I had managed to find a ship with accommodation for horses. The thought of leaving Raymond behind was unbearable; not only was he invaluable for traversing the countryside quickly, but he was my only reminder of home. Although my memories of Little Dunmow had been tarnished, and I knew I could not return whilst my father and brother still lived, I was determined not to forget about it. I was not the strongest of men, and nor did I think of myself as a natural leader, but I knew that if I stayed patient, and kept my wits about me, then an opportunity would one day present itself for me to retake my birthright.

Such were the thoughts I used to distract myself from the torments of ship travel. It was not a long journey (certainly, I would undertake much longer naval ventures in the years to come) yet I still felt an immense relief washing over me as we approached the small port town of Calais. Although the town was technically a part of the Kingdom of France, I knew that the arrival of our ship would not attract any hostile attention, as Calais was exceedingly popular with English merchants thanks to its close proximity to the English coast. This became apparent as I gently coaxed an unsettled Raymond down the gangplanks of the ship – he had evidently enjoyed the journey as much as I had – as the harbour was a hive of bustling mercantile activity. I heard hundreds of clamouring voices, many speaking a language I assumed to be French, although I was later informed that the inhabitants of the town predominantly speak Dutch. France was – and still is, in many regards – a strange and divided country.

Having led a jittery Raymond through the swarm of traders at the harbour, I paid for a night's stay at one of the plentiful wharfside inns. I was immensely grateful for the town's close ties with the English, for the innkeeper both spoke fluent English and accepted my shillings as payment. Having purchased hard bread, cured beef and white cheese from the kitchen's stores, I set out at dawn the next morning on the eight-day southerly ride to the town of Châteauroux.

The journey itself was largely uneventful, but it provided an opportunity to assess the mood of the French-held countryside following the years of relentless conquest by King Henry. Indeed, a mere fifty years ago this territory had formed the heartland of north-eastern France, yet now it was not too far from the fiercely fought border with English forces. Were it not for the recurrent infighting between the King and his sons, I do not doubt that the Kingdom of France would have long ago been forced to submit to the rule of the Angevins. Of course, I knew better than most that family conflicts, caused by simple jealousy, could have devastating consequences. It may seem strange for me to feel this way, but perhaps the King's sons, Richard included, were not so different to my brother Robert. They rebelled against their father not because of any great wrongdoing on the King's part, but simply because they were trying to secure as much land as possible through inheritance. Until recently, Richard had actually been allied to Philippe, the King of France, and had eroded much of Henry's territory. So many nobles in Europe would happily backstab their kin if it were to gain them a morsel more land or power.

Yet another reason why chivalry is a deception.

As I approached Châteauroux from the north, I noticed quickly that the town was dominated by two structures: a pristine church with an imposing bell tower in the east, and a fortress in the west which commanded the skyline with its high walls and ramparts. Gaining access to the town was fairly easy, as it lacked outer fortifications, which was understandable given the impregnable look of the fortress. As I entered the outskirts I called out to a group of nearby tanners to confirm that this was indeed Châteauroux, and received only sullen looks in reply, as if to suggest I was no more appealing than the turds they applied to their leather. Given that the town was currently in the possession of the English, I had expected my accent to attract open hostility. Yet the disapproval of the townspeople was silent, and, in many cases, non-existent. It seemed that what Alice had said was true – the war really didn't affect civilians, at least in towns. For that, I was grateful; I certainly didn't want any prying English nobles recognising the name of Fitzwalter.

For now, though, the only person on my mind was Henry Fox, as he was my one hope of survival in this alien land. Going to the fortress was pointless; I likely wouldn't be allowed in, and even if I was, the commander of the garrison would be some self-righteous knight who would ask too many questions. Instead, I directed Raymond through the meandering streets towards the church, as a place of God is always the centre of any community, and the priest would surely know of Henry Fox. Given my past experiences of priests, I wasn't particularly looking forward to the meeting.

All thoughts of priests and butchers vanished from my mind as I stepped through the great wooden doors of the church of Saint Martial. I had never been in any church except that of Little Dunmow, which was a tiny, barren place with few ornaments and even fewer colours. This, in contrast, was the most grandiose building I had ever seen. Construction had only finished in the last few months, so this was no doubt one of the most pristine churches in all of France. Vivid stained glass shone across every wall with an almost ethereal glow, and the altar was bedecked with golden candlesticks and chalices which proudly boasted of the church's wealth. It seemed almost that the townspeople gathered inside were praying to the flamboyant ornaments on display, and not to God.

Yet, of all the splendour inside the church, it was neither glass nor gold which caught my attention. Lining the walls were several stone-carved statues with inscriptions and candles, each one honouring a saint who was apparently treasured by French culture. Many of the saints held peculiar poses; the statue surrounded by the most candles, *Saint Denis,* stood with his dismembered head held in his hands. This was not the statue I was drawn to, however. At the near end of the church, farthest away from the altar, was *Saint George,* riding a magnificent stallion and illuminated by one candle. To this day, I do not know why the church of Saint Martial contained a statue venerating the patron saint of England. Perhaps it demonstrated the confused identities of England and France.

As I gazed at *Saint George,* pondering this, a gruff voice spoke from directly behind me. "Now what would a young Englishman be doing in a French town, in the midst of a goddamned bloody war?" it said. I spun round, startled not only by the English the man spoke, but also by his English accent, which was not dissimilar to mine. But that, it seemed, was where my likeness to Henry Fox ended.

It was not the man's voice or appearance which revealed his identity, but rather his smell. A faint scent of blood accompanied his presence, and I remember thinking that such an attribute could only belong to a butcher or a serial murderer. He certainly could have been the latter, judging by the snarl etched upon his heavily lined face. I estimated his age to be around forty years, most of which had been spent performing hard physical work. His hands were rough and calloused, his stocky frame muscled.

Although I was already fairly certain that this was Henry Fox, I did not want to appear presumptuous to a man who seemed angered by my very existence. "I'm looking for an Englishman named Henry Fox. A butcher," I stated politely. "Do you perhaps know him?"

"No," he replied bluntly, and turned to the church's exit.

I frowned, puzzled. "Well, what's your name then?" I called after his retreating back.

"My name? I'm bloody Saladin," he growled, pushing on the oak-beamed doors. "Good day."

I pursued, following him into the streets of Châteauroux, which were now bathed in the light of a crimson sunset. "But you're English," I persisted. "Surely you'd know the other Englishmen in this town?"

"There are no other Englishmen in this town, aside from those pompous arseholes up in the castle," he asserted. "Good thing too. Believe it or not, but I left England to get away from English people. I much prefer talking to these halfwit French. They don't talk back, because they don't talk English, and they don't act like they have a thorn up their arse when I swear at them. Speaking of which, please sod off."

"Does the name Gilbert Peche mean anything to you?" I asked desperately.

He paused and turned to face me, his expression softening slightly. "The Baron? Aye, I know him. Fine man. What of it?"

"I know… well, I don't know him, I've never met him, but I'm under his protection," I stammered, floundering for the right words. "I was told you might be able to help me, or at least shelter me for a while."

Henry Fox stopped and swivelled to face me, an incredulous expression on his face. "You've come all the way to Châteauroux just to beg the friendship of an old butcher, claiming to be under the protection of a man you've never met?"

Now that he said it, it did sound rather farcical. "I had no other choice," I replied miserably. "But I do think Baron Gilbert would value my safety – he's my future brother-in-law. I was told to show you this to prove it." I delved into my pockets and produced the locket.

Flipping the locket open, Henry's face took on a look of genuine surprise. "Never thought I'd see that sour old crone again. I can still hear her berating Gilbert for his 'disreputable acquaintances' like me," he mused. Snapping out of his reverie, the butcher turned his gaze to me. "I suppose that I can tolerate somebody who's a friend of Gilbert's," he said grudgingly. "We'll sort this out at my house. Follow me."

"Wait a moment," I interrupted him. "I need to fetch my horse." I had left Raymond tied up outside the church and did not wish to leave him alone for too long.

Henry's eyebrows shot up in disbelief. "Your horse? Oh, bloody hell, don't tell me you're the son of a noble? I should have known from your soft hands and scrawny body. What's your name?"

I hesitated slightly, then decided I had no choice but to tell the truth. If I could not trust Henry Fox, then I could not trust anyone in Châteauroux. "Alistair Fitzwalter," I answered. "But my father banished me, and probably wants me dead, so I'm not sure I have a right to that name anymore."

"A Fitzwalter, eh? You are full of surprises, boy," he said, examining me with a new interest. "I saw your father once, when he visited Bourn about a year ago. He looked like a right grouchy bastard. Aside from Gilbert, I've never met a noble who looks cheerful. They all have expressions like they're constantly smelling shit."

I smiled. I had never imagined such attitudes towards nobles existed, as I had never been exposed to them during my sheltered life as a baron's heir. Henry Fox was quickly forcing me to revise that view, and I found his sardonic bluntness amusing. "So, do I look like I'm constantly smelling shit?" I asked with a grin.

He laughed. "Ha! Never thought I'd hear a noble arsehole talk like that! No you don't, my boy, but you smell a bit like shit yourself, so you're probably used to it." A week in the saddle hadn't exactly improved my hygiene, so that was fair enough. "Now," he said, changing the subject, "you said your father banished you. Why did he do that? Because of your foul mouth?"

We collected Raymond from the church, and as we wove our way through Châteauroux, I told him what had happened. Our path took us south through the eastern side of the town, away from the castle, and for that I was grateful. Henry listened attentively to my tale, but if I had expected sympathy, I was disappointed. "So, you surrendered your inheritance without a fight?" he asked when I was finished.

"What could I have done?" I exclaimed, angered by the question. "My father has knights, men-at-arms, councillors and justices on his side. I have nothing."

"You should have at least shown some defiance, some spine, so that the people of Little Dunmow remembered you," he retorted. "Meekly running away would hardly have gained you any support." He was right, of course, but there was nothing I could do about it now. "Regardless," he continued, "I reckon this'll do you some good. People who have everything handed to them on a plate, like most nobles, have weak characters. You'll have to make your own way in the world now. Speaking of which, what are your plans? To become my assistant?"

"If you'll have me," I responded. I was not sure how a butcher's apprentice was going to garner enough strength to take Little Dunmow, but I was hardly in a position to complain. As we spoke, Henry led me onto his land, which consisted of a moderately sized butcher's shop adjoined directly to living quarters. The building was constructed from sturdy timber, with great cuts of meat hanging from meat hooks around the shop's entrance. Much of the butchery's interior was filled with large barrels filled with salted pork and beef. I would later learn that a great deal of Henry's trade came from the need of French and English armies to provision themselves for campaigns which contributed to the incessant warfare of this region of France.

"I suppose I could use someone to chase away the mice and man the shop when I'm drunk," Henry said gruffly, as he produced a candle which lit up the shop's murky interior. "You can have my bed, my lord. I, of course, will sleep on the floor."

"Really?" I asked hesitantly.

He guffawed so loudly that it probably woke the entire street. "No, you pompous imbecile! You can fight with the dog for the pillow on the kitchen floor. I expect you up at daybreak tomorrow. I have plenty of carcasses which need their offal scraped out!" With that, he bade me a cheery good night, still chuckling to himself.

Thus, I became a butcher's apprentice, and my new life as a commoner began.

Chapter 4

The days and weeks after coming to Châteauroux I remember with great clarity, as they were a remarkable departure from the privileged and aloof life I had led previously. You might assume that my most tangible memory is that of missing my family or plotting revenge against my brother. Yet what I recall more than anything is the aching. By God, how my muscles ached by the end of the day! The lifting of barrels and carcasses, the constant treks which ranged all over the town and the rigorous cleaning of the shop were all tasks for which my body was hopelessly ill prepared. I even tried to enlist Raymond as a draught horse, but when my makeshift harness broke on the first attempt and spilled a leg of beef into a sewage ditch, Henry growled that I had better use my bloody arms next time because my brain was clearly non-existent. Of all the arms in Châteauroux, mine were probably the weakest, because manual labour was so alien to me. Looking back on it, I can now appreciate the immense patience that Henry showed in employing such an inept labourer. Perhaps he simply saw the political advantages that the gratitude of an exiled baron's heir conferred. Regardless, it was a mutually beneficial relationship, and my physique rapidly improved to meet the demands of the butchery.

Fortunately, there were other aspects of being a butcher's apprentice for which I was better suited. In particular, my lack of knowledge of the French language was alleviated by the similarities between the French names of meats and the language used by the English nobility. Of course, my family had never reared its own animals, but merely eaten the meat which we either hunted, took through tax or purchased at the market. As such, animals known as "sheep" to commoners were referred to only as "mouton" by us, and a peasant's "pig" was known only as "porc" amongst my family. Because of this, I was able to pick up the dialect of a French butcher fairly quickly as I unwittingly already had an excellent knowledge of the French names of meats. I asked Henry why this was, and he informed me that the French nobles who conquered England over a hundred years ago used their own language to describe meat, in order to show their superiority to the Anglo-Saxon peasantry. Of course, he didn't use those exact words; I imagine the phrase "aristocratic arseholes" was used more than once in an attempt to rile me. Yet it struck me as peculiar that the most powerful men in England, who had so recently been of French background, were now so determined to distance themselves from French allegiance. I suppose this was, and still is, just another violent consequence of the baffling contradictions of Anglo-French identity.

These contradictions were also evident in the characteristics and mannerisms of the men who governed Châteauroux – who were ostensibly of English allegiance. The castle garrison's commanders usually sent squires and servants to purchase meat for themselves and their soldiers, but occasionally the nobles put in an appearance. English seemed their most natural language, yet they spoke in thick French accents. Most of their parents were minor aristocrats of English descent, but they had spent the majority of their lives in France. This last instance was fortunate for me, as none of Châteauroux's Englishmen were familiar enough with domestic English families to recognise the name Fitzwalter and ask uncomfortable questions.

Yet I was not to experience the company of such men for long. As late spring stretched into early summer, and the days warmed considerably, the change in season and climate precipitated a shift in the war's fortunes. Although I was, at the time, unaware of what caused the ebbs and flows of the conflict, I shall attempt to explain them here – although in truth, I am not sure that I understood those peculiar wars.

To classify the struggle as an Anglo-French war would be somewhat misleading. It is certainly true that King Henry had slowly absorbed much of the Kingdom of France into his Empire due to a weak French monarchy, and his aptitude for siege warfare. However, a complete breakdown of trust between Henry, his sons, and his wife led to almost constant civil war amongst the Angevins. Of course, much of this took place whilst I was very young, so I do not know the full details. What I do know is that by 1188, the year I was exiled, King Henry did not take responsibility for any of the actions of Prince Richard, who had made quite a name for himself as a bold and daring leader during his conquests in France.

There were three major factions in France's political sphere at the time: King Henry of England, his son Prince Richard, and the French king, Philippe. None of the leaders had any great affection for each other, all of them had been allied to each other in the past, and all of them had besieged Châteauroux at some point over the last two years. All three had forged an uneasy peace in January 1188, in order to prepare for the Crusade which was supposed to override all secular concerns. Unfortunately for the Pope, his designs for a peaceful France had been dashed by a lightning campaign which Richard launched into the Quercy region, occupying numerous strongholds including the formidable fortress town of Toulouse itself. Consequently, Philippe was furious that the treaty of January had been so rudely broken, and he organised an enormous campaign of his own to take revenge, with his focus squarely on the province of Berry.

As such, on a rare overcast day in the midst of a bright June, the military might of France came to bear on the placid town of Châteauroux.

I remember the day as vividly as if it were yesterday. Henry – the butcher, not the King of England, to be clear – had reluctantly decided to grant me full responsibility over the day's trading. He was, of course, closely supervising, "just to make sure you don't mistake rump for ribs," in his words. I'm not sure what was less helpful, his disapproving glances or frequent sniggering. He was certainly guilty of the latter as I spoke to the town's cobbler, trying to explain in my stilted, halting French that it wasn't my responsibility if his pork loin became inedible after a week out in the sun. My fierce determination to see off the hysterical man was interrupted by the cries of a small girl, who ran past the butcher's shop shouting "The King! The King has come! From the west! The King!" The news was greeted by a rush of townspeople who scrambled towards the town's western perimeter.

I glanced at Henry whose brow was furrowed. He smiled when he saw my own worried expression. "Nothing to fear, lad," he said reassuringly. "You'd be surprised at how often this happens. Maybe Philippe's just visiting to sample my sirloin. Go on. Go and see what all the commotion's about. I'll take over here."

Ducking out of the shop, from where I could hear the cobbler renewing his complaints – he clearly wasn't awed by his King's apparent arrival – I briskly walked west, passing the fortress, which I now knew was named Castle Raoul. It had ramparts curiously absent of any military activity, considering an enemy assault could have been imminent. I shrugged off that anomaly amid the excitement I felt at seeing an armed force for the first time. Looking back on it, I now realise how much that moment revealed about my true nature. I had never revelled in fist-fighting as a child, unlike my brother Robert. Yet something was tugging me, drawing me to the thrill of armed combat.

Naturally, when I laid eyes upon the French royal army, I was immensely disappointed.

What was I expecting? I had been reared on tales of shining hordes, of ranks of men resplendent on horseback, with armour glittering like a sun-bathed ocean. Any accounts of battles in France, even to this day, intricately link the effort of combat with the splendour of chivalry. Splendour, I suppose, is what I was expecting above all else.

The impression I received instead was one of chaos. A huge grey swarm of men writhed across the western plains in a ragged column, which seemed absent of any sense of organisation. Some mounted men – presumably minor nobles – rode in circles, frantically attempting to round up groups of mercenaries and men-at-arms who wandered away in seemingly random and errant directions. The great swathe of soldiers was followed by an even more immense artillery and baggage train, which was trailed by families, merchants, and the diverse mixture of opportunistic camp followers which seems to materialise around every army. If I had been closer to the French force, I would have been repulsed by the muddy, fatigued appearance of the weary foot soldiers, as well as the stench of sweat, horse dung and disease, which my nose has thankfully become resilient to over the years.

What did awe me was the sheer number of men approaching the crowd of townsfolk and the quiet town behind it. Growing up in Little Dunmow, I had thought that the gathering of a hundred people in the marketplace was a remarkably large number. On that peaceful summer's day, though, it seemed as if half the population of France was marching towards me. However, I now realise that the French force could not have consisted of more than three or four thousand men, and in time, I was to face much larger and more threatening foes.

I intently watched the lumbering horde for about half an hour, unhappy at the fact that it did not appear nearly so magnificent as I had imagined it would be. What puzzled me more than anything, however, was the fact that the army barely seemed to be moving at all – it might have travelled about half a mile in all the time

I watched it. In my young and idealistic mind, this was merely another disappointment. I now know that an army only travels as quickly as the slowest man, wagon or artillery piece.

Impatient and agitated, I left the murmuring throng of townspeople and sprinted back through Châteauroux. Seeing a French army in the flesh had awakened some instinct inside me, some animalistic drive to fight which I do not think I can explain, and I had never felt before. It was a raw and untempered feeling – I had barely picked up a sword before – yet it was all I could think about.

"It's true! The French are here!" I shouted as I barrelled through the front door.

Henry lifted his gaze from the sheets of vellum littering his desk. I had insisted over the past weeks that I begin recording his transactions, so that he could not be fleeced by folk who claimed poverty when they visited, and then failed to pay him back later. I had also been attempting to teach Henry a few letters so that he was not utterly reliant on me, but he had little enthusiasm for such "priestly nonsense". I dare say my intervention had increased his profits substantially, but he would never have admitted as much.

"And?" he now replied, raising an eyebrow. "What does that have to do with us?"

I was stunned by his failure to match my fervour. "We have to fight!" I exclaimed. "We still have time to make it to the castle before the enemy arrive – they were moving at a snail's pace! Do you have a sword? You must have a weapon somewhere!"

Henry seemed genuinely bemused by my attitude. "Swords? Fighting? Enemies? What in the name of sheep's bollocks are you on about, lad?"

I gaped at him, unable to articulate my disbelief.

The butcher gave an exasperated sigh. "This may be difficult for you to comprehend, seeing as you're barely weaned from your mother's noble teat, but war isn't about dashing, heroic knights and blushing maidens." He was becoming angry now. "It's about trying not to notice when all the men around you shit themselves. It's about staying on your feet when your friends are spilling their guts all over you. It's about killing men who have never wronged you, because some poncing lord wants to boast about owning an unimportant village."

I said nothing, wondering how he knew all this.

Crossing the room and placing a hand on my shoulder, Henry's expression softened slightly. "Look, lad. This isn't our war. Armies come and go from Châteauroux as often as the wind changes direction. We leave the soldiers alone, and they leave us alone, whether French or English."

Although his words had dampened my fervour, I was still internally conflicted. "Do you not feel any patriotism?" I asked. "Do you not feel any attachment to your country at all?"

He shrugged. "How can anyone be patriotic in a country where no one seems to know what their bloody national identity is? I'd only put my life on the line for someone who I genuinely feel would return the favour. Baron Gilbert, some of my neighbours here in Châteauroux, though not that stuck-up cobbler. Perhaps even you, if I had nothing better to do," he added indifferently.

"I assume 'better things to do' includes scraping offal from carcasses," I remarked with a smile.

He laughed and thumped me on the back enthusiastically, causing me to wince at his overbearing affection. "That's why I like you, lad. You don't seem to mind that I'm an arsehole!" Still chuckling to himself, he crossed the room and closed the entrance to his shop. "To keep your mind off the commotion outside, why don't you try to hammer some more of these damn letters into my head? I'll even pretend that some of it's useful, if it makes you feel better!"

And so Henry and I spent the remainder of the afternoon poring over the few vellum sheets I had managed to acquire. Whilst the butcher struggled over any word of more than one syllable, I pondered ideas such as loyalty, patriotism and valour. Perhaps the chivalrous tales of my childhood hadn't provided me with the realistic education I'd thought.

When I emerged from the shop later that evening, Châteauroux belonged to the French. Slumbering armies stirred all over France, and the path of my adult life was thus laid.

Chapter 5

It was, of course, not the norm for a fortress as feared as the Castle Raoul to fall within a single day. Sieges of modern castles could drag on for many months, as even armies with mighty siege trains would hesitate before high ramparts and crenelated towers which spat crossbow bolts and a torrent of other lethal missiles. So safe were the bleak grey strongholds across France that the majority of conflict was conducted as siege warfare. Field battles were simply considered too great a risk by both sides. Indeed, I have heard it said that King Henry never fought a pitched battle during his entire reign, and, looking at the dominating presence of fortresses such as Castle Raoul, I could understand why.

Yet the English commander holding the castle had submitted as meekly as a whipped priest. Most of the townsfolk, including Henry, surmised that the quick capitulation was down to mere cowardice fuelled by the sight of the immense trebuchets and other siege equipment that the French army had mustered. I was to discover later that the garrison had been bribed into opening its gates, and the English commander was rewarded with gold and swathes of land in south-west France. At the time, I would have been horrified to hear of such deceit and dishonourable tactics. I now realise the pragmatism of the French approach; they had just begun a rapid campaign to reconquer the Berry region, and could not afford to be held up by Castle Raoul's defences for the months it would take to whittle down the garrison.

King Philippe himself led the invading force, though I did not see him. In fact, a mere two days after it had arrived, the French royal army trudged out of its encampment surrounding the castle and marched east, intent on securing as many key strongholds in the region as possible before Prince Richard responded. I watched the army depart, gazing at the trebuchets still clearly visible on the horizon long after the main force had devolved into a murky, sluggish mass, once again struggling to maintain a brisk pace under the clear summer sky. Despite the heated conversation between Henry and myself, I still felt that persistent itch which could only be satiated by martial action. Although I certainly saw the sense in Henry's words, I was the son of a baron, however many bloodstains covered my threadbare butcher's apron. Perhaps the bull-headed desire for military life was, and still is, simply in my blood, and I had only realised that upon seeing the French army.

A substantial garrison remained, its sole aim to ensure that Châteauroux was never wrested from Philippe's control again. Henry asserted more than once that our lives would not change as a result of the French takeover.

I sensed from the start that he was wrong.

The garrison's commander was a man named Guillaume des Barres, a knight reputed to be one of the finest soldiers in all of Philippe's kingdom. A keen jouster and popular leader, des Barres was fanatically loyal to his King and devoted his entire being to pushing the English out of France entirely. He was unlike the previous French commanders of the town, in that he did not accept the neutrality of the townspeople and believed that a total purge of the English from Châteauroux was imperative to ensuring that it did not fall again to Anglican forces, as it had so many times already. As such, he issued an edict which demanded that any English natives should be delivered to the castle. In truth, taking such action was probably sensible in terms of holding the town, as a multicultural Châteauroux was not one that would effectively resist English occupation. Yet his stance placed both myself and Henry in a very dangerous position.

"We're not moving," Henry said flatly when I nervously informed him of the peril we were in. "I'm not a young man, Alistair. I've already run away from too much in my life, and I'm too old and tired to relocate again. I intend to live out the rest of my life in this town, however long that might be."

"So what do we do when the French soldiers kick down our doors to take us to the castle? Just meekly submit?" I asked, exasperated.

He smiled grimly. "They won't take me without a fight." Sighing, he left the cow's leg he was butchering and sat heavily beside his desk. "You're young, lad. If that bastard des Barres does come knocking, there's not much I can do to protect you. You should ride north, maybe to Normandy. You'll be safe from any French patriotism there."

I briefly considered his suggestion, then hated myself for doing so. Henry had taken me in at no real benefit to himself, and I at least owed him a little loyalty. Besides, there was no guarantee I would be safer in English territory, as the wrath of my father and brother would be much more likely to find me there. "No," I said stubbornly. "I'm not going anywhere. I'm fed up with running as well."

"You really are as stupid as I first thought," he replied gruffly, but I think I saw a small smile on his lips. "Anyhow, I don't think they'll find us quite as easily as you think. The people round here know me. I think some of the poor sods even like me, though God knows why. They don't know des Barres from a snail's mother. Why would they turn us in? Why would they favour him over me?"

I raised an eyebrow. "Did you just use the word 'anyhow'?" I asked.

"Oh, sweet Mary, it seems I did," he said, his eyes widening in surprise. "It seems your lordly priggishness is rubbing off on me. I'll be stealing grain from peasants and perfuming my arse next."

Henry was right about the attitudes of the townspeople. It seemed that months of having Henry in the community was much more important to them than the demands of a hot-headed knight whom they'd never met, and nobody was willing to turn us in. I was especially grateful for this when I heard what became of the English civilians who were captured by des Barres's men; each day, rumours came of men and women deprived of food and water in their seemingly permanent captivity. Some weren't even native to England – they might have just been overheard speaking fluent English. Yet still Henry refused to leave, and I would go nowhere without him.

Our greatest danger was the soldiers who visited the butchery in order to purchase supplies for the garrison. Henry always dealt with them personally, speaking in his passable French accent to allay any suspicions the soldiers might have. We were also both wary of strangers, because we did not know if their allegiance lay with Châteauroux or with the occupying soldiers. One such stranger entered the shop three weeks after King Philippe had departed. He arrived on an afternoon when Henry had crossed the town to harangue the blacksmith who was late delivering an order of new cleavers – the poor man was obviously overworked by the French soldiers, but Henry saw his new butchery tools as the blacksmith's greatest priority. The stranger was an altogether unremarkable looking man, with a round face and neat black moustache, who dressed in a plain black linen tunic with matching hose. What caught the eye, however, was his cloak of deep purple, a colour which denoted high status and above all, wealth. It was without doubt that this individual had money to spend freely, and so would be looking at the finest cuts of meat. Knowing Henry would be tremendously disappointed if I did not make a sale, I opened the conversation reluctantly; if my French was bad, then my newly adopted French accent was awful.

"Good afternoon," I said as pleasantly as I could. "Are you looking for anything in particular?"

The man gave me a peculiar look, probably triggered by my irregular speech, but he chose not to comment on it. "Just looking for something refined to please the wife," he informed me cheerfully. "Not that my pockets are as well lined as a few weeks ago. All these soldiers tramping through the market, demanding my fine cloth for a fixed price! It's terrible for business! The name's Estienne, by the way."

"Alistair," I replied, detecting a faint scent of garlic about him as I shook his hand. "All of our prices are fair," I continued evenly, determined not to be ruffled by his sob stories.

"Oh, I don't doubt it. But soldiers! Wearing my fabrics! You may as well give my wares to Englishmen!"

Estienne almost seemed as if he were about to cry, but he managed to compose himself. "Ah well. *Amissio nihil aliud quam mutare, et mutari naturae gaudet*, as my priest always used to say."

"Loss is nothing else but change, and change is nature's delight," I translated automatically.

"Goodness me!" Estienne cried, "you know your Aurelius! Even the butchers are more educated than I am these days!"

I shrugged, suddenly aware that it had probably been unwise to reveal my knowledge of Latin to this complete stranger. "My priest was keen about quoting people more intelligent than himself," I said, in attempt to appear light-hearted. I was telling the truth, although Father Geoffrey had believed the quote to have come from Jesus Christ.

"Aren't they all like that?" Estienne agreed amicably. "Though if change is nature's delight, I wish the soldiers would change back into their old clothes." He sighed dramatically. "Ah well, can't be helped. Good day, young Alistair." Bowing slightly, he retreated back into the street and swept off westwards with a swirl of his cloak, leaving me more than a little bemused.

He hadn't purchased, or even asked about, any cuts of meat.

Upon his return from the blacksmith, Henry dismissed the irregularity of my encounter with a nonchalant wave of his hand. "We get all sorts of wacky types in here. I once had a customer who barked like a dog and tried to run off with a leg of mutton in his mouth. I swear, it's the peculiar French food which has an impact on these people. If your cheese smells that bad, what sort of strange things must it do to your brain?"

I tried to brush the incident aside, but the atmosphere within Châteauroux was making me increasingly worried. Henry and I weren't exactly inclined to espionage, and the soldiers of des Barres were becoming increasingly relentless in their search for English men and women. Houses were broken into, innocent folk were interrogated, and rewards were offered for the successful delivery of English captives. We heard little of the war's progress, because although the townspeople hid us from des Barres, they became distant and unwilling to share information with us. The few locals I knew stopped speaking to me entirely, and even the cobbler, who I knew had a firm friendship with Henry despite their frequent arguments, apologetically told Henry that they could not be seen together.

It was in those days that I began to miss my family. I would have given anything for one more horse ride with Alice, or one more hour of my mother's futile attempts to teach me to play the lyre. I wondered if I would ever see them again, and I wondered whether Alice's engagement to Baron Gilbert had been finalised yet. I hoped so; one of us deserved some happiness. I even surprised myself by missing Robert a little, although I doubt the feeling was ever reciprocated. During the evenings, if I couldn't distract myself by continuing Henry's writing lessons, I spoke softly to Raymond or gazed at Gilbert's locket, even though I had never met the woman whose picture was inside it, or her son. Those were the only ways I could remind myself of Little Dunmow. On one star-speckled night in mid-July, I swore that I would make it out of Châteauroux alive, and so would Henry. I had never held any fanatical devotion to God – Father Geoffrey had seen to that – but I prayed that something, anything, could stop the horror that was spreading over the town. I prayed that someone could challenge the brutal rule of des Barres.

Three days later, it seemed my prayers were answered.

Prince Richard came to Châteauroux.

Chapter 6

"Well, it looks like you got what you wanted, boy," Henry commented sourly as he stood beside me, arms folded, frowning at the Prince's army as it lumbered towards Châteauroux from the east. He was pretending indifference, yet it was remarkably rare for him to leave the butcher's shop unattended, and so he must have been intrigued by the army's arrival. In truth, it was little different in appearance to the force Philippe had led a month earlier. What made it unique was the colossal banner flying above the vanguard, which depicted a roaring golden lion, majestic against a red background. It was the first time I'd seen that banner, and I cannot describe how much I came to love it. Henry had seen it plenty of times before, and so had known that Richard himself was present.

I peered into the distance, trying in vain to locate the Prince in the dying evening light. Even if the army had been fully illuminated, it would have been impossible to distinguish anything in the midst of the churning grey mass in front of us. "Surely you'd prefer Richard Plantagenet to Guillaume des Barres?" I asked.

"Hmrph. I suppose," Henry grumbled. "Either way, it doesn't matter. Even if he successfully sieges the castle – and many have failed – he'll be gone again a few days after, and the French will return. It's been that way since long before I arrived here. Still," he mused, "at least he might take des Barres out of the picture."

To examine Castle Raoul on that evening, a French defeat did not seem a likely prospect. Even from a distance, we could both see spear points bristling from the ramparts like spines from a hedgehog's back. It seemed des Barres was determined to live up to his exceptional military reputation by fighting off the English for long enough so that Philippe could reinforce him. Of one thing I was certain; the castle would not yield as easily as it had done when Philippe took it.

The next day, Châteauroux was a hive of frantic activity. French soldiers scoured the town to garner provisions for the siege, paying paltry amounts for food which was essentially taken at sword-point. Henry reluctantly yielded two sides of beef to the men-at-arms who belligerently demanded cuts of meat, although not without spitting at their shoes as they left. Richard's army was yet to surround the castle, and milled about a mile from the city outskirts, presumably collecting timber to construct giant siege engines. Occasional groups of knights and mercenary cavalry separated from the Angevin forces and roamed close to the castle, only to clash bloodily with French cavalry detachments. It was after the third such engagement that Henry handed me one of his new cleavers and ordered me to wear it under my tunic. "We're to stay out of the fighting," he informed me firmly, "but it doesn't hurt to have insurance."

I slept uneasily on those nights after Richard's army arrived. My burning desire to be in battle had once again flared up, and I was finding it extremely difficult to contain. Yet I did not possess any weapons or armour, and aside from my equestrian skills I had few attributes necessary in a modern fighting man. I could not couch a lance, parry a sword thrust, or hurl a heavy spear. The hardened troops in Richard's army would laugh if I asked to fight alongside them. It was after a night of such galling thoughts that I arose early on the third morning since Richard's arrival. I breakfasted on stale bread and cheese, and in a futile attempt to calm my thoughts, I tallied the previous day's sales. Although transactions had been decreasing recently, especially in the last few days, it was a task that had be performed to avoid Henry's sardonic remarks about lazy aristocrats, which I did not think I could handle on top of the turmoil in my head.

I have probably forgotten many details of my time spent in Châteauroux, yet I remember that morning with perfect clarity. A fly buzzed incessantly around a leg of venison hanging next to my desk, and my frequent shooing did nothing to deter it. Henry's snores rumbled like an imminent avalanche throughout the shop. From outside, children squealed in delight as they pursued each other through the streets. It almost beggared belief that they could play so normally in a time of such turmoil, but their tangible joy brought a smile to my face, nonetheless.

Then a knock came at the door.

I frowned, swivelling in my seat. Dawn had only broken a couple of hours beforehand, and the townspeople knew that we never traded this early. "Sorry," I called in my questionable French accent. "We open later this morning, please come back in a few hours."

"Open this sodding door, or I'll kick it down," a coarse voice growled from outside.

A pool of anxiety began to well in my stomach as I rose and cautiously opened the door, only to be roughly shoved back into the butchery by a soldier with foul-smelling breath and a pugnacious expression. "There. Wasn't so hard, was it?" he snarled, glaring into my eyes.

Despite the soldier's intimidating appearance, I managed to keep my composure. "We've paid our due to the garrison," I said in a level tone which belied my nervousness.

"Oh, we know you have," said a familiar voice from the doorway. "We're here for something else. Something even more valuable to the war effort."

When I saw who had spoken, I knew I was in deep trouble.

It was Estienne, the self-proclaimed cloth merchant who had visited just a week ago. Yet now, there was no doubt that his claims and attire had been little more than an elaborate charade. Standing before me was not a merchant, but a man-at arms, who wore a studded leather brigandine and nasal helmet, both of which were scarred and dented from extensive use. A sword and knife were strapped to his waist. A sickly smile of triumph was etched upon his face.

"You!" I exclaimed, trying to understand his deception. "What are you doing here?"

Estienne's smile grew broader still as he slowly sidled across the room towards me. "What I always do," he replied. To my astonishment, he spoke in English. "Obeying my lord. Guillaume wanted all the English rats in this town to be sniffed out and exterminated. I'm just a little more subtle than the regular thugs he employs." The other soldier, who had entered first, frowned, but did not speak. "At first, I thought you were just another sorry Englishman with an atrocious accent," Estienne continued, "but then you showed an understanding of Latin. A butcher's apprentice! Speaking Latin! Now that was quite a rarity." He stepped closer, leering at me with pale blue eyes. "You're a nobleman, aren't you? An English nobleman. What a valuable prize to find."

I stepped backwards against the butchery's rear wall, too flustered to form any coherent thought. "What... what are you going to do with me?" I stammered.

He laughed as if it had been a stupid question, which, I suppose, it was. "We'll take you up to the castle, of course. A nobly born captive is priceless in times like these. The only reason it took us so long to collect you was that we needed to weed out all of your associates. When we're finished with you, we'll put that uncouth butcher out of his misery as well."

I opened my mouth to shout for Henry but was silenced as a third man entered the room. I am considered tall, but this newcomer towered over myself and everyone else present; had we been outside, he probably would have blotted out the sun. He was bedecked in full war gear, sporting a pristine chainmail hauberk and coif covered in a red-and-yellow checked surcoat. Heavy chausses encased his legs, and a polished great-helm was tucked under one arm. I was looking at a brutal machine built only for war, a killer with flint-dark eyes and an unforgiving demeanour, who could swat me down with his colossal great-sword without breaking a sweat.

I had no doubt that this was Guillaume des Barres, one of the most feared knights in all of France. Despite my apprehension, a small part of me was in awe of his dominating presence.

"What's taking so long, Estienne?" des Barres asked in a voice that sounded surprisingly refined for one whose appearance was so intimidating. "The English cavalry are everywhere. We don't have time for your games."

"Sorry, sir," Estienne replied deferentially. Together with the other foot soldier, he roughly grabbed my arm and began dragging me towards the exit of the shop. I struggled, frantically trying to reach the cleaver, which was still concealed under my tunic, but a firm strike across the head from Estienne's armoured glove almost knocked me unconscious. "We'll have no more of that," he told me in a voice that was almost cheerful. "If you behave yourself, we might even give your senile butcher friend the pleasure of a quick, painless death!"

Roaring with anger, Henry burst through his bedroom door, clutching a rusted but sharp sword in his left hand. Immediately setting eyes on the soldier who had entered the shop first, he shouted in rage as he thrust his blade into the back of the thickset man, who convulsed, mewed like a kitten, and sank to the floor. Recovering from his shock at the demonic butcher's appearance, des Barres unsheathed his monstrous great-sword as Estienne threw me to the floor. Emanating an animalistic growl, Henry hurled himself at the armoured giant, spitting insults as he slashed left and right with surprising speed. Des Barres calmly deflected some of these strikes, letting the rest scrape off his chainmail, before thrusting Henry back with a mighty blow of his sword's pommel. Estienne was slowly sidling around the room behind Henry. I tried to gain my feet to help, but my head was still spinning, and I could only watch in paralysed horror.

"I will not fight an unarmoured man," des Barres declared ponderously.

Bruised but not beaten, Henry hefted his bloodied sword. "Then you'll die an idiotic prick!" he shouted, then stopped and gasped as I cried out in anguish.

Estienne had plunged a knife into his back.

His steps faltering, Henry tried to turn and face his assailant, but his legs crumpled as blood gushed from the wound near his shoulder blade. Scrabbling against the floor, he dragged himself into a sitting position and breathed heavily as his eyelids fluttered. Estienne advanced towards him, knife raised and a gleeful smile on his face.

"Estienne!" des Barres's voice cracked like a whip. "I told you, we don't have time for this." He wrinkled his nose at the sight of the charnel house which the butchery had become. "Get the boy. We have business to attend to at the castle. If you hadn't forgotten, we're fighting a war here!" With that, he swept out the butchery without looking back once. Sheathing his knife, Estienne seized my tunic as I beat at him limply with my fists. My last sight as I was dragged out the door was Henry, slumped against the wall, his ragged breathing becoming ever more erratic.

As I was pulled into the serene morning sunlight, I saw that des Barres had brought a contingent of around thirty mounted men to capture me; why he thought I was so important, I had no idea. Two of these men were ordered back inside the butchery to "clean up" as I was tossed on the back of a soldier's horse like a sack of potatoes. I forced myself to think clearly. My main priority was escaping my captors so I could return to Henry. Perhaps, I thought, it would be beneficial to pretend a greater state of inertness than I actually felt, so I could surprise the Frenchmen by rolling off the horse and escaping when they least expected it. It was a feeble plan, but given what I had just experienced, it was a miracle that I could think with any sobriety at all.

Des Barres's men set a brisk pace as they cantered through the streets of eastern Châteauroux. I tried not to think about Henry; it was extremely unlikely that he still lived. Yet it seemed that any thoughts of escape were equally futile. I was surrounded by French men-at-arms who would surely notice if I tried to slip away. My only advantage was the concealed cleaver, but if I produced it now, I would be struck down in an instant.

Then, as we neared the grassy clearing outside the castle, my luck turned. From the head of the small column, I heard des Barres shouting frantic commands and the horsemen sawed on their reins, coming to a disorganised halt. Wriggling into a position so I could see what lay before us, I spied the cause of the French consternation. A small group of English heavy cavalry, about equal in number to the French contingent, was pounding towards us from the direction of Richard's encampment. Evidently, they had seen des Barres's coat of arms and had resolved to capture the Capetian commander. Just a few weeks beforehand, I had been determined to avoid any contact with English nobles, because I feared their possible connection to my father. Now, my heart lifted at the sight of them, and I inwardly willed them to cut off the Frenchmen.

Estienne spurred alongside des Barres and spoke quietly but intensely in his ear, gesturing emphatically in the direction of the castle gates, which could not have been more than a thousand yards away. The gist of his words soon became clear. "Retreat?" cried des Barres incredulously, wheeling to face Estienne, "If I am seen to be fleeing the English, what will that do to the spirits of the men on the ramparts? Why should they fight for me if I won't fight for them? You," he pointed at the soldier escorting me, "Get the boy into the castle. The rest of you," he called, slotting his great-helm onto his head, "follow me!" Without waiting to see if his men were following, des Barres spurred his destrier towards the English.

Crying "Saint Denis!" and "Sir Guillaume!" his troops pursued, scraping swords from scabbards, eager to close with the enemy before their lord. Meanwhile, my captor steered his horse towards Castle Raoul's imposing timber gates. Knowing I would not get a better chance to free myself, I sprang up from my motionless position, grabbed the man-at-arms and succeeded in tipping him from his mount. To my dismay, his foot caught in the stirrup, causing his horse to swerve and toss me from the saddle. Landing heavily, I quickly scrambled to my feet and saw that I had fared better than the Frenchman, whose bloodied head was still sickeningly bouncing on the ground as his terrified horse ran in circles. At that moment, my ears resonated with an almighty crash as the two groups of French and English cavalry collided at full gallop, spilling men on both sides to the sun-scorched ground. I saw the red-and-yellow surcoat of des Barres emerge from the far side of the fracas, his sword sheeted in blood, before he turned and charged back into the melee.

In that moment, I faced a choice. I could have so easily slunk into a side alley, made my way back to the butchery, and fled the town if Henry was dead, or I could have simply hidden until the French were defeated. Alternatively, I could follow des Barres and Estienne and enter a horrific brawl, unarmoured and untrained, in which I would probably die.

Or perhaps I had no choice at all. I certainly did not stop to think about it.

Reaching inside my tattered tunic, I produced the cleaver which Henry had given me, and stumbled towards the fight. A Frenchman wheeled away from the melee, pale faced and clutching a horrendous stomach wound, but I did not hesitate. Blood was roaring in my ears, and sheer adrenaline was forcing my feet to take one step after another. A tiny voice in my head complained that this was pure idiocy, and I think I almost listened to it.

Then I saw Estienne.

He was a few feet away from the main engagement, dismounted, and locked in single combat with a mounted Englishman dressed in war gear as fine as des Barres's, although this man wore no helmet. The Englishman, whose auburn-haired head was drenched in sweat, was having the better of the exchange, driving Estienne backwards with arcing swings of his blade. Desperately defending himself, Estienne dropped his shield and drew his knife, whilst dodging a lunge that missed skewering him by an inch. As I lumbered towards them, I saw exactly what Estienne was planning to do, and shouted a warning which went unheard in the cacophony of battle.

Ducking low, Estienne plunged his knife, still red with Henry's blood, into the neck of the Englishman's horse. The beast screamed and reared, despite its rider's best attempts to control it, and tipped him heavily onto the ground. I increased my pace to an awkward run as the Englishman's horse collapsed on top of him, pinning him to the ground in his cumbersome armour. Estienne drew his sword back, preparing to strike at his helpless opponent, and I screamed. Whether it was a battle cry or a wail of terror, I do not know to this day.

Estienne began to turn at the sound, and I raised the cleaver over my head, putting all the strength of my arms into one massive blow.

I did not miss.

True to its name, the blade connected with Estienne's skull and almost cleaved it in two, sinking down into his head as blood fountained upon me. The Frenchman spasmed twice, wrenching my hands off the cleaver, and flopped to the ground, causing me to grimace with equal satisfaction and revulsion. Turning away from the sight, I suddenly fell to my knees and vomited, gasping for air as I voided my stomach. I stayed in that position for what seemed like an eternity, trying to comprehend the enormity of what I had just done. Eventually, a strong hand clasped my shoulder, and drew me upwards to face the Englishman whom Estienne had so nearly killed. He had a strong, square face, a face lit up by a genial smile, and expressive eyes which seemed to understand my situation and sympathise with it. When he spoke, his voice was powerful and reassuring at the same time. "It seems, my friend, that I owe you my life. What is your name?"

"Alistair... Alistair Fitzwalter," I replied, too dazed to give any other answer.

"I am forever in your debt, Alistair Fitzwalter. My name is Richard. Some call me the Lionheart."

Chapter 7

To my credit, I didn't faint. Although I think I may have been close.

"R... Richard?" I spluttered. "Prince Richard?" I could not take my gaze from his strong, confident eyes. It seemed remarkable that such a self-assured man was almost killed by a weasel like Estienne.

"The very same," he confirmed, his eyes crinkling with amusement at my apparent stupor. "That's an interesting battle attire, I must say," he continued, observing my blood-drenched tunic and filthy shoes. "Perhaps I should try it myself sometime." How he could be so calm after a near-death situation staggered me. The Prince waited for me to speak, but I was struck dumb by shock. I had never suspected that the Angevin commander himself would be so close to the fighting. I was to learn that participation in combat played a crucial role in Richard's leadership style; much like des Barres, he needed his men to see him in the thick of battle, in order to either shame or inspire them into more impressive martial feats.

The Capetian leader himself had gambled and lost. Richard had evidently been accompanied by a personal retinue of elite men, mostly young knights and lordlings who sought to make a name for themselves in his service. However, these nobles did not look to be the mincing aristocrats that Henry stereotyped them as.

They were beings of metal, scarred and battle hardened, mounted on huge English destriers. It was no wonder that they had routed the French soldiers, who had been mostly mercenaries, many of whom now fled towards the castle. Others lay scattered in pools of their own blood, some still occasionally moaning or twitching. Riderless horses grazed contentedly at the grass, seemingly unaware of the horror around them.

Des Barres alone remained standing. The French giant looked more fearsome than ever; his helm had been torn off to reveal a bloodied head and vicious snarl, which he directed at four Englishmen who were slowly closing in, wary of the wild swipes of his great-sword. The end came quickly. A helmeted knight, equally as tall as des Barres, swept his companions aside and directly confronted the battle-crazed Frenchman, calmly deflecting the scything blade as if a child swung it. Whilst des Barres was distracted, a shorter, red-haired man rode behind him and almost casually clouted the French knight with the hilt of his sword, causing the latter to topple unconscious to the ground with a resonating crash.

Having watched the confrontation with a measured expression, Richard now turned back to me.

"It is not often I say this, young Alistair, so listen well." I could not have listened to anything else if all the spawn of Hell were screaming in my ear. "Thank you for what you did today. I would be honoured if you would accompany us back to our camp, so I can speak to you properly."

I had never been in awe of anyone so much in my life. "Yes, of course I will!" I exclaimed, finally finding my voice. "Thank you, Your Highness."

"Your Highness!" a voice echoed me from a few yards away. It belonged to the red-haired man, who was now frantically gesturing in the direction of the castle, where a column of horsemen was streaming out of Castle Raoul's gate in a desperate attempt to rescue their commander.

Richard was quick to respond. "Oliver! Take care of our prisoner!" he called, and the Englishman who had faced down des Barres dutifully slung the French knight onto the back of his horse, with the help of two comrades. "Everyone else, mount up and ride. By God's legs, we've given them a bloody nose today, my good fellows!"

They cheered and hauled themselves into their saddles as the red-haired man led a stray horse over to me. "We can't have our hero being left behind, now can we?" he said with a wink. "Name's Harold, by the way."

I smiled my thanks as we spurred our mounts to catch the others.

After a few hundred yards, our party slowed to a walk. It seemed the French cavalry had no real enthusiasm for the chase, and had halted beside the remains of our skirmish, evidently intent on looting the dead. Now that the turmoil in my head had subsided a little, I remembered something very urgent. Summoning what courage I had remaining on that day, I drew my unfamiliar horse up alongside Richard. "Your Highness?" I asked tentatively.

"Yes, Alistair?" he responded, immediately turning all his attention to me. "How can I help?" It genuinely seemed as if he wanted nothing more than to assist me in that moment, despite all of his responsibilities. He didn't know it, but by that time he had already gained my unwavering loyalty. It is perhaps strange that in ten minutes of acquaintance I felt more attached to him than I ever had to my father.

"I have a friend in the town who was badly injured by the French soldiers earlier today. I must go and help him... that is, if he's even alive." It had not occurred to me until that moment that Henry might be dead. I prayed fervently that it was not so.

Richard's eyes creased with concern. "Of course, of course. I would accompany you, but I fear that my mercenary captains will start a civil war if I do not return to them soon. Harold will escort you, and make sure you return to our camp safely." The red-haired man nodded his acquiescence. "You must promise me something, Alistair," Richard continued. "You must promise to come to my tent before the end of the day."

"I promise," I replied instantly.

Smiling, Richard turned and led his companions away from Châteauroux's outskirts, leaving Harold and me alone. I sat motionless for a few moments, once again overcome by the enormity of the day's events.

"So," Harold said, snapping me out of my reverie, "where are we going, exactly?"

I turned to face my new companion. In terms of appearance, Harold was quite unlike any other member of Richard's personal retinue. He was short for a warrior, with a chubby, jovial face which was constantly sporting an impish smile. His lively blue eyes stood out from a pale complexion, which was rare in the bright climate of France, but his most noteworthy feature was a shock of bright red hair which could be seen easily from across a crowded marketplace. He seemed unwounded from the earlier clash; I surmised that he had just hung back from the fighting. As I mentioned, he did not look to be a lethal fighter in the mould of Richard or des Barres. Certainly, he was younger than most warriors — perhaps a year or two older than myself.

"The butchery on the east side of town. Come on. We have to hurry!" I replied. Sensing my urgency, Harold did not ask any further questions as we thundered through the town, although he fell behind more than once. His lack of knowledge of the town's layout was exacerbated by his lack of natural horsemanship — he undoubtedly rode more clumsily than myself or any other in Richard's group. Not for the first time, I wondered how he'd become a member of the Prince's elite bodyguard. I tried to dismiss such critical thoughts; I would hardly be suited for the role myself. Drawing up outside the butchery, I steeled myself and prepared for the worst as I ducked through the doorway.

Henry was alive. I had expected to see him lying lifeless where I had left him, but instead was greeted by the sight of a swarm of townspeople who had crowded into the shop and stood murmuring in small groups. Confused, I pushed my way through the throng and into Henry's bedroom, where I saw him lying almost peacefully on his bed, clearly unconscious. Although pale and heavily bandaged, his breathing was strong. One of the town's senior doctors stood over him.

"Will he be all right?" I asked in a garbled rush. "And what happened? I saw the French soldiers come back in here. I was sure they'd kill him!"

The doctor stemmed my flow of questions with a raised hand. "He'll be fine," he assured me, "although he was extremely lucky. The knife missed his lung by an inch. As for what happened," he turned and gestured to the cobbler, who stood at the end of the bed, "this fine man apparently heard the commotion and led a group of his friends to subdue the French soldiers. They then found me, and I was able to patch him up." He gave a wry smile. "It would seem that this town is loyal to community over patriotism. How des Barres would hate to hear that."

I thanked the doctor, and then the cobbler, who sheepishly waved off my compliments in embarrassment. I assured both of them I would return on the morrow, and re-joined Harold outside the shop, pausing only to replace my French mount with Raymond.

"So how did this happen?" Harold asked as we wound our way through the subdued streets of Châteauroux. "I've been all over France in the last few years, and for the most part, civilians in towns have been left alone."

I recounted the attack and reflected that it could not have taken place more than two hours ago. The day already felt a hundred times that length. "We weren't the first, either," I explained. "In fact, I feel we were lucky to have lasted this long. Most of the English population of the town is currently enjoying the hospitality of the castle's prison cells."

"So much for France's flower of courtliness, eh?" Harold said lightly, referring to des Barres. "To be honest, Alistair, I wouldn't much like to live anywhere in France at the moment. I seem to be the only person in the country who doesn't speak the language, most of their food is highly suspicious, and the women are too busy hiding from soldiers to keep me company."

"Aren't you a soldier?" I asked, an eyebrow raised.

He chuckled loudly, causing his horse's ears to flicker in surprise. "Good question! Depends who you ask, I suppose. Either way, the women still don't seem interested in my obvious charms. The only reason I joined Richard's little band was so the noble ladies of the court would swoon over me, thinking I was some delicate, noble knight. But, alas, they have somehow resisted." He dramatically wrung his hands at the apparent futility of the situation, as if his romantic failures were somehow the greatest issue faced by anyone in France. Looking back on it, it may appear strange that Harold wanted to discuss women, of all things, after what had just occurred. Yet I was to learn that he was an excellent reader of body language and demeanour. As such, he could detect that I was still somewhat shaken and sought to distract me with seemingly meaningless talk, rather than discuss the skirmish and further worry my troubled mind.

I decided to probe further into Harold's background. "No noble English lady waiting for you back home?" I asked.

"Oh yes, because all the titled women in the country are queuing up to marry the son of a minor landlord from a town on the Welsh border," he replied sarcastically. That was an interesting revelation. From what I knew of Harold already, he was a young man of imperfect physique and modest birth who had trouble sitting on a horse. What his role could possibly be amongst the battle companions of a prince, I had no idea. "I'm not even sure that I'm English," he continued morosely. "My father undoubtedly is, but my mother always said she liked the idea of having a little bit of Welshman inside her. Of course," he grinned, "she never said it quite like that in front of my father. He might have taken it the wrong way."

I surprised myself by laughing. I liked Harold already.

Once we'd arrived at Châteauroux's outskirts, I didn't need to ask for directions to reach Richard's camp, for it covered the plains south-east of the town in a sprawling mass. I had expected some sort of fortified palisade ringing the encampment, complete with a ditch and perhaps timber watchtowers. Furthermore, I had imagined the interior of every military camp was clearly organised with regimented tent lines and defined boundaries.

What I saw instead was unfettered chaos. As was typical of Angevin armies in France, it predominantly comprised large mercenary contingents. Although probably better trained – and certainly more disciplined – than armies of knights and squires, mercenary groups famously do not cooperate particularly well as a cohesive force. As such, the different mercenary captains bivouacked their men in different places, which gave the impression of several miniature armies coincidentally camped together, rather than the whole encampment of a single royal army.

"Welcome to the most feared military force in all of France," Harold announced sardonically as he noted my bemused expression. "It's an absolute mess down there. But don't worry; it's even more confusing at night. It's usually impossible to find your own tent." He smiled impishly at me. "One morning I awoke to find myself in a tent with a strange Pisan man and his wife. I tried to be nice to them, but they didn't even offer me breakfast!" He sighed at their apparent rudeness. I wasn't quite sure whether I believed him, so instead I asked where all the mercenaries had come from.

"Where haven't they come from is more the question," he replied as we passed an indiscernible boundary into the camp's perimeter. The sentries, who evidently recognised Harold's distinguishable fiery hair, waved us through. "The Prince is famous for his aptitude for siege warfare. Successful sieges yield copious amounts of plunder, and copious amounts of plunder yield hundreds of delightfully loyal mercenaries. We have men from Brabant, Burgundy, Navarre, and all sorts of Italians. A real mixture. The only thing that unites them is their dislike of the English, which is probably caused by the fact that we steal their cheese. Don't tell Richard I said that."

"I somehow doubt it will crop up in our next conversation," I said drily. Glancing back at Châteauroux, I felt a strange pang of affection for the town that had only been my home for two months.

"Has Châteauroux ever been sacked?" I asked. I knew that it had changed hands many times during the past few years, but none of the buildings looked particularly devastated.

"Not to my knowledge," he replied. "In military terms, it's too valuable to devastate. Although I'm sure some of the more bloodthirsty mercenaries would disagree." Now that I was in the midst of a horde of soldiers for the first time, it was impossible not to notice how brutal they looked. Many of the mercenaries had faces engraved with a thatch-work of scars, some had missing teeth, and the entire camp was pervaded with foul smells. I tried not to think about their source.

Winding our way through the chaotic bustle of the camp, we eventually arrived at Richard's central pavilion, an enormous red tent which dwarfed the structures around it, even the abodes of the Angevin nobles accompanying the army. It was there that Harold left me, in order to return to his tent and change out of his military equipment. I did not want him to go, but I also knew that a baron's son could not be dependent on others; not that I had any intention of revealing my true heritage. Harold had been kind to me, but I doubted that the other proud nobles in Richard's entourage would be quite so welcoming to an unknown butcher's apprentice.

Ducking into the pavilion, I was initially surprised at how plain its interior was. It was littered with tables, many of which were covered with maps and hastily sketched diagrams of Castle Raoul. However, the space was dominated by a huge oaken dining table – how it was transported on campaign was always a mystery to me – around which ten men and four women lounged. I recognised some of the men from the earlier skirmish; evidently, this was where Richard, his retinue and their wives took their evening meal. Of course, few wives came on such campaigns, and those that did were hardy women indeed. Richard himself was not present.

Unsure of how to conduct myself in front of such high-born people, I took a few steps forward as muttered conversations ceased and gazes swivelled to meet mine. Glancing around the room for a friendly face, I wondered if I should speak, and perhaps introduce myself.

Evidently, there was no need. "Well, if it isn't our mighty butcher," the knight closest to me sneered, a haughty expression on his regal face. "Come to teach us all to carve steaks, have you?" A murmur of laughter sounded from the men and women around him.

"Prince Richard asked me to meet him here," I explained, refusing to rise to his provocation.

His eyebrows shot up in disbelief. "Do you really think our lord has nothing better to do than nursemaid lost boys?" he asked derisively.

"Be quiet, Sir Baldwin," another knight from across the table snapped. "Unless you want to explain to the Prince why you were rude to the brave young man who saved his life?"

Scowling, Baldwin turned back to his drink, and my rescuer beckoned me to sit beside him. Unlike Harold, this knight looked every inch a man of martial prowess. He was immensely tall and broad, with well-muscled arms and legs which resembled small tree trunks. Contrary to the fighting men I had seen outside, he was far from ugly, with high cheekbones, deep brown eyes and a mop of sandy hair. An equally attractive and refined-looking woman sat alongside him.

"By God, it's a pleasure to meet you," the knight said enthusiastically, shaking my hand as vigorously as a terrier shakes a rat. "I am honoured to introduce myself as Sir Oliver de Burgh. This," he gestured at the woman beside him, who inclined her head with a friendly smile, "is my wonderful wife Joanna." Without waiting for me to return the introduction, he ploughed on. "I can only apologise for Baldwin. He seems to disapprove of anyone having Richard's attention besides himself."

"I'm fairly sure every knight in Richard's retinue has that flaw," Joanna commented dryly.

"Not I, my dearest, not I!" Sir Oliver proclaimed, seeming genuinely shocked at the suggestion. "I am simply as loyal to Richard as I am to God. Just like this young warrior. Andrew, isn't it?"

"Alistair," I corrected him. "And I doubt I'd call myself a warrior. I've never killed a man before today. I barely know anything about fighting."

"Nonsense!" Sir Oliver reproved me. "That was a fine blow you delivered. You may not have experience, but I can tell already you have a fighter's spirit." His words stirred a cauldron of emotion within me: trepidation, uncertainty, but no small amount of pride. "Anyhow," he continued, "we'll need all the fighters we can get. We've received word that the King's brought his army from England to Normandy. Once we join forces with him, we mighty English will crush these French lice once and for all!" He slammed a meaty fist on the table to accentuate his words.

I was spared the need to match Sir Oliver's overbearing patriotism by the arrival of Richard, who swept through the pavilion's tent flap, accompanied only by his chaplain, a worried-looking man with constantly fidgeting hands. All those present began to rise, but Richard waved them down, then beckoned me to follow him to the far end of the room, away from curious ears.

"I'm not a man who generally has time for pleasantries, Alistair, so I'll cut straight to the important part," Richard told me in his deep, strong voice. Strangely, I had not noticed until now that he spoke in a thick French accent. He leaned forward intently. "Do you wish to serve as a part of my royal bodyguard?"

If I did not think anything else could have shocked me on that bizarre day, I had evidently been wrong. My mind whirring like a hummingbird's wings, I struggled to form a coherent answer. "Your Highness, I... I'm honoured, but I have no experience as a fighter. I'm sorry, but... I'm sure there are men better suited to the role." It was true. Every man – and most of the women – in the room had ten times the military experience and battle prowess I did.

"I disagree," Richard said emphatically. "Your intervention today was a message from God. You were meant to guard me, and from now on, you will. I suppose I shouldn't have framed it as a question," he said with a rueful smile.

There wasn't a lot I could say to that, although part of me was elated by his words.

"I do have one question, though," Richard continued, his thick brows furrowed. "How does a young Englishman with a noble name like Fitzwalter end up working as a butcher's apprentice in a French town? You even have your own horse!" He had clearly seen Raymond tied up outside.

I suddenly had a sick, plummeting feeling in my stomach. I was convinced that Richard would never allow me into his bodyguard if he knew I was an exiled son of a baron. In fact, I reckoned he would probably punish me for angering a baron in the first place.

And so I lied. I hated myself for it, but I lied. "I'm a distant cousin of a noble family from Cambridgeshire," I explained nervously. "My parents both died in a fire, so I set out for France in order to make my fortune, and this is where I ended up. I'm a nobody, Lord Prince."

Richard smiled broadly. "Well, we'll have to do something about that, won't we, my friend?" He grasped my hand. "Welcome to my bodyguard, Alistair. What's mine is yours. If you stay at my side, and stay loyal, you'll do well in my service."

I swore loyalty to Richard that evening. Thus, based on a lie, I entered into the royal retinue.

On that day, I became a soldier. Since then, it is all I have known.

Chapter 8

"I always knew you were a damned fool," Henry said scathingly. "Soon you'll be a damned dead fool, and the world will be a little less stupid." Evidently his wound had done little to dull his tongue. Indeed, to look at him, you would never have known that he'd received such a terrible injury just the day before. Although the butcher was still bed ridden, his face was full of colour and his voice full of scornful energy.

"You're probably right," I sighed. "I doubt I'm cut out for this. But who am I to refuse a prince?" Richard himself, along with Sir Oliver and a few other knights, had ridden to Castle Raoul to parley with whoever now commanded the garrison. The Prince had received word from an exhausted messenger in the early hours of the morning who carried news that King Philippe's army had advanced into the Loire Valley, apparently escaping the clutches of King Henry, and now pushed further west towards Richard. As important as Châteauroux was, the movements of the French King were far more significant. If Philippe was near, then the siege could not continue.

As such, Richard could not expect a full surrender from the castle. Rather, he demanded concessions pertaining to the way the townspeople were treated by the French soldiers. I had explained to Richard that the English had been hunted and vilified throughout

Châteauroux, and the bruised des Barres had apparently corroborated my story. Therefore, Richard's sole condition for leaving Châteauroux was that the English prisoners in the castle cells be released, and that the English townsfolk never be molested again. The French garrison agreed to his terms, though not without repeatedly demanding the return of des Barres, which Richard refused.

Henry didn't seem particularly grateful for these negotiations. "Interfering elitist pricks, all of them. The town was much better off before any of them came here."

I smiled. "I thought Châteauroux was being fought over long before you arrived?"

Frowning, he changed the subject. "So, I suppose you'll be leaving with the English army when it departs, being the seasoned warrior that you are?" he asked sarcastically.

"Yes," I confirmed. "I'm sorry, Henry. I don't like leaving you in this state." He snorted scornfully at that. "I'm sure the townspeople will look after you," I continued.

A look of amusement appeared on Henry's face. "I wonder if the cobbler will regret saving my life if I ask him to wipe my arse," he chuckled, wincing slightly as the movement aggravated the pain in his chest. When I did not reply, the older man noted my troubled expression and placed a reassuring hand on my shoulder. "Look, lad. You probably don't think you're ready for whatever it is you'll be doing. And maybe you're right. But you have a quick mind, and that's more than can be said for most of the useless lumps strutting around in battle. Just try to stay out of any politics – they can be more lethal than the meanest French soldier – and don't get killed. You might be an air-headed aristocratic wimp, but you're also a good man."

I smiled, grateful for his support, and hopeful that I would return to Châteauroux one day to see him again.

"Now go on," he said, returning my smile. "I'm sure the Prince needs his latrine emptied. You'd best get back to him."

I stood and walked reluctantly towards the door, turning back once as I neared the exit. "Thank you," I said simply.

Henry inclined his head slightly. "Good luck, Alistair Fitzwalter." It was the very first time he had called me by my name.

I looked away and walked briskly out into the street, not because I wanted to leave, but so Henry wouldn't sense the lump in my throat.

***

If I'd thought the day-to-day running of a military camp was disorganised, then the dismantling of such a camp was sheer pandemonium. Swarms of men and women clustered around the wagon park, frantic to store their belongings before the wagons were deemed too full. Mercenaries fought each other over meaningless items before their captains angrily bellowed for them to cease their stupidity. Wayward cattle and sheep meandered between partially dismantled tents, followed by agitated provisioners who had seemingly no control over their animals.

Harold, whose tent I'd shared the night before, stood alongside me with a wry expression as I surveyed the chaos. My few possessions, including Gilbert's locket, were already stored in Raymond's saddlebags. It seemed Harold was similarly unburdened; aside from his long, narrow-bladed sword and a bag stuffed with parchments, he travelled as lightly as I did.

I winced as a nearby Italian woman shrieked at her husband in her native language, presumably for forgetting to pack a small cooking pot which she now used to ferociously beat him. "This is madness!" I exclaimed. "How can an army so disorganised achieve anything?"

"They certainly don't mention this in your knightly stories, do they?" Harold commented mildly. "Though, in truth, the Prince's army isn't half as bad as some others I've seen. Last year, an army of King Henry set out on campaign with a hundred barrels of horseshoes, but not a single loaf of bread. I'll bet they didn't put that in the chronicles," he chuckled.

It was a full four hours before the army had assembled in marching order, and under the blinding radiance of a midsummer sun, Richard's three thousand men finally departed from Châteauroux, moving north-west towards Vendôme. Riding in the vanguard alongside the rest of the royal retinue, I twisted in the saddle to give the town one last wistful look, knowing that my civilian life disappeared along with the church spire and castle towers.

However, I did not dwell on such thoughts for long. Sir Oliver had insisted that I ride in full battle attire, and so all my concentration was required to simply remain in the saddle under the immense weight of hauberk, coif, and chausses. The chainmail was old and a little rusted – I suspected it had been taken from a casualty of yesterday's skirmish – and the indescribable weight of it caused me to ride hunched over. It was in those hours that I understood why foot soldiers never marched armoured; exhaustion would quickly set in, especially whilst enveloped by such searing summer heat.

"You know, I doubt Richard will be particularly impressed if his newest recruit dies of heatstroke within a day of joining up," Harold said dubiously, noting my drooping posture. He himself rode in a simple linen shirt: even the day before, I had not seen him sporting anything heavier than a leather brigandine.

"I think you underestimate our new friend, Harold!" Sir Oliver replied heartily. "He's coping just fine! Isn't that right, Alistair?"

I mumbled something incoherent, unable to articulate a proper sentence whilst my brain was being so thoroughly roasted.

"See, he's doing wonderfully!" Sir Oliver boomed, clouting me with what was supposed to be an encouraging pat on the back, but ended up throwing me against Raymond's chestnut mane. "Soon, this will feel like a second skin to him, and mounted on a horse as fine as his, he'll be as noble as any man who rides into battle with our Prince." Many of the knights in Richard's retinue had already noted how well-bred Raymond was, though most of them probably doubted I had the capability to ride him with any skill. Sir Oliver had even offered to buy the gelding for a princely sum, which I had declined as politely as possible. Harold had simply rolled his eyes at the thought of Sir Oliver purchasing my only means of travel.

"Even if he does survive the ride," Harold spoke as if I were not there, "how exactly is he going to survive his first battle? Richard seems to think he's blessed by God – and I'm not about to argue – but will God's blessing be enough to stop a French pole-axe from splitting him in half?"

"Thanks for that," I murmured, swaying slightly in the saddle. "Your confidence is ever so inspiring."

"Oh, you leave all that to me," Sir Oliver said confidently. "In any case, the best training for battle is battle itself. Now that Richard, Philippe and King Henry all have armies in the field, we'll have plenty of those." He spoke with relish.

I knew enough about Richard to be aware of the tensions between him and his father, which had been strained immensely over the years. "So, whose side will we fight on?" I asked them.

"No idea," Harold replied unhelpfully.

Sir Oliver frowned indignantly. "Richard will fight for his father, of course!" he asserted, his strident voice ringing across the French countryside. I was fairly certain we were out of Richard's earshot, but Sir Oliver was so deafening that every soldier in the column probably heard him. "Blood ties are more important than politics. If we can't trust kings and princes to respect their family, then what can we trust?"

"You know it's more complicated than that," Harold commented dourly. "Especially if the King continues to favour Prince John."

He was right, of course. We like to think that royal power derives from family, and the continuation of God's chosen bloodline. However, that idealism crumples before the stark reality that land is the greatest source of power in the world. Land allows for greater taxes, widespread purveyance, and a greater host of knights to be called upon in times of conflict. King Henry's favouritism of his youngest son, John, was carried out on the belief that Richard would continue to offer his full support due to family loyalty. By indicating that John might inherit the Angevin Empire, Henry shook Richard's support because the Lionheart's desire for land and power was so great. Indeed, Richard's inner conflict between his faith in his family, and his hunger for land, would shape the war to come.

But I am getting ahead of myself. For now, I was hot, exhausted, and about to be beaten to a pulp.

As the sun crawled reluctantly beneath a horizon of deep crimson, Richard's army came to a fatigued halt, having marched almost unceasingly for the last twelve hours along winding country tracks of uneven terrain. Knights and squires slid gratefully from saddles, and mercenary foot soldiers slumped wearily on the grass, not bothering to erect tents. Personally, I was looking forward to relaxing around a fire with my evening meal and removing that wretched armour.

Sir Oliver had other ideas. As soon as I had dismounted, he hailed me from a small, forested clearing which lay a hundred yards from the track we traversed. Trudging towards him, I noticed to my bemusement that his squire was dressing him for battle, although I was quite certain that there were no hostile forces for at least ten miles in any direction. I glanced back quizzically at Harold, who shrugged, although I think he knew what I was about to endure.

"As you've probably guessed by now, the Prince has entrusted me with the task of making you battle-ready, young Alistair," Sir Oliver explained as I approached. He held a blunted sword effortlessly in each hand, and a sinking sensation began in my stomach as I realised what he intended. "Wearing the armour all day was a good start," the knight continued, "but we often have to ride equipped for battle all day, and then still have energy to fight at the end of it." He offered me the hilt of one of the swords. Reluctantly, I accepted it with leaden arms and a heavy heart, knowing how hopelessly I was outmatched. Not only was Sir Oliver five or six years older than I; he was vastly experienced and strong as an ox. Although two months of manual labour in Châteauroux had toughened me slightly, the strength in my arms was still pathetic compared to the hulking warrior I faced.

Having equipped me with a lion-emblazoned shield, Sir Oliver first showed me his basic combat stance for fighting on foot: legs apart, shield held close against the body, shoulders hunched slightly. "The two most important features of a warrior are his strength and his armour. Strength allows you to beat your enemies into the ground, no matter how well-versed they are in the art of sword-fighting. Strong armour prevents the same from happening to you, and increases your weight, which makes you even stronger. As I shall now demonstrate." Without warning, Sir Oliver gave an almighty shout and barrelled into me, thrusting me clear off my feet with his shield. I crashed into the undergrowth at the edge of the clearing, head ringing and body throbbing all over. Wincing, I hauled myself to my feet, trying to ignore the protest of my battered muscles.

"How can I defend against an attack like that?" I asked dejectedly. Even if I had been prepared, the sheer weight and power of Sir Oliver would have been unstoppable unless I was a similar size.

"I'm afraid there's no easy answer to that," Sir Oliver replied with a small smile. "You just have to work on your physique. If you're bigger and stronger than your opponent, you've half won the battle already." I nodded at that truth and understood why Henry had stood no chance against des Barres when they'd fought in the butchery. "Now, see if you can stop my sword blows with your shield. If you can do that, I'll be open to a counter-strike."

For half an hour, I tried to do ask he asked. Although I managed to block some of his more half-hearted blows with my shield, the majority of his attacks melted my defences and dealt a crunching blow to my shoulder or midriff, which would flower into a ripe bruise overnight. Only once did I try to strike back, and Sir Oliver swatted my lunge aside with such force that my blunted sword was wrenched from my hand and spun into a hedge.

It was then that I heard a familiar sardonic voice from the edge of the clearing. "Enjoying yourself, Sir Oliver?" Harold asked casually, sauntering up alongside me. "Part of the proud de Burgh heritage to batter untrained butchers into submission, is it?"

I began to protest that such methods were necessary if I was to grow stronger, but Sir Oliver overrode me. "I'm not doing this for my own pleasure," he replied ponderously, drawing himself up to his full height so he could gaze down at Harold. "We're in the middle of a war, if you'd forgotten. I'm trying to help Alistair to survive. Rather a bruise or two now than a fatal wound when he first sees battle."

"So why are you teaching him that standing still and bashing each other's brains out is the only way to kill your opponent?" Harold demanded, exasperated. "Clearly your head is pure skull with nothing inside, so maybe it works for you, but other methods work better for other people."

I gasped involuntarily. Never in my life had I heard a knight insulted so brazenly, and I feared Sir Oliver's response. "Look, it's not really important..."

Sir Oliver cut me off once again. "What would you suggest then, Harold? Wetting yourself and hiding behind the nearest knight, hoping he'll save you?" To my astonishment, he was smiling. It seemed that such affronts were commonplace in the conversations, and the friendship, of these two.

"I suggest," Harold said mildly, "that we let Alistair watch you try to land a blow on me." He picked up my fallen sword and gave it an experimental swing, his bright blue eyes gleaming mischievously in the decaying evening light. If my contest against Sir Oliver had been unfair, it seemed this would be a complete mismatch; Harold was short and somewhat portly compared to Sir Oliver's magnificent physique. Yet in the short time I had known Harold, I already suspected that he had a remarkably sharp mind, and so I was intrigued to discover how he intended to reverse the odds.

Sir Oliver did not pause to consider his opponent's strategy. Determined to prove the merit of his methods, he attacked as I knew he would, by thundering towards Harold with shield outstretched, seeking to subdue the shorter man with his weight alone. Instead of attempting to match his brute strength, Harold nonchalantly twisted aside from the knight's charge, before swivelling with incredible speed to tap the back of Sir Oliver's chainmail coif. Turning with a deep growl, Sir Oliver swung his sword in a massive cleaving arc that could have concussed any enemy, but once again, Harold moved aside nimbly and touched his blade to Sir Oliver's left forearm before dancing backwards.

Harold's swiftness took my breath away. Unhindered by heavy armour, he was able to delicately step away from every cumbersome blow that came his way. By refusing to play to Sir Oliver's strengths, he had the knight struggling to land an attack. Yet Sir Oliver was a fearsome and experienced fighter and was not prepared to submit. Approaching Harold more cautiously, the knight feinted left and immediately withdrew his lunge to strike with a powerful overhead blow on his right. Unfazed, Harold dropped his sword entirely and rolled forward, grasping Sir Oliver's leg, his bright orange hair a stark contrast against the dull steel of Sir Oliver's chausses. Grunting with the effort, Harold gave an almighty heave, and like a colossal tree being felled, Sir Oliver toppled to the ground, landing in an ungracious heap of limbs and metal.

Leaping to his feet, Harold flashed me a broad smile. Aside from a slight sheen of sweat on his brow, he seemed utterly unperturbed by the rigorous fight he had just won. "You see, Alistair?" he said. "If you have awareness, and use your brain a little, no fight is impossible. Now, I think I've earnt a double portion of Richard's finest venison." With that, he turned back to the encampment, leaving me to haul Sir Oliver to his feet.

"I'd like to see him fight like that on horseback, or in a narrow street," the knight grumbled. I supposed he had a point.

I had thought that those few minutes had aptly answered my question as to why Harold had a place in the Prince's retinue. He was a remarkably fast swordsman, and that, surely, was why he had been plucked from his obscure background and placed in such a prestigious position.

Later that evening, I discovered the true reason.

Long after the sky's grey murkiness had dissolved into a black blanket, Richard and his companions sat in a loose circle around a crackling fire, exchanging stories and jests, as was their custom. Perched upon a tree trunk, and finally clothed more comfortably, I quietly enjoyed the evening, gazing in awe at the company I now kept. Sir Oliver, who had evidently recovered his spirits, embarrassed me by extravagantly telling the tale of how I'd rescued the Prince by cutting down four French soldiers single-handedly. I haltingly tried to explain the reality of the situation but was drowned out by the cheers of the knights around me, which were led heartily by Richard himself. I noted that a few men did not cheer; Baldwin, who had mocked me previously, was one, and another sullen soldier glowered at me from beneath a fringe of dark hair.

As our fire began to wither and fade, Richard held up a hand for silence. "Harold, would you bless our ears with your voice before we turn in for the night?" he asked solemnly. I looked in surprise at my companion, who had been as quiet as I had in the last few hours. Harold nodded, took a deep drink of water, and cleared his throat. Not knowing what to expect, I imagined he would sing some sort of bawdy soldiers' song.

When he opened his mouth, I was transported to another world.

To this day, I find it impossible to adequately describe the atmosphere which Harold's singing created. It was certainly the purest voice I have ever heard, more flawless even than the choirs in the great abbeys and cathedrals of England. Yet it was more than that. It created a certain stillness within you, and indescribable tranquillity which lifted you out of your present situation and floated you gently in a sea of thought. It was a chilling song of loss, of family left behind, of the desperate inevitability of change. A merest whisper of wind brushed against my cheek as I listened, and with it a plethora of memories drifted in and out of my consciousness like ghosts, impossible to grasp, but painfully tangible, nonetheless. I saw the malicious glare of my father whose gaze penetrated my soul like needle-sharp icicles. I saw Alice's goodbye, her belief in me shaken by my own overwhelming self-doubts. I saw the knife slicing into Henry's back, my failures obvious as his eyes begged me not to leave him.

But then the song changed. I do not remember the words. I doubt anyone did. The melody was still haunting and solemn, but the sense of tragedy had vanished, replaced by a swiftly flowing current of hope and possibility. Although the final embers of our fire flickered out, the field, the forest and my future suddenly held no darkness. I was entirely unaware of the shivers down my spine or the wetness on my cheeks as I allowed the song to take me, to lift me soaring through the fields and up into the sky, glorious in its mission to disintegrate my worries, and imbue that beautiful night with an aura of magical calm.

Chapter 9

The next three days of the army's march were basked in exquisite sunlight, the crystal blue sky unblemished by any streaks of cloud. On the first morning of this fine weather, Sir Oliver jovially declared that he wished to lead a foraging party. Although Richard always established supply trains to follow his troops, these were often unreliable, especially in enemy territory. As such, several groups of soldiers per day rode out into the arable French farmland in order to secure grain which could supplement the supplies trundling in from the west. Despite the fact that these expeditions were usually led by mercenary captains, Sir Oliver insisted that he take on the responsibility; I think he disliked the slow pace of the column's march, and wished to explore the surrounding countryside. I eagerly volunteered to accompany him, partly to provide Raymond with some proper exercise, and partly to escape the hostile glances which were constantly levelled by certain members of Richard's bodyguard.

Thirty of us rode eastwards, ranging off the well-established paths which armies typically followed, and venturing into the local manors which were held by French lords of dubious allegiance. In fact, the majority of nobles in the Berry and Loire regions had switched sides numerous times in the past few years, according to the whims of the war.

"How do we know that it's enemy grain we'll be stealing?" I asked, drawing up alongside Sir Oliver. "Surely if the lords here are friendly to us, we risk angering them by plundering their land?" Although still weighed down by heavy armour at Sir Oliver's insistence, I had been allowed to remove the compressing mail coif, so I could at least articulate my thoughts clearly.

"I wouldn't worry about that too much, Alistair," Sir Oliver replied diffidently, looking down at me from atop his mighty black destrier. "I doubt that anyone who occupies these manors knows who they fight for. Both sides gather supplies from the region, so they probably don't feel a great allegiance to anyone. Regardless, every time an army passes, they'll lock themselves up in their grand houses and keeps, so I doubt we'll meet any resistance."

He wasn't wrong. A mere twenty minutes into our expedition, Sir Oliver's squire spotted a dilapidated grain warehouse which stood at the edge of a cluster of golden-carpeted barley strips. We saw no animals, but that was hardly surprising; the horses and oxen used for such farming were usually kept on the lord's common pasture, which was nowhere in sight. The granary was in poor repair, and the timber creaked ominously as a group of mercenaries wrenched the doors open. A meagre pile of barley was stored inside – which was unsurprising, given that the last harvest had been ten months ago – but Sir Oliver still whooped with joy at the discovery.

"I thought we were the royal bodyguard, not royal foragers," Harold grumbled as his horse ambled up behind me. He had only reluctantly agreed to come because of my dogged insistence; he had seemed subdued since his unforgettable song the night before, and I was determined to question him about his talent.

"Royal thieves, more like," I said wryly as I watched the mercenaries gather huge armfuls of grain and stagger to their horses. "I assume this sort of 'foraging' has become common for the French people. I can't imagine it ever happening in England." The idea of marauding armies plundering the fields surrounding Little Dunmow seemed somehow inherently wrong. Such was the peace in England itself that I never imagined a war occurring there, at least not in my lifetime.

Oh, the naivety of youth.

"Well, if soldiers came to my home town, they'd be severely disappointed unless they were in the market for sheep dung," Harold told me with an amused smile. The granary empty, the mercenaries were laboriously remounting, complaining to each other as they were impeded by stuffed saddlebags.

"Your home town? I suppose that's where you learnt to sing?" I asked in a deliberately offhand manner.

Harold's smile vanished. "I taught myself to sing, and I taught myself to fight. That's all you need to know." He spoke bluntly, without a trace of sarcasm or mirth.

Sensing that I trod on uneasy ground, I rapidly changed the subject. "What's got him in such a chipper mood?" I enquired, indicating Sir Oliver, who was chattering happily at a bemused-looking Italian mercenary about the best way to cultivate barley. Not only was the knight clearly clueless on the subject, but the mercenary didn't speak a word of English.

The grin returned to Harold's face instantaneously, as if our last exchange had never happened. "I got up early this morning – your trumpet-like snores made certain of that – and thought I'd seek out Sir Oliver so I could steal some of his breakfast. Instead, I overheard him talking to his wife Joanna. It seems that he's been sticking his great-sword in more than just Frenchmen, because she seems fairly certain that she's pregnant." Disregarding Harold's crudeness, I smiled at the news and the great elation which it had evidently brought Sir Oliver. I had known him for barely two days, but his happiness was simply too infectious to ignore.

"Between you and me," Harold continued quietly, "some of us had been starting to doubt whether or not this would ever happen. They've been married for four years now, and that's a long time to wait for a first child. If Sir Oliver wasn't so loyal, and so attached to Joanna, he probably would have replaced her by now."

He spoke bluntly, but he spoke an unfortunate truth. Infertility is a desperately sad situation for a noblewoman, especially a noblewoman married into a family as prestigious as the de Burgh line, as it removes the only real power they have in our society. I have heard it said that women control all Christendom, because women control men. If that is the case, then all of those women are mothers and fertile wives.

I hoped sincerely that Joanna's pregnancy turned out to be genuine.

Our foraging party discovered one more warehouse that day, built next to a deserted French monastery, which Sir Oliver piously refused to take any grain from, as he was unwilling to risk God's displeasure.

"Don't you always say that God is on our side?" Harold asked him as we turned our horses back towards Richard's army. "So surely He wouldn't mind us taking a few kernels from the fat monks here? I'm certain He'd prefer that to robbing starving peasants."

"Oh, do stop asking such impertinent questions," Sir Oliver said impatiently, though not aggressively. "My mother always told me not to associate with redheads. Heads dyed with the fires of hell, she said. It seems she was right. You want to be careful about questioning God, or it might just be that you'll never meet Him!" He had not, I noticed, addressed the point that Harold had been making. I myself was surprised at Harold's cynicism. Although I said prayers, attended mass, and respected God's power, I did not devote my entire being to pointless genuflections and mind-numbing piety, which was an attitude probably fostered by Father Geoffrey's spiritual negligence. I wondered what Harold's reason was.

We returned to the Angevin army as the sun reached its zenith in the sky, having traversed a land that seemed utterly absent of civilians. Clearly, there were people who still lived here, as the fields had been sown, and the hovels we'd seen had still been standing. I imagine that the peasants had simply become adept at hiding.

Over the next few days, Richard kept his column moving northwards at a brisk pace, forcing a relentless march from dawn until dusk, pausing only briefly in the early afternoon to avoid the worst of the blazing heat. I assumed that his rapidity was caused by a desperation to catch and destroy the army of King Philippe, and so finally end the war which had caused so much instability and turmoil in France over the past decades. Indeed, when the Prince received word that Philippe had sacked the Angevin-held settlement of Trou, burning the town and taking a group of knights captive, he urged the army to increase its speed even further. I pitied the foot soldiers whose blistered feet must have ached insufferably by the end of each day. To their credit, however, I did not see a single squire or mercenary drop out of the line of march; evidently, Richard's force consisted of only seasoned campaigners.

I now understand that Richard was not chasing Philippe at all. Doing so would have drawn him ever deeper into French territory, where he could have easily been cut off from his supply lines and surrounded. Instead, he was attempting to link up with his father's army in Normandy, so that the two of them could combine forces and conquer the remainder of Philippe's land together. Of course, if family cooperation had been that easy, then the French kingdom would have been vanquished many years beforehand. Yet it was a constant feature of those wars that father and son could not effectively pursue a shared goal. Evidently, Richard now believed that could change.

What did not change were the tireless sessions of mock combat I continued to endure with Sir Oliver. Every night without fail, I would garner a new patchwork of bruises as I struggled to evade the hammer-blows of his sword, which would barely have time to heal before my next beating. I tried desperately to replicate the quick, deft movements which Harold had shown me, but I was hampered by the weight of my armour, my inexperience, and Sir Oliver's uncanny ability to read my position and know what my next movement was going to be. To his credit, the knight's words were patient even if his blade was not. Indeed, since he had discovered his wife's pregnancy, Sir Oliver had not spoken a word in anger. "It's just about practice, Alistair," he sighed on the third evening of the march. "I have a lot more experience than you, and I wasn't lying when I said that battle is by far the best way of becoming a more proficient fighter. Trust me, ten minutes of actual combat is worth ten months of messing around with toy swords." I seriously doubted I could survive my first minute of battle, let alone ten, but I was grateful for his supportive words, nonetheless.

Unsurprisingly, not everybody in the camp was so encouraging. The following morning, Harold, Sir Oliver and Joanna rode three abreast, discussing which barons in England were likely to pledge support to Henry or Richard if the two ended up fighting each other. Wary of any conversation which might involve my father's name, I drifted back towards the rear of Richard's bodyguard, where I encountered Eustace de Quincy, the man who had glowered at me over the campfire before Harold's song. He was a Scot, the second son of a loyal companion to King William of Scotland. A greasy-haired man with a sour disposition, de Quincy had been accepted into the royal guard on political grounds, in order to foster positive relations between King William and Prince Richard – or so Harold told me. He certainly wasn't included for his glowing and friendly personality; indeed, he had only grown more acrimonious since he had been tasked with guarding the captive Frenchman des Barres, who sat sullenly on a small palfrey.

"Hiding from Sir Oliver after he humiliated you again?" de Quincy mocked me in his slimy voice, lisping slightly from his bulbous lips.

I attempted to ignore him, turning my gaze to the rolling hills and fields to my left.

"I think he's too lenient on you," he continued, persistent in his attempts to needle me. "If I had his job, I'd batter you into the ground until you couldn't walk. That might teach you that pathetic peasants have no place guarding a prince."

Unable to dismiss his taunts any longer, I turned to face him, forcing myself to look in his cold, grey eyes. "What exactly is your issue with me, Eustace?" I asked. "Of course, it's going to take time if I'm to become a proper warrior like you or anyone else here. Bad attitudes like yours aren't going to help." I think I already understood why he was so quick to criticise me. He was a very young man, perhaps nineteen years old, and before I arrived he had been the youngest member of the royal guard. As such, he was determined to assert his dominance and show everyone that he was no longer the weakling of the group.

"Help? I don't want to help you!" he exclaimed petulantly. "I want you gone, and I'm not the only one. Sir Baldwin doubts you, and so do most of the others. I would rather fight alongside a woman than you. I would rather fight alongside a Frenchman!"

"I can assure you that no Frenchman would be proud to call you a battle companion," des Barres muttered, addressing de Quincy, and surprising me by speaking English. The huge knight had been slumped over in his saddle but stirred at the insult to his countrymen.

De Quincy stared indignantly at his previously docile captive. "And what would you know of battle prowess, French pig?" he sneered. "I'll remind you that it's not me riding swordless! It's not me who idiotically rode out of his castle during a siege!"

Des Barres drew up to his full height. His presence was dominating, even though he wore only a plain leather jerkin. "And I'll remind you, good sir, that this young man," he gestured at me, "cut down one of my finest soldiers while you skulked at the back of the fight. You are ever so aggressive with your tongue, but your sword has barely been drawn in anger. Every man here is a greater fighter than you, and more honourable as well."

Eustace's nostrils flared as he fired a hostile glance at des Barres. For a moment, I thought the hot-headed Scot would draw a weapon, but instead he scowled and turned to me. "It's your turn to nursemaid this arrogant fool, butcher's boy," he snarled. "I've had enough of his stench for one day." Oblivious to the curious looks his stinging words had attracted, Eustace thrust his heels into his horse's flanks and pulled ahead of us.

"If that sort of man is the future of knighthood and chivalry, then I should weep," des Barres sighed. "If I had sword or lance, I'd show him how a true knight conducts himself." He turned to me and gave a hint of a smile, which seemed an unnatural expression on such a rough and battle-scarred face. "At least you seem to be respectable, my young adversary; as humble as a monk, and as brave as that butcher back in Châteauroux."

I frowned, puzzled by his tone. "But I killed Estienne, your soldier," I reminded him. "You must feel some animosity towards me."

He shrugged. "I try to judge men by their character, not by the side that the tide of war has carried them to," he told me, running a hand through his copper-brown hair. "I have immense respect for your prince, for example, and knights such as William Marshal. Yet if I met either of them on the field of battle, I would attempt to kill them, if that is what my king wished."

"You would certainly kill me without breaking a sweat," I said wryly.

Des Barres gave me a long, measured look. "Yes, I would," he said eventually, "but you do not know the true measure of yourself until you have been tested in battle. Until you have seen the enemy's terrified eyes, until you have heard their dying screams, until you witness your friends being butchered around you, you do not know if you are a destined to be a simple soldier or a genuine warrior. I suppose you will discover that for yourself soon enough."

I struggled to sleep that night; such was my intense contemplation of his words. What if I faltered and ran at the first sight of an enemy? What if I could not look a man in the eyes and take his life? The itch for battle I had felt before still wriggled through my veins, but it was now mingled with a persistent feeling of doubt.

I did not have long to mentally torture myself over such issues. The next day, the fifth of the march, our scouts brought news that the Count of Vendôme, who had been doggedly neutral throughout the war, had now declared strongly in favour of Philippe. His town, Les Roches, and his castle, the Château Lavardin, blocked our path north. We could have found a route around and continued on to Normandy, but that was not the way of Richard the Lionheart.

Des Barres had been right. My first battle was upon me.

We would fight.

Chapter 10

Les Roches fell into our hands without a sword being raised.

Of course, the Count of Vendôme would have been a fool to attempt to protect it. The town itself was completely indefensible, as it was a tiny settlement of trade and commerce built on a wide, flat plateau. Instead, the Count had pulled all of his soldiers inside his fortress, and the townspeople had evidently followed.

As soon as Richard's army arrived, bathed in the withering humidity of a July afternoon, it set about the arduous business of establishing a camp, much like the one I had witnessed outside Châteauroux. Tents were raised in a rough semi-circle, animals were driven into makeshift pens, and siege engineers began the laborious task of preparing their mangonels for battle. They would certainly be necessary for the daunting task that lay ahead.

I rode alone to a small hillock outside Les Roches to examine the defences of the fortress which Richard was so determined to capture. If I had been concerned about my first taste of combat beforehand, then the sight of what lay ahead filled me with a sickening sense of dread.

The Château Lavardin was a modern fortress of terrifying proportions. It was constructed upon an enormous rock promontory towering over Les Roches, with sheer, insurmountable slopes to the sides and rear which made anything but a frontal assault impossible. Such an attack would have to be carried out against the forty-foot curtain wall which ran along the promontory lip and was dominated by an imposing stone gatehouse and covered in high battlements. Even if an army fought its way past such intimidating defences and into the inner enclosures, it would then be faced by another curtain wall and a brand new keep almost a hundred feet high. Protected by three monumental towers, the keep loomed over the rest of the castle, the town, and indeed, the whole of the Loire Valley. It was truly a marvel of contemporary architecture and one of the most frightening castles in all of France.

"Impressive, isn't it?" a deep voice said from behind. I glanced back and saw Richard approaching; he had somehow escaped his permanent flock of knights, priests and clerks, and now walked his horse alongside me to stare thoughtfully at the Château Lavardin.

I nodded, too nervous to look Richard in the eye. Instead I gazed at the white lion and golden lily emblazoned on the flag of the Count of Vendôme, which flew proudly above the gatehouse. "When I saw the castle at Dover on my way to France, I thought it must be the most magnificent in all the world," I told Richard. "But then the castle in Châteauroux, and now this? It seems these strongholds are more common than I thought."

"It's true," he said, "monstrosities like this are springing up all over Europe. I sometimes think my father only taught me two useful things in my entire life: how to build castles in stone, and how to tear them down to rubble. He certainly didn't teach me how to be a good politician. Or a good father, or husband."

I wondered if he talked to all his soldiers so intimately. I was unsure whether I should respond, then bravely surged ahead. "I think you'd be better than your father at all those things," I said. Naturally, I did not know at the time whether I spoke the truth, but they were the words of a young man in awe of his chivalrous hero.

Richard laughed. "Some would consider those words treason!" he exclaimed. "But I'm not inclined to disagree." Modesty was never an attribute he claimed. Smiling, the Prince moved a few paces forward so he could turn and hold my gaze. "So, Alistair, how would you go about sieging Château Lavardin?" he asked.

I couldn't have been more surprised if he'd just asked me to become the Pope. Richard had at least a decade's experience of siege warfare, so the notion that he needed the advice of a clueless eighteen-year-old was ludicrous. Determined to earn his respect, I gave the most logical answer I could think of. "I suppose I would use the catapults to batter down the outer walls," I ventured, "and then surround the keep, and try to force the French to surrender?"

Richard acknowledged this with a nod. "I'm glad you said that, for that's exactly what I want Vendôme to think I'll do. But we don't have time for that," he was talking faster now, "so instead we'll set up the artillery, fire a few shots, and then storm the walls with an escalade." He slammed a palm with his fist to accentuate his point. "After that, we sweep up the hill. As for the keep, we'll storm that too, and kill everyone inside who lifts a blade against us!" He had spoken with a furious passion, as if his words themselves could force the walls to crumble. It was difficult not to share his infectious enthusiasm for battle, and I felt a small shudder of anticipation down my spine.

My zeal was soon to be dampened. "I have an important task for you, Alistair," he said, speaking intently. "Once the battle commences, I fear that des Barres – who I know you are acquainted with – will attempt to escape. He has accepted parole, and surrendered his sword, yet I fear that the tug of patriotic loyalties will prove too strong if he sees and hears his countrymen dying." I could see the sense of his words. Des Barres had the reputation of being amongst France's greatest knights for a reason, and it was difficult to imagine him staying docile throughout a battle. "That's why I'd like you to guard him during the attack tomorrow," Richard continued. "I need someone strong, and someone responsible, who won't allow him to make any mischief. Can I rely on you to do this? I'm not sure who else I could ask."

I eagerly accepted, thrilled to be entrusted with such an important task.

"Oh, and one more thing," Richard said as he was turning to leave. "I've been meaning to return this to you. I hope it reminds you of the great service you have already done to me, and of the immense faith I have in you." To my amazement, he produced the cleaver I had used to save his life and handed it to me. I spent the rest of the evening with a warm, satisfied glow pervading every inch of my body, content in the knowledge that I was both valued and needed.

It was only later, much later, that I realised how cleverly Richard had manipulated me. Watching over an unarmed man was not a difficult or honourable job. Richard's reasons for choosing me were twofold. Firstly, he knew I was utterly unprepared for battle, and would likely get myself killed, having served no real purpose in his army. Secondly, and more importantly, Eustace de Quincy, who usually guarded des Barres, was a more experienced and valuable fighter than I, and he could not be wasted as a camp guard. Yet instead of merely informing me that I was not allowed to fight, which would have certainly caused a great deal of resentment between us, Richard had appeased me by discussing his battle plans, asking my opinion, and then offering me the role of the French knight's warden by dressing it up as a noble duty.

Richard may have been an expert at managing battles, but he was also a master of managing men. The priests and the chronicles will not tell you that, for they do not know him as I did.

The morning of our assault dawned grey and dreary, as if God was sickened by the prospect of bloodshed and had cast a looming shadow over Château Lavardin. Although I did not expect to see any combat, I had struggled to sleep at all through a night punctuated by the sharp cracks of mangonel stones striking the castle's outer wall. As Richard had explained, he did not expect his catapults to create a breach, but merely trick the defenders into thinking that we were settling down for a long siege. Many men had not tried to sleep at all, but instead sat drinking and talking with their companions in a futile attempt to take their minds off what was to come.

Sir Oliver and Harold came to speak with me half an hour before the escalade was to begin. Sir Oliver, fully encased in steel, looked every inch a man of immense combat prowess, but Harold wore only a studded brigandine and leather skull-cap, and could have easily been mistaken for the knight's awkward squire.

"I see you're looking after our pampered Frenchman for today," Harold greeted me with an indecent level of cheerfulness. "I suppose it's no bad thing that you'll be watching us from back here. When Sir Oliver falls off his ladder, you'll be there to scrape him off the ground and dry his tears."

"Oh, please," Sir Oliver scoffed, "I'm not the one with Welsh blood. The first sight of a French crossbow will send you scampering back to whatever barbaric valley you came from."

Harold's eyes widened with surprise. "I seem to have taught our metal lump some semblance of humour! Unless, of course, he's being serious, and he genuinely hates me."

I smiled nervously at both of them. "Both of you, just... try to be careful, all right? I would hate to have to tell your mothers that you died in some meaningless skirmish." In truth, it was much more than a skirmish, but I was trying to keep a level head.

"My mother's probably forgotten my name by now," Harold laughed. "The French should be grateful that she's not here. I swear, that woman could knock down a castle wall with her fists if she were angry enough."

"Don't worry about us, Alistair," Sir Oliver reassured me. "We've both been in plenty of scraps and come out with nothing more than scratches and bruises. We'll do some more sword practice this evening, and Harold will be there, making immature remarks, and you'll wish some Frenchman had bashed his head in."

I waved them off with a heavy heart. Knowing that they could die today was an awful feeling and knowing that I could not be there to help them was even worse.

The mangonels, lined up next to a priory of St Martin which sat at the bottom of the promontory slope, continued to fire their projectiles as Richard's forces quietly deployed for battle. Eight ladder parties, each consisting of a hundred men, huddled behind the priory, out of sight of the defenders. These groups, one of which was led by Richard himself, would attempt to scale the outer wall, leap over the parapet and open the gate. A mixed force of knights, squires and mercenary cavalry waited in the streets of Les Roches to flood into the castle once the gatehouse had been captured. It all seemed so simple.

I stood outside Richard's pavilion and watched the catapults hurl their last few shots. Most soared harmlessly over the outer wall, but one connected solidly with an arrow loop on the gatehouse, which must have been poorly constructed, for the slit crumbled into a small hole. I prayed that the sentries on the wall were tired and unobservant, for it would take only one alert Frenchman to spot the ladder parties early and bring a horde of soldiers to pack the ramparts full of crossbows and spears.

At two hours past dawn, Richard gave an almighty shout and his ladder parties swarmed from behind the priory and charged directly at the right-hand section of the wall.

The battle for Château Lavardin had begun.

At first, it seemed as if Richard's plan was proceeding perfectly. His troops jogged closer and closer to the wall, towards a seemingly oblivious enemy who were still ducking down to dodge the catapult shots. I willed the French to stay ignorant of their impending doom, and they may not have reacted at all were it not for one brave soul who peered between the merlons on the wall and gave a panicked cry of warning as he caught sight of the Angevin soldiers. In response, the leaders of the ladder parties urged their troops to increase their pace, although it seemed they crawled up the slope, as if they were slogging through thick mud. Richard's soldiers were a hundred paces from the gate as the first crossbow bolts flickered towards them and an alarm bell screamed its warning from the gatehouse.

"He's failed," said a grim voice from beside me. Startled, I turned to see des Barres watching the assault with folded arms. "He'd hoped to be at the wall before the garrison noticed his presence. Now, they'd be lucky to gain any foothold in the castle." There was a note of satisfaction in his tone.

Filled with nervous energy, I wrenched my borrowed sword from its scabbard and levelled it towards the knight. "Get back inside the pavilion! Now!" I shouted.

He laughed. "What, and miss all the excitement?" he said, apparently unfazed by my bravado. "I want to see for myself if this 'Lionheart' lives up to his reputation. Besides, what exactly am I going to do? All the horses are guarded, and if the castle falls, then I'll be stuck in the middle of enemy territory." He peered over my head, looking at the promontory. "I don't envy whoever's going first up those ladders," he said mildly.

I spun back around and saw that the eight ladders were indeed being thrust against the walls. An ever-thickening crowd of French soldiers fired crossbows and hurled axes into the throng of Angevins who were horribly exposed at the wall's foot. The catapults had ceased fire for fear of hitting their own men. This had emboldened the enemy and convinced them to raise their heads and rain projectiles on the attackers. A few Italian crossbowmen attempted to fire back, but they could not properly target the French defenders who had the benefit of the rampart's cover. In spite of the increasing intensity of the missile barrage, Richard's men bravely scaled the walls in order to close the distance to the Frenchmen, who attempted to heave the ladders away from the battlements. I saw Richard, his bright golden circlet making him a target for every French missile, being forcibly hauled from a ladder by one of his bodyguards. The knight proceeded to climb himself and spasmed madly as an axe cut his skull open. He was followed by the distinguishable red and white surcoat of Sir Oliver, who climbed one-handed, sword aloft, before a piece of masonry was hurled from the ramparts, plucking him off the ladder and tumbling him into a group of friendly troops.

Although the groups of mercenaries close to the promontory escarpment were having some success in scaling the walls, the Brabant mercenaries who comprised the leftmost ladder party, closest to the gatehouse, were taking horrendous punishment. Crossbow bolts spat from arrow loops with merciless and rapid efficiency, turning the Brabant force into a charnel house of blood, dead flesh and crying men. Unwilling to see his entire unit turned into carrion, the Brabant captain screamed for his men to abandon the ladder, and his mercenaries fled, pursued by the missiles and jeers of the French.

The defeat of the Brabants sent a visible shudder through the ranks of Richard's army. Other groups of mercenaries looked nervously over their shoulders as the Frenchmen manning the gatehouse turned their attention to attackers further down the line. However well-trained, mercenaries are always loyal to money and not men, and most of them were probably doubting whether their salary was worth the cost of their lives. Richard roared at them to hold, to gain a foothold on the wall, and his knights dutifully thrust their way up the ladders into the maelstrom of French projectiles.

Meanwhile, my gaze drifted to the abandoned Brabant ladder, and then the hole in the gatehouse wall which had been created by the catapults earlier.

Suddenly, I saw an opportunity. Time seemed to slow, and I knew exactly what I had to do.

"You will stay here," I ordered des Barres. "If you try to run, you will be hunted down, and the whole of France will know of your cowardice."

If he was taken aback by my new surge of confidence, he did not show it. "I would never dream of besmirching my honour in such a way," he said haughtily. "I would never break parole. You have my word."

Without waiting another moment, I turned and sprinted away from Richard's pavilion, towards Château Lavardin and the cauldron of death which it had become. My sword and cleaver, both strapped to my belt, thumped against my rusted chausses as I ran, and I remember my certainty that the metallic clinking counted down the last seconds of my life.

Yet I did not care. In a golden moment of clarity, I had realised why some men choose to be warriors. It is not for friendship, nor self-fulfilment. It is for reputation. I was the true heir of Little Dunmow, I was part of a proud line of barons, and if I was to take back my title, then I had to forge myself a name as a warrior. But I could not do that by dawdling at the back of the field whilst other men built their reputations. Richard's concern for my safety was touching, but it was not what I needed. I will not claim that I was not afraid; indeed, it felt as if my legs had the consistency of freshly churned butter. Yet I was able to turn that fear into energy which propelled me inexorably towards those dark ramparts which spat an unrelenting torrent of death.

Sprinting past the catapult crews, I fixed my eyes on the fallen ladder which lay in a slight ditch beneath the gatehouse. Astonishingly, not a single crossbowman turned his weapon towards me, so fixated were they on Richard's ladder party and the other mercenaries who were struggling to force their way into the castle. My mind screamed warnings as I approached the gatehouse, alone and exposed, yet still I was ignored. Stunned that I was alive, I scrambled down into the ditch and attempted to wrestle the ladder into an upright position, but it was simply too heavy for me alone to lift. Looking around frantically, I saw a familiar shock of orange hair at the base of the nearest ladder party.

"Harold!" I shouted hoarsely, struggling to be heard above the clamour of battle. "Help me!"

Somehow, he heard me and ran over to assist, hugging the wall so that he would not be spotted by eagle-eyed defenders. "What are you doing here, Alistair?" he asked, exasperated. His eyes had a wild, flickering look to them that I had not seen before, and his helmetless head was smeared with blood. "You have to get back to the camp. There's no way to get up to the walls!"

"I think I've found a way," I told him, trying to stay calm despite the feeling of sick nervousness which enveloped my stomach and bowels. "Just help me get this ladder upright, and..." I gestured at the hole which had been blasted through the gatehouse arrow loop.

He understood instantly and his eyes widened with shock. "That's suicide!" he exclaimed. "There's only two of us, and there must be fifty Frenchmen in there!"

"I'm going," I said with the stubborn pride of youth. "Are you with me?"

For a second, I thought he would argue or refuse, but instead he gave a laugh which bordered on hysteria. "We're all going to hell sooner or later, so why not?" he said, and together we hauled the ladder up, propping it against the hole in the gatehouse; the gatehouse filled with enemy soldiers, who, for the moment, were still oblivious.

Inhaling a massive breath which I thought might be my last, I drew my sword and began to climb, with Harold panting as he scaled the ladder behind me. A crossbowman on the walls finally noticed our escalade, and his bolt whistled past my head, missing by no more than a foot. I could see nothing of the gatehouse interior, but I imagined a group of Frenchmen with crossbows trained towards the breach, who would turn my head into a pin-cushion as soon as it emerged.

My slippery hands frantically grasped at the last few rungs, and suddenly, the fear had vanished. I was no longer a frightened boy who had never seen battle. I was Alistair Fitzwalter, heir to Little Dunmow, and I would make the poets write glory-songs of the slaughter I brought to Chateau Lavardin.

I screamed once and hurled myself into the breach.

Chapter 11

I have been asked countless times how I've survived so many battles. Men will attribute martial success to all sorts of factors; faith in God, endless practice, sound strategy, the list goes on. What tends to be overlooked is the role that luck plays in both survival and success. The most experienced warrior, with the most tactically astute mind in the world, can be struck by a stray crossbow bolt, which snuffs out his life like a nonchalant breeze extinguishing a candle.

Without doubt, luck was on my side as I scrambled through the ruined arrow loop and into the gatehouse of the Château Lavardin. Not only were the Frenchmen in front of me oblivious to my escalade, but they were few in number; most of the crossbowmen assigned to the gatehouse had filed out onto the wall-walk in order to shoot at Richard's ladder parties. Twenty men-at-arms stood before me, protecting the precious gate winch that could unlock the castle's outer defences.

I took the first enemy unawares. The shrill battle cry still emanating from my lips, I thrust my sword two-handed into the back of a leather-clad soldier, who stiffened, arching his spine, before collapsing forwards. Knowing that maintaining the element of surprise was crucial, I spun around and clubbed a moustached Frenchman on the head with the blade. His face barely had time to register shock before he sank to the floor, inert.

By now, the remaining Frenchmen were realising with horror that an Angevin soldier had invaded the gatehouse, although most simply stared at me with appalled expressions. Two were quicker to react than their comrades and advanced on me with hefted shields and grim expressions, intent on pinning me in the corner of the room and butchering me. Desperate not to be trapped, I swung wildly at one of the Frenchmen, who staggered slightly as he caught the blade on his shield. Taking advantage of the fact I was unbalanced, the second enemy thrust at my midriff, and I instinctively twisted aside with a speed which stunned me as much as anyone else, causing the sword to merely graze my mail. Grimacing, the man-at-arms drew back his dented blade for a second attack but screamed instead as Harold's sword severed his right hand, then swept up in one fluid motion to spear him in the throat. Without pausing, my red-haired companion stepped lightly forward towards the first Frenchman, who was now recovering from my assault. Harold feinted once left, once right, then whipped his blade forwards to impale his foe through the neck, in the exact place he had struck the other soldier just seconds before.

Taking a shield from one of the fallen men-at-arms, I stood beside Harold, who slid his sword out of the

Frenchman's gullet with a sickeningly wet sound. When I had killed my first man, back in Châteauroux, I had been horrified by the viscera and vomited uncontrollably. I had almost wept at the thought of taking another man's life. Yet now, a mere week later, I felt different. The battle-fervour was upon me for the first time, and it was a glorious sensation. I knew that I would live through that day, that luck and God were with me, and that my sword had only had its first taste of enemy blood.

We were still horribly outnumbered by the Frenchmen in the gatehouse, but they were alarmed by the rapidity with which we had dispatched four of their comrades and were reluctant to attack. I could hear men climbing the ladder we had erected, but I was in no mood to wait for reinforcements. Bellowing "Richard!" at the top of my voice, I charged clumsily towards the soldiers protecting the gate winch. Dimly, I heard Harold echo my shout and match my pace, and I also faintly heard the clangour of the battle which still raged on and beneath the walls. But that conflict could have been a thousand miles away, for I was focused solely on a short, bearded Frenchman directly in front of me, and how I was going to kill him.

I realised later that the soldiers in the gatehouse were probably amongst the weakest in the French garrison. They had stayed to protect the winch because they thought themselves safe. None of them wore chainmail, and few boasted weapons of quality. In truth, they were probably farmers who had been drafted into the service of the Count of Vendôme unwillingly. They were not warriors.

In my eyes, they were only dead men.

Implementing the strategy that Sir Oliver had taught me, I presented my shield and hurled my weight into the bearded Frenchman, thrusting him back so that he sprawled into his allies. Utilising my momentum, I drew my arm back and lunged the blade into his belly, gritting my teeth with the effort. Ignoring his screams of anguish, I withdrew the sword, only to be struck on the arm by a wild-haired man whose weapon was evidently blunt, for it left no mark but a bruise. As I turned and savagely attacked my assailant, Harold whirled past in a flurry of steel, leather and flesh which left one man stabbed through the eye and another forlornly clutching his chest.

Learning from their mistakes, the French soldiers began to fan out and surround us in a menacing semi-circle. I had killed four men in total, and Harold at least that many, but we were still outnumbered five to one and the overwhelming number of our enemy forced us to back away from the winch. Sweat ran in rivulets down my forehead as I tried to summon the courage for another attack. I glanced at Harold, who breathed heavily, saw my look, and gave me a tiny nod. I steeled myself, raised my blood-spattered sword, and readied myself for an impossible fight.

But then, quite suddenly, the enemy were running. One moment, they had been advancing implacably, spitting insults, seeking to avenge their dead comrades. Then they had faltered, eyes wide with panic, and sprinted down the stairwell which led to the castle enclosures. My confusion at their flight evaporated as I saw Brabant mercenaries behind us, climbing into the gatehouse via the route we had used. Evidently, the captain had seen us manoeuvre the ladder into position and had come to reinforce us. We certainly needed his men, because the Frenchmen who had relocated to the wall-walk had now realised that the gatehouse was under threat. Intent on re-taking the guardroom, scores of Frenchmen were now trying to force their way back through the doorway. The long oval shields and short-shafted spears of the Brabants held them off.

I did not have time to thank the Brabant captain, for I knew that Richard's men were still dying on the walls. We had to end the battle for the outer defences quickly, and there was only one way of achieving that. Joining Harold by the gate winch, we heaved the enormous handle together in a circular motion. Gradually, the ropes attached to the portcullis below became taut, and my shoulders shrieked agonised protest as we wrenched the gate's immense mass upwards. Knowing they stared defeat in the face, the French soldiers on the rampart became even more desperate, and several fell to the sharp, precise thrusts of the Brabants who gleefully avenged their earlier casualties.

I did not see the wave of allied cavalry thundering towards the portcullis, but I definitely heard it. Sir Baldwin, who led Richard's cavalry contingent, may not have had the gentlest tongue, but his instinct in battle was as sharp as a needle. The moment that we began turning the lever in the guardroom, he gave the signal to his men. Hundreds of horse hooves drummed against the floor as they charged towards the promontory, sounding akin to an almighty avalanche.

As soon as they passed through the gate, the fight for the outer ramparts was over. Once the French defenders were aware of enemy troops behind them, they melted off the walls, all except a few foolhardy men who were swarmed and cut down by spiteful Angevins. Scrambling downstairs from the guardroom, I saw the Frenchmen attempt to flee the knights and mercenary cavalry who ruthlessly cut them down. Some ran towards the residential areas in front of me, and a few others bolted into side-enclosures which contained kitchens and underground storerooms. However, most retreated directly towards the keep, as the imposing towered fort must have seemed to be the only safe haven from the Angevin horse. Indeed, the keep appeared utterly impenetrable, and so we would have to settle down for a long siege after all. We had merely secured a tool for the inevitable negotiations which would now take place.

Exhausted from my exertions on the winch's crank, I leaned against the wall's interior and took several deep breaths. Suddenly, I was aware that I was terribly thirsty, but Harold had brought nothing to drink, and nor had any of the Brabant mercenaries. Now that my part in the fighting had drawn to close, I wanted nothing more than to eat, drink, and sleep for a day. I certainly did not want to speak with Eustace de Quincy, who had spied me and now sauntered over. Although fully armed and armoured for battle, his sword was unbloodied and his armour unscathed.

"Disobeying the Prince's orders already?" he asked mockingly. He seemed to be unaware of the human carnage strewn around us. "I've been protecting Richard with my life, and what do you do? Leave des Barres unguarded! He's probably riding straight to King Philip now, laughing at your idiocy!"

"Protecting Richard?" Harold said. "You couldn't protect a fortress from an unborn fetus!"

De Quincy ignored him. "It seems you have a lot to learn about serving a prince," he told me, although he had not accompanied Richard for much longer than I. In truth, I was now feeling a little nervous about the fact I had abandoned my duty. Would Richard embrace me for my impulsive actions, or punish me for refusing to respect the chain of command in my very first battle?

Pushing such thoughts aside, I asked de Quincy about the welfare of Richard and Sir Oliver. Unhappy that his taunts had failed to provoke me, he sniffed and reluctantly answered. "The Prince is unharmed, God be praised, but Sir Oliver took a savage beating. He scaled the ladder four times, trying to prove that he's some sort of hero, but he never even made it to the ramparts. His wife's seeing to his wounds now. I have no idea what she's doing here. It seems all the women came to the front lines without orders."

I admired Joanna's adventurous spirit. "But Sir Oliver will be all right?" I persisted.

"Worried that the only man in the army who tolerates you won't be around much longer?" he sneered. "He'll be fine. He took a big knock to the head, but there's nothing in there of value anyway, so I doubt he even felt it."

I turned to Harold, expecting him to enthusiastically agree, but instead he was staring intently at the keep's fortified entrance. "If you have a moment, gentlemen, it seems the day's entertainment is not over," he said mildly. I followed his gaze and saw instantly what had captured his attention.

The Count of Vendôme had blundered, and it seemed my sword's work was not yet complete.

The second gateway leading to the keep was wide open. Evidently, the Count had seen the outer wall's defenders streaming up the promontory's slope and had left open a path of retreat so that they could reach the keep. Yet the Angevin cavalry were amongst the fleeing Frenchmen, and I watched with astonishment as the mixed crowd of defenders and attackers were allowed to rush through the entrance in the secondary curtain wall. If the Count had simply shut his gate, he would have doomed the outer wall's defenders, but protected his fort against enemy incursion. Now, groups of knights, squires and mercenary cavalry were inside his final defences. Unless the remaining French garrison could eject these horsemen from the keep, Château Lavardin was on the brink of falling within an hour of the assault commencing.

Richard was quick to seize the initiative. From within a group of Angevin infantry huddled fifty paces away, I heard his voice roar: "To the keep, men, to the keep! By God's legs, charge the fools! We can end this right now!"

I did not expect many of his warriors to respond. Their horrifying experience of scaling the walls had left even the hardiest soldiers shaken and battered, with blood caked on their armour and sweat plastering their faces. Yet those who could walk rose to their feet, given renewed energy by the Prince's encouragement. Richard himself led a thick wedge of armoured knights and mercenaries, which myself and Harold scrambled to join. Together we surged towards the second curtain wall, intent on reinforcing our cavalry who were now embroiled in a fierce melee around the gates that still remained open. De Quincy was nowhere to be seen, but I did not care. All I knew was that my lord was headed into the part of battle where the conflict was fiercest, and I had to fight by his side.

Finally, Richard's finest troops were released to the slaughter, and how they excelled at it. Pent-up frustration and anger, garnered during their struggle to take the outer walls, now transformed itself into a bloodthirsty rage which was brutally exacted on the French soldiers attempting to secure the keep. I ran shoulder-to-shoulder with Harold, and a foul-smelling squire whose name I did not know, as we crashed into the flank of the enemy troops gathered in the small space between the keep and the inner curtain wall. Stumbling forward to find a target for my sword, I tripped on a dead horse and landed heavily on the corpse of an Italian cavalryman. Trapped in a forest of legs, I struggled to regain my feet, deafened by the grating sound of steel on steel, the confused commands which nobody heeded, and the piteous screams of the wounded. This was not a tournament fight of glittering lances and extravagant courtesy. It was a pushing match between two sides of frantic men whose only thought was to kill before they were killed. My sole focus was to not suffocate, as I was pinned to the rocky ground by the tight compression of Angevin and Capetian soldiers alike.

My suffering was alleviated only by the retreat of the French into the keep itself. They had been holding and had begun to cut down the intruding Angevin cavalry, but Richard's charge had broken their resolve. They now arrayed themselves for one final stand in the keep's ground floor, outnumbered immensely, but protected from outflanking by solid stone arches and walls. A few crossbow bolts were discharged from the keep's massive corner towers, but most of the remaining Frenchmen waited in front of us, spears levelled, shields held firm, prayers forming desperately on cracked lips.

Eventually scrambling to my feet, I grabbed the nearest discarded shield and followed the crowd of Richard's troops through the keep's main entrance arch, and into the barracks which comprised the ground floor. The Count of Vendôme himself stood at the centre of his battle-line, fearsome in his torn white surcoat, blood-encrusted mail and intimidating great-helm. Surrounding him were an elite bodyguard of burly, well-equipped soldiers who looked ready to fight and die for their lord.

The Count could have – and probably should have – surrendered. Despite his mistake in leaving the gates of the keep's curtain wall open, he and his men had fought bravely and well. Intent on securing their submission, Richard took a step forward, his armour clinking heavily in a room which was suddenly permeated by a tense quietness.

Before he had a chance to speak, the Count screamed at his men to charge, and they obliged. Vendôme himself made a beeline for Richard, and the two clashed blades in the centre of the barracks as their soldiers hurled themselves into the fray once more. Locking eyes with a helmetless Frenchman, I took three steps forward and flailed at him with a sudden energy, forcing him to duck behind his shield. He retaliated with a heavy strike from his spear which jarred my arm as I wrenched my own shield up to halt the blow. Leaning backwards instinctively, I brought my sword across and scythed it onto the Frenchman's sword arm, causing him to reel away in pain. I tried to follow, but the press of men was simply too tight. Instead, I was forced to ram my blade into the indiscernible mass of enemies before me, hoping to connect with something. I was rewarded with a howl of anguish as I felt my sword enter flesh. I could not see Richard, Harold or Vendôme, but all three still lived.

In the end, it was Sir Baldwin who decided the issue. Gathering his remaining cavalry, he ordered them to dismount and led them onto the curtain wall. Using a narrow wall-walk, his men crossed into the first floor of the keep and fell on the flank of the French troops with triumphant shouts of glee. Assailed from all sides and hopelessly outmatched, the Capetians began to drop their weapons and shout their surrender. Some of the Count's bodyguard fought on ferociously but were quickly surrounded and dispatched with multiple sword thrusts.

Yet the Count of Vendôme was not prepared to submit to English captivity. Leaving the remainder of his retinue to fight to the death, I watched the French commander flee down a small stairwell which led to chambers under the keep. Knowing the renown that his capture would bring, I shouldered mercenaries and squires aside and pursued. I was not the only one who had witnessed his flight; Harold too was chasing the Count and was a good ten paces ahead of me.

The gap between myself and Harold widened as we reached the foot of the stairs and sprinted through several murky underground corridors which were held up by timber supports. I realised that these tunnels led away from the keep, presumably to a secret exit on the promontory's steep slopes. My breath came in short gasps as I forced my leaden limbs to continue the chase; Harold was now out of sight, and I did not want him to face the Count alone. The twists and turns of the underground path sapped the remaining energy from my legs and I dropped my cumbersome shield to reduce the weight I carried. Forcing myself through sheer willpower to push on, I suddenly heard an echoing clash of swords, and saw a dim light as I rounded the tunnel's final corner.

Harold and the Count were locked in combat at the end of the underground path. From what I could make out, Harold had caught the Frenchman just as he was about to leap on a horse tethered by a small shed. The ringing of blades grew louder and louder as I lumbered towards them, and I was a mere thirty yards away when Harold ducked under the Count's sword and sunk his weapon into Vendôme's thigh. The Frenchman roared in anger as Harold's eyes widened with fear; the sword was stuck in the Count's flesh, and he had no time to react as Vendôme's mailed fist connected solidly with the side of his head. Instantly knocked into unconsciousness, Harold collapsed to the ground as the Count agonisingly extracted the blade impaled in his leg. I drew up in front of him and pointed my weapon at him with all the confidence I could muster.

"Submit," I said hoarsely, my throat dry with thirst. "You don't have to die today. We have Sir Guillaume des Barres captive in our camp, and you know his reputation. There is no shame in being captured by Richard the Lionheart."

"No shame?" he hissed. His leg was streaked with blood, his shoulders were slumped with fatigue, but there was a feral edge to his voice which unnerved me. "There's no shame in failing my king? No. You're all that stands between me and freedom. It's time for you to die, boy." He stepped towards me, swinging his sword in a huge overhand arc, which I barely stepped away from, narrowly avoiding being disembowelled. Knowing that I had to fight or die, I lanced my sword with as much swiftness as I could muster towards his great-helm, but the blade merely grazed off the thick steel. Growling, the Count rained three quick blows at me in succession, which I barely managed to parry. Desperate to escape his reach, I stumbled backwards into the daylight, then came forward with a lunge that the Count swatted aside contemptuously.

We were evenly matched. Both of us were exhausted, and the Count's leg wound hindered his mobility, which compensated for my lack of experience. For what seemed like hours, but must have been no more than a minute, we strove against each other, weapons either clashing or scraping against armour. Sweat poured off our faces and our breaths were ragged as I put all my strength into a clumsy sequence of looping sword strikes which Vendôme easily managed to deflect.

Eventually, the matter was decided by the quality of our equipment. Countering my attack, the Count placed both hands on his sword and swung a huge, graceless sideways blow at my head. Intuitively, I held my borrowed blade upright to parry, and the two weapons connected cleanly.

My sword broke. It simply could not stand up to the castle-forged steel of Vendôme's expensive sword, and it shattered in two, leaving me holding a useless stump.

Implacably, the Count raised his blade above his head for the killing blow. Out of nowhere, my mind's eye saw how Harold had defeated Sir Oliver during our practice, the day after I met them both. For the second time that day, I saw my opportunity and took it.

Using reserves of energy I did not know existed, I sprung forwards and ducked down, inside the reach of the Count's heavy sword. Drawing the cleaver from my belt, I twisted rapidly and struck the Frenchman's arm. The cleaver crunched through mail, flesh and bone, half severing the arm, and Vendôme gave a grunt of surprise as his sword fell from nerveless fingers. He dropped to one knee as I withdrew the cleaver, and blood spurted onto the summer grass.

"I... submit," he said weakly, gritting his teeth as pain wracked his body. "You have bested me. Please, take me to Richard." Hugely relieved that my ordeal was over, I placed my cleaver on the ground and stepped forward to help the Count to his feet, remembering that dignity and honour comes from helping a defeated foe.

It was then that I learnt the first rule of chivalry.

Never show mercy without good reason.

Roaring his defiance, the Count rose to his feet, snatching a jewelled knife from his belt and lunging it at my throat. Instinctively, I held up a hand to protect myself, and pain seared through my body as the knife sliced through my forearm, cutting into flesh as if it were butter. I staggered backwards, blood pouring from the wound, as Vendôme brought the knife up for the killing blow. If Richard hadn't struck from behind, I wouldn't be writing this tale.

The Prince's sword took Vendôme's head from his shoulders in a single, clean blow. The body stood still for a moment, as if puzzled, then flopped to the ground, blood fountaining from the truncated neck. The Count's head gently rolled down the slope we'd fought on and came to rest in a patch of dry grass.

I looked up at Richard, tried to speak, and then fainted.

Chapter 12

Reading back what I have just written, I make it sound all so straightforward. I found a way into the gatehouse, I helped to storm the keep, and I fought against the Count of Vendôme as he attempted to escape. All of this happened, but I could never adequately relate my exact experience in that battle, or any other. It would take a much greater wordsmith than me to properly describe the mental struggles that torment you in the midst of combat. Trepidation, horror, determination, pride; all of these emotions swirl through your head in an instant and are gone so swiftly that you are unsure whether they existed in the first place. It is like a perpetual nightmare, and although you are certain you keep waking up, the realities of battle swallow you again immediately. Yet it is an addictive nightmare that keeps pulling you back, keeps demanding that you test yourself and improve yourself both physically and mentally. For how else are we to gain recognition from our peers, and build the reputations that grant status and power in our society?

It is easy to forget just how young I was in those days. Youth can be both a blessing and a curse in a soldier; young men think themselves invincible, but their rash decisions can have a high cost. I was incredibly fortunate to survive the battle for Château Lavardin, and afterwards, I felt ten years older. This was not because I'd killed, or proved myself a hero, or served Richard and God faithfully, or any of that poetic nonsense. I felt older because I was beginning to understand the true nature of men, of war, and of power. I was beginning to understand that winning is everything.

It certainly did not feel like I had won anything when I awoke from my stupor after the battle. Even before I had fully regained consciousness, I felt the throbbing pain of the knife wound in my arm and inadvertently pictured the Count of Vendôme towering over me, poised for the kill. Snapping my eyes open, I did not pause to take in my surroundings, and instead scrabbled desperately with my left hand, trying to find a weapon. What if the battle was not over? What if there were still Frenchmen who sought to cut me to pieces?

"Calm down, Alistair, calm down, you're safe now," said a soothing female voice to my right. The first thought of my utterly addled brain was that the voice belonged to Alice, and that all the events of the past months had been a wild and unsettling dream.

Gradually, my eyes focused, and I found myself looking into the concerned face of Sir Oliver's wife, Joanna. I surmised that I must be in Sir Oliver's tent, a theory confirmed by the sight of the knight's sword leaning against the end of my makeshift bed. Wriggling into a sitting position, I noticed my arm was bandaged in a crude sling, though it did little to stop the pain which pulsed relentlessly into every corner of my body.

"I'm sorry, Joanna," I said, offering a weak smile which became a grimace. "I didn't know it was you. I suppose I'm still a little disorientated." I nodded towards my bandaged arm. "Did you do this?"

"Attack you with a knife? No, I don't think so," she replied mischievously. She was dressed unlike any noblewoman I had ever seen before; indeed, her tunic and hose looked distinctly practical and masculine. "I did bind up your arm, though. Luckily, the knife missed any major arteries, so I didn't have to cauterise."

I raised my eyebrows curiously. "You sound like you have some experience treating battlefield injuries," I observed. "I thought women of noble blood were only taught how to sew and stitch."

Her shrewd blue eyes crinkled as she smiled. "When you follow someone like Oliver for as long as I have, you tend to become a walking medical centre. I remember when he was your age, he was so clumsy, but he insisted on sword practice with experienced warriors every day. His skin was a permanent bruise."

I could relate to that. "Is Sir Oliver all right?" I asked, suddenly worried. "And Harold? Last I saw he..."

"They're both well, God be praised," Joanna assured me. "Just a little concussed. Trust me, they were the lucky ones. Twelve members of Richard's retinue were killed scaling the walls, and many more have nasty injuries. I've had a busy few hours."

I shuddered inwardly at the thought of the horrendous wounds I had seen during the battle. I did not envy Joanna's task at all. Throwing myself at the French blades had taken a great deal of willpower, but comforting weeping men who stink of rotten flesh required a different sort of bravery, a bravery I did not think I possessed.

It seemed her thoughts followed a similar pattern. "Physical wounds are bad enough – trust me, I would know, but..." she hesitated, frowning.

I was intrigued. "Go on," I prompted.

"Well, I sometimes worry about the mental wellbeing of those in this army," she confessed. "You all act as if you're the toughest and most loyal soldiers in the world, not fazed by anything. But there are human beings inside you too. You aren't just killing machines!" She spoke the final sentence loudly to emphasise her frustration. "I'm concerned that the stress of battle has adverse effects on all of you. I know you haven't been here for long, Alistair, and I apologise if this is too forward, but how are you coping with it all?"

I was touched by her concern. It was certainly true that I would be reluctant to talk to Sir Oliver or Richard about any mental weaknesses I had, and Harold would probably brush it off with a sarcastic quip. I decided to answer her as truthfully as I could. "I don't know, if I'm honest," I replied. "I think I'm still in a state of shock. I'm just trying not to think about it. If you do stop to think, then taking another man's life probably becomes impossible. It certainly isn't as easy as they make it sound in the stories." I shrugged. "I suppose it's too early to tell whether the life of a soldier will change me or not."

Clearly, my answer hadn't satisfied her, and an agitated expression crossed her face. "But do you think constant exposure to battle is more likely to make someone prone to anger? More likely to… react poorly to bad news?" She had begun to pace up and down the tent and was becoming visibly stressed. I was starting to think that her concern hadn't been for my sake at all.

"Bad news? What are you talking about, Joanna?" I queried with a frown.

"News that would cause Oliver a great deal of displeasure," she whispered, now barely able to look at me. "I shouldn't be saying any of this… I mean, I barely know you, but… well…"

"And how's the champion of Château Lavardin doing?" Sir Oliver boomed, erupting through the tent flap unannounced. Joanna, who had seemed to be on the verge of tears, turned away to regain her composure. Although Sir Oliver usually showered attention on Joanna, he now didn't notice her discomfort, as he was entirely focused on me. "God has truly blessed us with your presence, my friend. First your heroics in Châteauroux, and now you storm a fully guarded gatehouse by yourself! You've got to leave some room in the chronicles for me, Alistair!" I very much doubted, even at that young and naïve age, that any songs or chronicles would detail the battle of Les Roches and Château Lavardin. There had been hundreds of such engagements over the last twenty years, and the monks would run out of ink before they could describe every one.

"I wasn't even supposed to be there, Sir Oliver," I reminded him, shifting my arm to a slightly more comfortable position. "And I wasn't alone. Harold was with me, and I wouldn't have survived without his help." I was certain that I spoke honestly.

"I suppose the Welsh runt does have some skill with a sword, however unorthodox his technique," Sir Oliver grudgingly admitted. "He's still unconscious, but Joanna assures me he'll wake soon. Isn't that right, my love?" He turned, then a perplexed look crossed his face as he realised that Joanna had slipped out the tent while we had been talking. I considered telling him of his wife's peculiar behaviour before he had entered but decided against it. I did not want to be responsible for ruining Sir Oliver's ebullient mood, which in itself was impressive given his pained expression when he moved, and the scrapes and bruises which plastered his body.

In an attempt to distract the knight from his wife's disappearance, I asked him whether des Barres had caused any mischief after I left him unattended. Regardless of my actions on the battlefield, I knew Richard would be furious if such a notorious captive had been allowed to escape.

Sir Oliver seemed taken aback by the very thought that the Frenchman might break parole. "No, we found him in the Prince's pavilion, peaceful as a lamb. In fact, he was singing 'O Sacred Head Now Wounded' when I last saw him. Beautiful hymn, that; you'd have thought it was written by an Englishman."

"Maybe he was singing it to you specifically," I suggested wryly. Indeed, Sir Oliver's forehead now sported an enormous weltering lump, the size of half an apple. I winced at the thought of the damage he would have sustained without a helmet.

It soon became apparent that Richard did not intend to linger for long in Les Roches, as was his custom. Apparently unconcerned by the fall of Château Lavardin, King Philippe had marched to Paris to re-supply his troops and prepare for the conflict against King Henry, who still lingered in Normandy. Richard was therefore desperate to join up with his father as swiftly as possible, because together they would massively outnumber the Capetian royal army. Whether Richard and Henry could overcome their years of embittered disagreements remained to be seen.

For now, Richard was keen to see the back of Les Roches, and he left a garrison consisting of the Brabant mercenaries who had helped me secure the gatehouse. Their captain came to speak with me on the evening of our departure. He spoke a rapid and excitable French which I struggled to keep up with, but his pleasure was both evident and understandable; he was now entitled to a portion of the rents due to the new Count of Vendôme, an eleven-year-old boy who had watched his father's defeat and death from a room high in the keep.

Hearing that the Count had a young son was like a physical punch to the gut. I suppose it had been easier to dehumanise him when I had seen him only as a being of steel and sword, and I wondered how many fathers and husbands I had slain. I told myself repeatedly that I'd done what was necessary, and that I'd had no choice. Yet that weak justification rang hollow and untrue. Of course, I'd had a choice; I could have stayed in Richard's pavilion, and if I had, the new Count of Vendôme would still have a father. But Harold, Sir Oliver and Richard might also be dead. To put it simply, I had prioritised the life and wellbeing of myself over that of any Frenchman in Château Lavardin.

I didn't try to make excuses. I just knew I'd have to live with the guilt.

Such emotions did not prevent a surge of pride when Sir Baldwin presented me with a new sword as reward for my service. I recognised it instantly. It was the Count's blade which had so nearly skewered me and had broken my old sword as if it were made of glass.

Unlike many swords carried by nobility, it was not a weapon of overtly decorative beauty. Rather, it was designed as a perfect killing instrument, forged to transform its owner into a proficient swordsman, not a beautiful, glittering knight who would soon be a beautiful corpse. In fact, the blade's only clear adornment was a snarling silver lion engraved upon the pommel, accentuated by two tiny eyes of jade which brought pinpricks of colour to an otherwise grey affair. The weapon was not a two-handed great-sword, which could only be carried by the strongest brutes on the battlefield, like Sir Oliver or des Barres, but nor was it purely one handed. Instead, it was a hybrid bastard sword which could be wielded with either one or two hands for maximum flexibility. Such weapons were rare indeed, and I was entirely in awe   of it.

My reverence must have been fairly evident as I gazed adoringly at the sword on our ride away from Les Roches. Pulling up beside me, Harold tried to drag me out of my enraptured state. "You're giving that lump of steel more attention than most fathers give their new-born children," he observed dryly. "I don't think such a total obsession with a sword can be healthy."

"I'm not obsessed!" I protested. "I'm just... studying it. I'm working out its balance, and weight and..."

"Right, right, of course," Harold interrupted, pretending to believe me. "So if you're not obsessed, you'll let me hold the sword for a bit? I did stop the

Count from escaping, so I reckon it's as much mine as it is yours." Although not as dramatic as Sir Oliver's head wound, Harold's severe bruising near his temple must have given him dreadful headaches. To his credit, he didn't complain; he always was adept at hiding his pain.

I instinctively clutched my new sword closer to my chest, and then smiled sheepishly as Harold laughed. "Don't worry about it," he said. "Well-made as that sword is, I think I'll stick with my Wife-Tongue."

"Wife-Tongue?" I asked incredulously. "You named your sword Wife-Tongue?"

"Why not?" he replied with his trademark grin. "Sir Oliver said I should name it something lethal, dangerous and unforgiving. So I did. I personally think it's rather inventive."

"But you don't even have a wife," I told him.

"Probably because he's the kind of person who'd name a sword Wife-Tongue," Joanna interjected from behind us. Since her emotional outburst the day before, Joanna had carefully avoided me, and had only changed my bandage whilst Sir Oliver was present, so I couldn't question her in private. Whatever the issue was, I was certain that it would cause a rift between herself and Sir Oliver if ignored, and so I resolved to gently ask her about it at the first opportunity.

Harold sniffed, but did not disagree with her comment. "So I suppose you're going to christen your sword with some horribly pious or sentimental title?"

he asked. "A few months back, Prince Richard committed himself to the recapture of Jerusalem, and Sir Oliver immediately renamed his sword 'Saracen-Bane'. He didn't seem to realise that we weren't setting out east instantly, so now it sounds ridiculous. I recommended that he change the name to 'Saracen-Bane-When-We-Eventually-Reach-The-Holy-Land-But-For-Now-It's-Going-To-Keep-Butchering-Christians' but he refused to acknowledge my brilliant creativity."

Returning my gaze to the miniature lion carved into my sword's pommel, my mind was suddenly flooded with images of Richard, and everything he had granted me in the mere week since we had met. He hadn't been obliged to risk angering his knights by admitting me into his bodyguard, and nor had he needed to gift me this magnificent sword, which could have been used so much more effectively by a more experienced warrior. My young, impressionable self idolised Richard and dreamed of forging myself a fearsome reputation equal to his. More than anything, I wanted to repay his undeserved trust in me. I wanted him to be proud.

"Lion-Pride," I said quietly, lifting the sword so that the sunlight shimmered gloriously off the thick steel blade and illuminated the lion's eyes into two dazzling circles of fluorescence. It was not the most original name, nor the most poetic, yet it perfectly summed up the state of my being at the time. To be as brave and proud as Richard was my ultimate desire. The priests tell us pride is a grave sin. If that is true, then Richard, myself and most of the knights in Europe will one day roast in hell together.

Harold didn't seem to appreciate the solemnity of the moment. "Great!" he declared. "Now that we've got that incredibly vital decision out of the way, how about we catch up with the rest of the bodyguard before they start wondering where we've got to?"

Startled abruptly out of my thoughtful trance, I realised that Raymond had stopped entirely and was grazing placidly by the side of the track. A group of passing mercenaries sniggered at the sight of a dazed-looking young man ogling a sword with a glazed expression, but I paid them no heed. Quite suddenly, I was happier than I had been in months. I had survived my first battle, I had the favour of a prince, and I could not wait to take Lion-Pride in a conquering swathe across France. Afterwards, I would return to Little Dunmow, confident and enriched, to cast down my father and brother and take my rightful title. Whooping with joy, I kicked a surprised Raymond into a gallop and thundered down the length of the column, enjoying the simple pleasure of the wind through my hair. I heard Harold laughing behind me, not because he understood, but because my pleasure was so infectious.

My joyful mood lasted the entire journey to Normandy. Where everything started to go wrong.

Chapter 13

I have been told numerous times that King Henry the Second, the founder of a mighty Angevin Empire and arguably the most powerful man in Europe, had once been a handsome young man with inexhaustible stamina and admirable enthusiasm for his work. Evidently, such commendable attributes had either been eroded by age or withered by years of conflict and antagonism with his family.

When I first laid eyes on the King in his makeshift throne room in Château d'Harcourt, my initial impression was that of tiredness and decay. Strangely, he reminded me of an old hunting dog my father owned when I was young. The ancient mastiff had once been the leanest and fittest of the pack, but age had deteriorated his limbs so that he walked stiffly, wheezed frequently and slept for most of the day. Robert had predictably declared the dog to be useless and had incessantly demanded that we kill it so that it no longer drained our resources. Alice had stubbornly refused and won the argument. The dog spent its last weeks peacefully sleeping on my sister's lap, bathed in the mild sunlight of an English summer.

It was obvious that King Henry had nobody to offer him comfort in his old age. He was one of the most foul-tempered men I ever met and was in particularly fine form on that oppressively hot mid-August day. The King had summoned the Prince and his retinue for an audience as soon as we arrived at the royal encampment, and it seemed that Henry intended only to lambast his son for his perceived failures.

I shuffled behind Richard's retinue down the length of Château d'Harcourt's grand dining hall, trying to appear inconspicuous. Although it was doubtful that any of King Henry's nobles who lined the walls would recognise me, I was not taking any chances, and instead observed the faces of my weary travel companions. Richard gazed intently at his father as we approached the end of the dining hall, his face betraying no emotion. Sir Oliver smiled at friends and family amongst the King's barons and captains, and Harold's eyes flickered from side to side, although I had no idea who or what he was looking for. Eustace de Quincy looked utterly bored and surveyed the room disdainfully as if every man there was beneath him.

King Henry glowered menacingly at us as we drew up in front of his temporary throne. The expensive fur and ermine which swathed his body could not disguise his mottled complexion and weathered skin, whilst his hair retained only a tinge of its auburn colour. His heavy, jewelled crown seem to physically weigh down his entire body, and I wondered if he could even sit a horse properly, let alone ride into battle against the French.

Aside from the music of a small cluster of lute and harp-wielding musicians, a tense silence pervaded the room. After only the slightest hesitation, Richard dropped to one knee, and his retinue rapidly followed suit. The King did not speak, although everybody present expected him to. Our host Robert Harcourt, and Henry's chaplain, who stood in positions flanking the King, frowned in confusion.

Eventually, Richard glanced up and broke the silence. "Your Majesty..."

"The elm at Gisors has been cut," King Henry spat, interrupting his son barely after he had begun speaking. Evidently, he had intended to wait for Richard to talk before he overrode him. Such was typical of the way Henry conducted himself; he was outwardly antagonistic in conversation in an attempt to assert his dominance. He never did learn that such aggressive techniques simply alienated potential allies.

The King's words had meant nothing to me, but they caused a murmur of consternation amongst the assembled nobles and soldiers. "I know, Father, and I think it unimportant," Richard replied calmly. "The gardening habits of Frenchmen concern me little."

A vein in the King's forehead bulged. "You are impertinent, as ever," he retorted. "The elm has been cut, and you have done nothing to end the war against the mongrel Philip!"

Sir Oliver later explained to me the significance of the tree at Gisors. The ancient elm had marked a traditional place of conference between the King of France and the Duke of Normandy, and so symbolised the merits of peace and discussion between the Angevins and Capetians. Frustrated at Richard's breach of the January treaty, Philippe had ordered the elm cut down. Doing this had sent a clear message: he now had no use for diplomacy, and fully intended to end the war through military force. Of course, this was a bluff, perhaps intended to drive a wedge between Henry and Richard.

If that was his plan, it was working. "Not a fortnight ago, I assaulted Château Lavardin and slew a strong supporter of the French King," Richard said, rising to his feet. He had clearly been riled by his father's unfair accusation. "Before that, I rampaged through Quercy and Berry, reconquering huge swathes of land which Philippe had attacked. Your army has been encamped in Normandy for over a month. Pray tell me, what have you done?"

For a moment, I thought the King would stand, so that he could berate his son from the steps of his throne. Yet the physical effort was too much, and Henry soon slumped back in his seat. "I have been trying to negotiate, and finally end this godforsaken war," he grumbled. "In case you'd forgotten, it was you who demanded marriage of Philippe's sister. How exactly do you intend to follow through on that if you're recklessly attacking his castles and burning his towns?"

Richard glared at him, and the King sighed tiredly. "John would never have gotten us into such a mess," he asserted.

That struck a nerve. Richard took a sudden step forward, and God knows what would have happened if Robert Harcourt, owner of the castle, had not stepped between them. "Your Highness must be exhausted from the ride," Harcourt said placatingly to Richard, "and Your Grace must be hungry. How about we sit and eat? My cellar full of wine isn't going to empty itself!"

Visibly inhaling to gain control of his anger, Richard murmured his assent. Henry did not provide an answer. He simply ignored Harcourt and beckoned a serving girl to sit on his lap, then laughed as he fondled her. Turning away in disgust, Richard retreated to the far side of the dining hall, and a general mumble of uneasy conversation broke out amongst the assembled nobles.

In truth, I had not been paying a great deal of attention to the dialogue between the King and his son. In fact, I had been completely enraptured by the lavish finery of both the people and decoration inside Harcourt's dining hall. It was certainly a far cry from the stinking, bloodstained interior of Château Lavardin, and I marvelled at how these men and women could daintily laugh and drink whilst such a terrible war loomed on the horizon. I am now old enough to know that the silks, velvets and food are not mere opulence; they are a display of power, a tool to keep the peasants in their place, a way of showing they are loved by God.

"Alistair?" Sir Oliver's strident voice interrupted my thoughts, and I turned to see him standing beside an older man and woman, whose attire was as flamboyant as any in the room, as well as a young man my own age. "I would like to introduce my parents, as well as my brother, Hubert," Sir Oliver said, beaming. "They're here to show their support for the King in these troubled times." In truth, I suspected his parents had travelled to Normandy to see their son, as they were landowners, not warriors. They greeted me effusively – his father gripped my newly healed arm so fiercely that I barely suppressed a yelp of pain – whilst Hubert simply nodded in my direction. He seemed as overwhelmed by the occasion as I was.

When the introductions were over, Sir Oliver's face assumed an apologetic expression. "I'm sorry I have to drag you away from this splendid occasion, but could you fetch Joanna from our quarters?" he asked. "She was feeling a little unwell earlier, but my family would love to see her, and congratulate her on the pregnancy!"

I gratefully accepted the excuse to escape the stifling grandeur of the dining hall. As much as I admired Sir Oliver, his overbearing praise could be a little embarrassing, and I did not think I could cope with the appreciation of four de Burghs at once.

As I walked to the quarters assigned to Richard and his bodyguard, I pondered whether it was futile to keep up my charade. Surely, sooner or later, Richard would discover that I was an exile. Indeed, I was certain that a number of men in the dining room knew that Alistair Fitzwalter had been hounded out of Little Dunmow; they simply had never seen me in the flesh before. I considered whether my deeds at Château Lavardin would persuade Richard to accept me, regardless of my past. The problem lay in the nature of the accusations against me. The Prince was fully committed to participating in the upcoming Crusade, so it would be a political disaster if he was seen to be sheltering the murderer of a priest. In addition, his own personal piety, whipped into a fervour by the prospect of a Crusade, would likely turn him against me. Perhaps, I thought, the revelation of my true identity should wait until after we had returned from the East. It would be easier to explain myself if we were not surrounded by a whirlwind of religious fervour.

I was so absorbed in my thoughts that I almost did not hear the gentle sobbing emanating from the chamber shared by Sir Oliver and Joanna. My hand froze a few inches from the door, reluctant to confront whatever was causing her such hardship. I imagined that her sorrow was somehow connected to her strange words a fortnight before, and it honestly surprised me. There are huge numbers of women who struggle through immense poverty and hardship every day, but Joanna was not one of them. There are also countless women who are subjected to demanding and abusive husbands and are viewed as nothing more than a producer of heirs. Again, Joanna was not one of them. Sir Oliver was not an outwardly sensitive man, but he treated his wife with a gentleness that touched my heart. Why, then, was she crying in her chambers instead of discussing her issues with her husband?

It may sound ridiculous, but walking through that door was as difficult as hurling myself through the breach in Château Lavardin. Intruding on private grief is never easy, and Joanna certainly had not been expecting visitors. As soon as I looked into those weltering red eyes, a flurry of emotions crossed her face: shock, guilt, and finally anger. "Get out!" she screamed, her sorrow transforming to rage almost instantly.

Immediately regretting my interference, I hastily backed out of the room's entrance. Before the door could close, however, I heard a resigned sigh. "You may as well come in," she said quietly, her breathing still irregular from sobbing. "You'll only go and tell Oliver about this, and that'll just make everything worse."

I tentatively re-entered the room and leaned against the door to ensure we were not disturbed. Joanna, who sat upon her elaborate cushioned bed, resolutely refused to meet my gaze. For at least thirty seconds neither of us spoke. I was frightened of speaking insensitively and shattering her fragile frame of mind. Yet I was determined to discover the source of her tears. Isn't that what chivalrous men do? Courteously assist ladies in trouble? I should have fetched Sir Oliver – he knew his wife far better than I did – but the accursed pride of youth drove me to try and help Joanna by myself.

"You must swear not to tell Oliver," she said suddenly, whipping her head up to stare me in the eye. Her face was tear streaked and utterly miserable, but defiant. "If you tell him, it'll be the end of our marriage."

"I doubt that very much," I scoffed. "Sir Oliver…"

"Is a good man, and I love him more than anything," she cut across me. "But his family and his honour are more important than I am. I'm worthless to him." I could see tears beading at the corners of her eyes again.

I knew that if I didn't say something, she would be reduced to incomprehensible tears again. "Look, Joanna," I said, trying to sound as calm as possible, "I haven't known you, or Sir Oliver, for very long. But it's already obvious that you're the single most important thing in his life. Whatever it is, I'm sure he'll stick by you. I'm sure…"

"I'm not pregnant," she spat. "And I never will be."
She hurled the words at me, as if by doing so she could
cast her problems away. "I'm barren, Alistair. Do you
have any idea what that means for me?"

I was too stunned to reply. Sir Oliver had been so
buoyed by her pregnancy, and Joanna had appeared so
joyful as well. Yet all this time, her happiness had been
a mere mask to hide her desperate deception. "Are...
are you sure?" I asked hesitantly.

She treated that question with the scorn it deserved.
"Am I sure?" she repeated incredulously. "I was never
pregnant in the first place, you half-wit!" She buried her
head in her hands and started sobbing again. "What
should I do, Alistair? If I tell him, he'll be forced to set
me aside and take up with a more fertile woman," she
shuddered visibly at the thought, "but I can't keep up
this deception forever. It's tearing me apart."

My mind raced as I considered what advice to give
her. It was true that Sir Oliver's family would never
accept the fact that the heir to their estates was
married to a woman who would never provide him with
a child. Joanna would be shunned for the rest of her
days, and probably forced into a convent. Yet the
practicalities of keeping the secret were almost
impossible.

To this day, I regret the words that I spoke next.

"Don't tell him," I urged her. "No one needs to
know. If Sir Oliver finds out, it'll only cause catastrophe

and heartache for everybody involved. You can be a good wife to him without having children; I know that, but I doubt his family do. For your own sake, don't tell him."

"But what about my pregnancy?" she wailed. "How can I explain the fact that I lied about it?"

"Don't reveal that you lied," I advised her, my mind racing. "Make up some accident – you fell off a horse, perhaps – which caused you to lose the baby. That way, you won't face accusations of falsehood."

I could tell that Joanna was reluctant to accept my advice. Keeping up such a deceptive and permanent lie gnaws away at you and can erode relationships much more viciously than a difficult truth. Yet she was also grateful for the suggestion that she wouldn't have to face up to an impossible confrontation with her husband, and so she nodded miserably.

In the two weeks prior to that conversation, I had received copious amounts of praise – much of it from complete strangers – for my courage and valour at Château Lavardin. Yet, in those few sentences, I had proved just how gutless I was. It was true that I was concerned for the happiness of Sir Oliver and Joanna, and that I was worried about Joanna's future if knowledge of her infertility became public. However, I also feared for myself. Sir Oliver was a steadfast and generous man, and the impact of such news could embitter him to the extent that he wouldn't mentor me anymore. He was one of the two men in the army that I could truly call a friend, and the thought of losing that friendship was an awful prospect. In that instant, when Joanna had asked me for advice, I prioritised my own needs over the truth.

Coward.

Reassuring Joanna that I'd excuse her absence in the dining hall, I left her bedchamber, only to be instantly greeted by an unwelcome face that was plastered with a sickly smile.

"It's incredible, the things you hear whilst idly strolling the corridors of a castle," Eustace de Quincy said triumphantly. Why he was near Sir Oliver's bedchamber – or away from the dining hall at all – I had no idea.

I felt the blood drain from my face. "How much did you hear?" I demanded, praying that he'd only arrived in the last few seconds.

"Enough to know that the de Burgh family tree won't be sprouting any new branches in the foreseeable future," he replied smugly. "It also seems like you've been a naughty boy, Alistair. Trying to keep this a secret from Sir Oliver, who's been so very tolerant of your failures? Disgraceful."

"You can't tell him," I pleaded. "Imagine what it would do to Joanna. She'd be forced to leave her husband, and pressured into a convent, or worse. You can't do that to her!"

"Why not?" de Quincy asked, seeming genuinely confused. "A noble man like Sir Oliver doesn't want to be stuck with a barren husk. She's of no use to him. Now's the best time to tell him — his whole family is gathered in that dining hall, so they can all hear it at once!"

Panicked into action, I stepped forward and grabbed de Quincy, pinning him against the castle wall. A dull pain throbbed from the almost-healed wound in my arm. "You will not speak a word of what you heard here, understand?" I growled, staring straight into his shocked grey eyes, which were inches from mine. "I slaughtered more men than I can remember two weeks ago, and I won't hesitate to do the same to you if you cross me."

It was all bravado — I would never attack another member of Richard's retinue — and de Quincy called my bluff. Hatred flared in his eyes as he spat full in my face, and as I recoiled, he thrust me backwards against the cold stone floor. I tried to scramble upright, but he pressed me into the ground with a heavy boot and fixed me with an icy stare.

"Who the hell do you think you are?" he hissed, crushing his boot harder into my chest. "Do you think you frighten anyone, with your pathetic words, your peasant's background and your scrawny body? My father is the closest companion to the King of Scotland, you worm. If you ever threaten me again, I'll have you strung up like the wretched felon you are."

De Quincy removed his foot and I scrambled to my feet, desperately gasping for breath. His words had caught me off guard, as they had reminded me that it would be a political disaster for Richard if de Quincy, the Scottish representative in his army, were to come to harm.

He now smirked at me. "Perhaps I could be persuaded to keep my mouth shut," he said lightly, "but my silence will not be free."

"What do you want?" I asked nervously. He had me perfectly ensnared for any type of blackmail he desired, and I awaited his demands with trepidation.

"Let's start with a little respect," he suggested sweetly. "I think you should show the deference to me that you should have shown since we met." He paused for a moment, twirling a lock of his greasy hair in his fingers. "Kiss my feet, or I go to Sir Oliver and tell him Joanna's filthy secret."

I almost lunged at him again, but barely managed to contain the instinct. I feared to fight him here, in such a heavily populated castle, where his political immunity would be at its strongest.

For the second time in the space of a few minutes, I demonstrated my feebleness.

Despising myself, I knelt. I pressed my dry lips to the filthy leather of de Quincy's boots, trying to ignore his chuckles of amusement. "We're not finished, you and I," he assured me as I rose and wiped the dirt from my mouth. "By keeping quiet, I'm damaging my honour and risking God's wrath. So I expect you to make it up to me. If I want you to shoe my horse, you'll do it. If I want you to clean my armour, you'll do it. You're a peasant, Alistair, and it's time you started acting like one." With that, he strode down the hallway, still sniggering to himself, leaving me utterly humiliated.

God had punished me for my cowardice, and thus I became a slave.

Chapter 14

The next few weeks were a flurry of frantic activity as the largest Angevin army in a decade prepared to move in a joint offensive against the French King. So many nobles, knights and squires were crammed into Château d'Harcourt's walls that some were forced to quarter in the mercenary encampment outside, much to their outrage. The castle kitchens worked incessantly to produce enormous sacks of twice-baked bread, barrels of salted beef, and colossal wheels of cheese which looked as heavy as horses. Harold once joked that we should have deployed those cheeses in battle by rolling them down a hill into the French. "Imagine King Philippe's tombstone," he chuckled. "Bravely took up arms against cheese and lost. He will be missed."

Whilst the logistical preparations were surprisingly efficient, the planning of the proposed campaign was a disaster. King Henry and Prince Richard constantly bickered about strategy, to the extent that the army did not march until a full week after it was ready to depart. Richard proposed a rapid strike into the heart of Philippe's territory to besiege Paris, in order to capture the French King and immediately end the war. This, he argued, would allow the Crusade to commence as swiftly as possible, which was the greatest priority of all Christendom. Unwilling to throw his men against the formidable ramparts of the French capital, King Henry demanded a more patient approach. His plan was to advance towards Mantes, burning and looting the French countryside, in order to undermine Philippe's authority and draw him out from Paris. If there is one trait that the King and the Prince shared, it was stubbornness. As such, not one of their discussions in Château d'Harcourt ended on a genial note.

One evening, the majority of Richard's retinue sat eating and talking quietly in the secondary dining hall which had been allotted for the Prince's personal use. Sir Oliver and his wife were not present, as Joanna had told the false tale of her miscarriage that morning, and Sir Oliver had spent much of the day either consoling her, or closeted in his chamber, wracked by personal grief. I was tormented by the guilt caused by the knight's suffering, but I consoled myself that his sorrow would be much greater if he were to discover Joanna's infertility.

"Do you think Sir Oliver will be all right?" I asked Harold anxiously as we ate.

He considered my question as he noisily chewed a mouthful of bread. "Yes, I think he will," he said eventually. "As you might have noticed, our friend tends to wear his emotions on his face. For a couple of days, it will seem that he'll never smile again, but then he'll suddenly return to his normal self like nothing happened. Last year, he vowed to give up the martial life and become a monk, such was his grief at his grandmother's passing. Obviously, that didn't happen, though I think he'd look quite dashing with a robe and tonsure."

As with so many of Harold's stories, I wasn't sure whether to believe him, but I was pleased by the news that Sir Oliver would recover quickly.

"No, I'd be more concerned about Joanna," Harold continued in a more serious tone. "I imagine losing a baby is a horrific situation for any woman, but it must be even worse for the noble wife of a first-born son. I told you before that there were whispers about her ability to carry a child. This will only worsen the situation."

A look of consternation must have crossed my face, and Harold frowned. "Alistair? What is it?"

I was saved by the arrival of Richard, who strode into the dining hall in a malicious temper, his face beaded with sweat and red with anger. He had evidently just arrived from a particularly unproductive discussion with the King and was ready to vent his frustration.

"Why has God cursed me with such a lazy and indolent excuse for a father?" he shouted at no one in particular, silencing the room instantly. We all knew that his relationship with the King was tense at best, yet he had never been so brazen in his criticism before.

Sir Baldwin bravely tried to pacify him. "Your Highness, your father is an ageing man. Perhaps his advanced years have simply made him wary of the bold and daring plans you favour."

Master Philip of Poitou, Richard's elegantly dressed clerk, added his voice. "He speaks true, Your Highness. Thirty years ago, I am sure that the King would have approved of your plan mightily. Yet all elderly men are prone to caution."

"Caution?" Richard scoffed, shaking his head vigorously. "No, this isn't caution. You don't know my father like I do." He stood tall at the head of the table and addressed us all, apparently unfazed by the prospect of publicly denouncing the King. "He disagrees with me for the same reason he won't let me marry Philippe's sister. The same reason he won't force John to join the Crusade. The same reason he imprisoned my mother. He's a weak, conniving man who fears any member of his family matching his power. He's terrified of the reputation I could gain by attacking Paris. In his mind, it's more important to undermine me than to win this war."

Another of Richard's most trusted advisers, Sir William L'Etang, responded to Richard's string of accusations. "Be that as it may, Lord Prince, what choice do we have? Do we declare war on your father and fight two kings at once? God has blessed you with a keen mind for battle, but turning against your father would be a terrible, terrible risk."

Richard made to respond angrily to the knight's words but managed to control himself. Instead, he simply sighed. "I know, William, I know. It just frustrates me that my father will never grant me the recognition I deserve. I apologise for my outburst; all of you are the finest companions a prince could hope for, and my anger towards you isn't justified at all." He turned wearily towards where I sat with Harold. "I can think of only one way to lighten my mood. Harold, would you sing for us?"

Because of my close proximity to Harold, I was probably the only one to notice, but he stiffened momentarily as that question left Richard's lips. Recovering almost instantly, he smiled. "It would be a pleasure, Your Highness," he said. Perhaps I only imagined the note of reluctance in his voice.

A hushed silence fell upon the room as Harold drew a deep breath. The enchanting melody which caressed the ears of every listener wove a tale of dreams and adventure, of the majesty and mystery of faraway lands. Yet this time, I was determined not to be swept away by the powerful feelings which Harold's song summoned. Instead, I intently gazed into my friend's face, trying to read his expression. The candles which lined the hall lit up his pale face and transformed his eyes into miniature pools of dazzling blue.

But they were eyes utterly devoid of emotion.

It suddenly dawned on me that Harold's song was a thing of beauty, but not warmth. His words brought joy to everybody in the room but himself. The realisation baffled me immensely. Why would he take no pleasure in such an incredible talent? Usually, Harold had more life and vigour than anybody else I knew. Yet when he sang, he became colder than the frost on a winter's grass.

As I pondered this, I became aware of a sharp, prickling sensation in the back of my neck. Turning to look at the source of this instinctive warning, I became aware that someone else wasn't fully focused on Harold's song. Eustace de Quincy was staring directly at me, a small smile playing on his lips. Our confrontation had only taken place two days beforehand, and he was yet to burden me with any demands. I shuddered to think of the demeaning ordeals he was mentally concocting, but if I was to keep Joanna's secret safe, I had no choice but to be a pawn in his game – for now, at least.

His first demand came the next day, and it was entirely predictable. Ever since he had been appointed as the guardian of the captive des Barres, de Quincy had complained incessantly that it was a role which was not worthy of him. As such, it came as no surprise when de Quincy insisted that I take over the Frenchman's stewardship. Richard was bemused by my offer, but he accepted, nonetheless. "Just make sure you're more attentive than you were at Château Lavardin!" he said heartily, clapping me on the shoulder.

In truth, guarding des Barres was not a particularly onerous task. The Frenchman was generally an affable prisoner, unless insult was delivered to his countrymen. He had a healthy respect for my feats in battle, and so our relationship was not unpleasant. Indeed, he even agreed to help draw Sir Oliver out of his grief, by challenging the knight to a session of mock combat. I knew that Sir Oliver would be unable to resist such a lure, and after the two giant warriors had battered each other for almost an hour, Sir Oliver was left with an enormous, childlike grin on his face. He gratefully thanked me for arranging the combat session, provoking a warm feeling which mingled uncomfortably with my ever-present sense of guilt.

Indeed, his spirits improved so much that he enthusiastically offered to teach me how to joust. "Tournament prowess is critical to the career of a knight," Sir Oliver told me effusively as he led me to the stables. "Proving ourselves in battle is all well and good, but we cannot constantly be at war, or there would be no men left in the world. Not only do tilts provide us with a chance to win glory in the eyes of God, but they are also excellent practice for actual cavalry combat."

"I had always wondered how knights coordinated with each other in battle," I confessed. "You're saying that tournaments allow them to practise cavalry charges and the like?"

"Precisely," des Barres chimed in from behind me. "Young knights are very keen to show off their flashing new armour and weapons, but if they don't know the proper stages of walking, cantering and galloping, then they're useless on the battlefield."

"And the pageantry, Alistair, the pageantry!" Sir Oliver exclaimed dreamily. "The bright colours, the flapping banners, the noble women! You're going to love your first tournament, I guarantee it. But you're not going to be able to do anything but watch if you don't first learn how to properly couch a lance."

Harold gave a more mundane viewpoint on tournaments when I spoke to him later that evening. "Tournaments are recruiting fairs, nothing more," he said, sounding bored. "Their main function is for poor knights to convince onlookers that they're worthy of joining a lordly retinue. In fact, they're more social than military affairs; they help men with few brains climb another rung on the ladder of power." Although I surmised that his attitudes were fostered by his own lack of horsemanship, I was to learn that he was predominantly correct. Indeed, powerful knights such as William Marshal would never have achieved any high status if they were not recognised as proficient tournament fighters.

Having gathered our horses, weapons, and armour, Sir Oliver led me to the flat, grassy area outside the castle walls, with des Barres trailing behind. "Are you certain this is a good idea?" the Frenchman enquired. "I hear your King has a peculiar disregard for tournaments."

I frowned. "My father told me I would never participate in a tournament, because King Henry had outlawed them." That hadn't stopped myself and Robert arguing over who would be a superior jouster, because our childhood stories were dominated by knights whose skill at the tilt was their greatest asset.

"It's true that tournaments are forbidden in England," Sir Oliver conceded, "which is a tragedy that I hope is one day reversed. Yet we are not in England. Trying to ban jousting anywhere in France would be like trying to stop the sun rising. I think we'll be quite safe." Although I agreed that the King was probably powerless to prevent jousting amongst his knights, that certainly did not make us safe. Indeed, Henry had only banned the sport because so many knights were becoming critically injured during tournaments, which reduced their capacity to serve in his armies.

Leaning against a tree, des Barres observed us as I shrugged on my heavy mail armour and placed a chamfron of boiled leather over Raymond's head, to protect him from wayward lance blows. The lance itself was enormous, over ten feet long, and shaped out of springy wood so as not to deliver a lethal impact. Holding it upright was easy enough, but keeping it level at a horizontal angle took an immense amount of strength. "Just aim it plumb at the middle of my shield," Sir Oliver explained. "It's simple, really."

Des Barres wasn't convinced. "Your faith in your student is endearing, Sir Oliver, but wouldn't it be wise to practise with a quintain first?" he asked. "I've become rather attached to young Alistair, and it would be a terrible shame if you impaled him on his first tilt."

"Perhaps we could find a quintain up at the castle?" I proposed hopefully. Facing a wooden post with a hanging target would be much less daunting than riding against Sir Oliver and his intimidating black destrier.

"Nonsense!" Sir Oliver boomed, as I knew he would. "You won't be jousting against a quintain in a real tournament, so why do it now? You're young, Alistair, and the young heal quickly. Your arm is in fine working order, and just a few weeks ago that dastardly Count almost cut it off! What could I possibly do to hurt you after that?"

"Break his neck?" des Barres suggested.

I shot him a withering look. "You're not helping."

He shrugged. "It's just that I've been involved in my fair share of tournaments, my friend. Believe me, they're more than just honourable jousts and sighing ladies. They're highly competitive and brutal, especially the melees. The blunting of weapons doesn't stop skulls being caved in, and sometimes, the swords and lances aren't blunted at all." He shuddered at the thought, and I considered the morality of a man who could treat the English civilians so harshly in Châteauroux yet show dismay at the violence of tournaments. I suppose that Guillaume des Barres was always a man of soldiers; civilians did not concern him, but the fruitless deaths of fighting men frustrated him greatly.

I reluctantly agreed to face Sir Oliver in a joust and hauled myself into the saddle. Once I was comfortable on Raymond's back, my nervousness dissipated slightly. Although I was somewhat uncomfortable fighting on foot, I had spent countless hours of my teenage years on horseback and was immensely proud of my horsemanship. If I could best Sir Oliver anywhere, it was here, in the saddle.

Following the instructions the two knights had given me, I coaxed Raymond into a walk, as Sir Oliver did the same from where he stood three hundred feet away. The lance weighed down my arm as if I carried a tree, and the stifling afternoon heat began to roast my armour. Two hundred feet, and I urged Raymond into a canter. All I could hear was my ragged breathing as I suddenly worried whether my tight-fitting conical helmet would provide any protection if I were flung to the ground. A hundred and fifty feet, and I wondered whether Joanna was watching from the castle ramparts. Was she hoping that her husband would provide her with a convenient fatal accident to make her secret safe again? At a hundred feet, I spurred Raymond into a gallop, and all thoughts of Joanna, Eustace de Quincy, Richard and King Henry vanished from my mind as Sir Oliver thundered towards me. I lowered the lance, straining to keep it balanced, and hefted my shield, bracing for the terrible impact.

Fifty feet from Sir Oliver, my instincts took over. Suddenly aware that a change of direction would throw the knight off balance, I dug my knee into Raymond's right flank and simultaneously raised my feet slightly in the stirrups. Sir Oliver's lance, which had been on target to crack my shield in two, was now pointing at thin air, and at the last second, I corrected my own lance's path.

To my own amazement, the lance connected cleanly with the centre of Sir Oliver's shield, and the momentum of the impact thrust me backwards as if I had ridden into a stone wall. I did not see, but rather heard Sir Oliver topple out the saddle and crash to the ground behind me as a jarring pain shuddered up my right arm. Dropping my lance and shield, I pulled sharply on Raymond's reins and scrambled off his back, not waiting for him to halt completely. Sprinting over to Sir Oliver's prone form, I saw him juddering slightly where he lay, and panicked thoughts flitted through my head. What had I done? Was he having some sort of seizure? As I reached him, I wrenched off his great-helm, fearing the worst.

God knows how, but he was laughing. His face, which I expected to be a rictus of pain, was filled with uncontrollable mirth. "Oh, you're a rare one, Alistair!" he cried as he saw my anxious face. "Put on my back like a helpless babe during your very first tilt! Don't tell my father of this travesty – the de Burgh name will be shamed forever!"

I grinned sheepishly as I pulled the chuckling knight to his feet. "I suppose I was lucky," I said modestly. "I didn't really know what I was doing."

Hearing polite applause behind me, I turned and saw des Barres approaching with a thoughtful expression on his face. During our joust, he had been joined by a few curious mercenaries, who had clearly enjoyed the spectacle. "I'm not so sure about that," the Frenchman said. "You were probably lucky to survive Château Lavardin, but this? This seemed different. Your control over your horse was superb. Both you and the animal seemed to know exactly what the other was thinking, which is a rare skill indeed. I hope I am not being presumptuous by saying this, but you may have the makings of a champion jouster."

Flattered by his words, I accepted Sir Oliver's offer of a rematch, and for the next half hour we rode against each other. I did not unseat him again, though he knocked me off Raymond's back twice. I barely felt any pain from my impacts with the ground, such was my enjoyment of the contests. Des Barres politely refused to couch a lance against me, saying that it would not be a fitting activity for a prisoner, although he watched all of our bouts with great interest. More and more mercenaries, who had been bored witless waiting for the army to march, came to spectate. Those who had never seen a joust before seemed baffled and enchanted in equal measure. Such was their enthusiasm that many of them ran to saddle horses so they could participate. Obviously, none of them had any great aptitude for the sport, but their pleasure was palpable as they gleefully knocked each other over with the blunt end of their spears. Sir Oliver even organised a small tournament, which naturally he won.

I have fond memories of that afternoon. For a few hours, I was free from the clutches of Eustace de Quincy, and I could forget about my guilt.

But only for a few hours.

The playful childishness of the knights and mercenaries in the Angevin army could not last. Three days later, in the dying embers of a glorious summer, the armies of Henry and Richard marched, intent on crushing the Capetian dynasty once and for all.

Chapter 15

It was clear from the outset that the clash of opinions between King and Prince had not been resolved at Château d'Harcourt. Both men seemed to believe that their strategy was the one that had been chosen, which led to an appalling lack of cooperation between the two forces. In total, the Angevin army numbered around seven thousand men, including several hundred battle-hardened knights and a lumbering train of siege artillery. I had no doubts that such an immense force would be able to assault and take Paris, though not without horrendous losses. At the very least, we could have stormed the frontier fortresses of Philippe's supporters, in order to apply pressure to the French King and force him to sue for peace.

We in Richard's army were keen to come to blows with the French, but we were hindered by Henry's force which trailed behind us like a corpulent slug, ravaging and burning every piece of arable French farmland for miles in every direction. Frustrated by the sluggishness of the King's troops, the Prince tried to push us rapidly towards Mantes, but we, too, were forced to slow to a crawl.

"We were riding at a much faster pace between Châteauroux and Normandy," I complained on the fourth day of the march. "We're never going to close on the French at this rate." As usual, I rode between Harold and Sir Oliver, but des Barres was now a constant presence at my shoulder. King Henry had wanted him to remain prisoner in Château d'Harcourt, but Richard feared that he would not receive any ransom money if someone else was made responsible for the Frenchman. As such, he would follow us on campaign, armed with a sword to show that he had accepted parole. I did not mind the company of des Barres, as his companionship deterred Eustace de Quincy from demanding favours from me. The Frenchman and the Scot detested each other, and so, unexpectedly, I had found a potential ally in my miniature war against de Quincy.

"It's the mercenaries, I'm afraid," Sir Oliver sighed in reply to my question. "They know that the King's troops are busily plundering villages, and they can't resist joining in, whether Richard agrees or not. It seems the lure of gold and grain outweigh the orders of a prince."

"Who would have thought that a mercenary would prioritise his purse above his pride?" Harold asked dourly. Indeed, our column of soldiers shrunk every day as they scuttled off to raid the countryside, inspired by the activities of King Henry's army. Richard's knights and squires remained loyal, but we amounted to only a paltry force which could barely assault a village, let alone a castle or city.

Enormous plumes of smoke dotted the landscape as the marauding Angevin soldiers annihilated every settlement between the Normandy border and Mantes. The impact of the devastation was exacerbated by the time of year; we were on the brink of harvest season, and stores of grain from the last harvest were almost entirely gone. As such, the French peasantry who weren't killed by bands of Angevin troops would almost certainly starve in the coming year. Acres upon acres of ripe grain, dried out by the recent arid weather, burnt in a ravenous wave of fire. Horses and oxen, crucial for ploughing, were driven back towards our army. Men were butchered outright if they tried to defend their holdings, and women were taken alive to be personal playthings. I saw one of Henry's most revered knights laugh as he slapped a crying French woman on the rump, as she screamed that the man had killed her husband and child. An angry growl rose in my throat as my hand automatically dropped to Lion-Pride's hilt. Harold restrained me with a strong arm and a sad shake of his head. It seemed that Alice had been wrong all those months ago, when she'd told me that the war didn't affect commoners. From what I saw, the mauling of peasants was far more prevalent than actual combat against enemy soldiers.

It was in those days that I learnt the second rule of chivalry.

Always strike your foe where he is weakest, even if that means targeting the most innocent.

Prince Richard seemed to be one of the few men in the army who did not pursue this goal. This was not due to any particular sympathy towards the French peasantry; rather, he was desperate to find soldiers and armies to fight. In his eyes, defeating foes in battle was the easiest way to secure land, and land was ever Richard's priority.

Belligerently ignoring his father's orders, the Prince ranged ahead of the main army, accompanied by his bodyguards and a few hundred cavalrymen. Although we were fairly certain that Philippe was still safely enclosed by the gargantuan walls of Paris, groups of his knights roamed the countryside, targeting isolated units of Angevin soldiers. Predators became prey as Henry's mercenaries hid rather than face these fearsome opponents. Yet Richard actively sought them out.

He came across his first quarry in the village of Vernon, a sleepy settlement filled with anxious peasants who awaited Angevin raiders with trepidation. Half a mile from the village's outskirts, two of Richard's scouts galloped up the track towards us, their horses lathered with sweat. The Prince, dressed in his worn riding leathers, trotted forwards to meet them. After a quiet conversation, he turned to address us.

"There are French cavalry in the village ahead," he announced, causing a murmur of excitement as the news rippled down the column. "It seems God has smiled upon us. Not only do we outnumber them, but they're not expecting us. Most of them probably won't even be mounted, because they're resting and watering their horses." He projected his voice a little louder so that the entire force could hear him. "My father thinks it apt to terrorise commoners, and shy away from a proper fight! Today we show him how wrong he is! Today we send a clear message to King Philippe that his finest soldiers, and not just his peasants, have reason to fear us!" His men, myself included, cheered uproariously, though I think he could have given a sermon praising Satan and they still would have celebrated. These men were his fiercest fighters, his most experienced knights and squires, and they would quite happily give their lives for their Prince, because they knew he would do the same for them.

Fifty men were chosen to stay and guard our baggage. Much to my frustration, I was one of them, although I protected something far more valuable than tents or forage. As he had done before, Richard rode over to speak with me briefly before the attack commenced. Although he was undoubtedly in a hurry, I still gained the impression that I was the most important soldier in the army when he spoke. Somehow, he made every man under his command feel this way simultaneously.

"I will never forget your heroics at Château Lavardin," he told me sincerely, "but you must trust me when I say that they won't be necessary this time. Let your new sword sleep in its scabbard." He smiled. "Give the French a fighting chance, eh?"

"Of course, Your Highness," I replied humbly.

"And as for you, Sir Guillaume," Richard said, addressing the man I was charged with protecting, "You're doing your countrymen a great favour by keeping this fearsome fighter out of the battle. I have your word that you won't try to escape?"

"If I was going to dishonour myself by breaking parole, I would have done it already," des Barres replied loftily. "You have my word, of course." A mutual respect had formed between the Angevin Prince and the French knight over the past months, and the two men spoke now as friends rather than as captor and prisoner.

Richard inclined his head amicably to us both, and rode to the front of his cavalry force, which was now fully armed and armoured for battle. It was obvious that urgency was key if the planned assault on the village was to succeed, for neither Sir Oliver nor Harold had spoken with me, such was their rush to prepare. I could see neither of them in the cavalry column, although I did see de Quincy loitering at the back. I prayed that some opportunistic Frenchman would conveniently gut him for me.

As the Prince's troops began walking their horses towards the village, I forced myself to turn away and head back towards the men guarding the wives and pack-horses. I was determined to follow my orders this time, and remain with des Barres, yet showing such restraint was not easy. The itch for combat was crawling under my skin once again. I knew that I should probably dismount, and perhaps speak with Joanna, who must have been feeling as uneasy as I did. Yet I simply could not force myself out of the saddle; what if Richard's men suddenly needed me to go to their aid? Even though I knew I would face no combat that day, my body was automatically ready for it, an instinct almost impossible to dispel.

"How about we go for a short ride?" des Barres asked gently, seeming to sense my restlessness. "I think it would do us both some good to get away from here until the Prince's men return."

I gratefully accepted his offer and we set out along a tiny, winding track through the sparse forest that lined the road. Sunlight permeated through the scattered canopy, reminding me of all the wonderful rides I had enjoyed with Alice outside Little Dunmow. Raymond, seeming to share my memories, snorted contentedly. The atmosphere was so tremendously tranquil that it seemed peculiar men were dying nearby in Vernon. As a soldier, I have been forced to look upon death casually my entire life. Yet at that time, I was painfully aware that dozens of individual existences, each with their own families and thoughts, were being snuffed out not a mile from where I rode. One of those lives lost could be Harold, Sir Oliver or Richard, and I was not there to protect them.

Although he could not see my troubled face, des Barres must have known what I was thinking. "I feel it too, you know," he said quietly. "In fact, I've felt little else over the past months. How many of my countrymen could I have saved if I fought alongside them?"

"How do you combat those thoughts?" I asked him. "How can you have any peace with yourself, knowing that you're unable to serve your king?" I imagined myself in his position; undoubtedly, I would have tried to escape captivity on the very first night.

Drawing up alongside me, he smiled. "I tell myself how important restraint is in a warrior. I'm almost thirty years old, Alistair. I haven't lived this long by hacking off heads and inviting danger at every moment. Knowing when not to fight is one of the greatest assets a knight can have, and it's severely underrated."

"So what would you say is the most important skill of a successful knight?" I asked curiously. As the question left my lips, I pondered how much our relationship had changed; Sir Guillaume des Barres had transformed from a hulking brute of metal and terror into an unexpected confidant. Perhaps, I mused, we could become friends with the French if only we sat down and spoke with them, rather than reverting to swords at the first opportunity.

"I suppose you expect me to speak about bravery, and martial prowess?" he replied offhandedly. "Any man can be skilled with a sword, if he has enough practice. Bravery is more difficult – you clearly have it in vast quantities – but it is not the only thing that advances a knight's career." He halted briefly to untangle his sword from a vicious patch of tall nettles. "No, loyalty is the most important trait for a knight," he continued. "Indeed, a knight who is brave but not loyal is more dangerous than any coward."

"So anyone can have worth if they are loyal?" I questioned, surprised.

"Absolutely!" des Barres responded emphatically, enthusiastic about the point he was making. "Every man has talents, and as long as he is loyal, those talents can flourish."

I nodded, completely absorbed in our discussion. "You mentioned restraint earlier. Is loyalty more important than restraint?"

A slightly glazed expression crossed the knight's face, gone in half a heartbeat.

Then, quite suddenly, des Barres sprung his trap.

Leaning down in the pretence of scratching his leg, he swiftly grabbed hold of my right foot, hauling it out of the stirrup. Before I had a chance to realise what was happening, the knight grunted as he wrenched my leg upwards and pushed, tipping me out the saddle so that I crashed down Raymond's left flank. I cried out as I fell, partly due to surprise, and partly because my left foot was trapped in its stirrup, and twisted painfully, as my body connected solidly with the ground.

"What?" I gasped, utterly shocked. "Why?"

Des Barres gazed down as me, and I think there was a tinge of regret mixed in with his satisfied expression. "There's the answer to your question, Alistair. Heed it well." With that, he kicked his horse forward, winding through the trees at the greatest speed he could muster.

Cursing under my breath, I clumsily regained my feet, gritting my teeth as agony arced through my twisted ankle. Raymond's eyes rolled uncertainly as I heaved myself back into the saddle and kicked the confused horse into a gallop. I could no longer detect des Barres through the undergrowth, yet I could see the trail that he'd left, and frantically urged Raymond to increase his pace. The thought of letting the Frenchman escape was unbearable. I would not be made to look a fool, not by a man who had claimed to be a friend only as a deception.

Utterly oblivious to the tangled roots and uneven terrain underfoot, I recklessly raced through bushes and around trees, occasionally catching glimpses of des Barres's blue cloak flitting through the forest. He had taken me completely by surprise, yet the knight did not hold all the advantages. Although he was undoubtedly an excellent horseman, his borrowed palfrey was no match for Raymond's strong muscles and nimble agility. A grim smile spread across my face as I realised that I was gradually closing the gap. Des Barres must have noticed too, glancing backwards as Raymond soared across a small river, reducing the distance between us even further. The first few delicate, golden leaves of autumn were trampled underfoot as the chase became ever more frantic. My focus on catching des Barres was so absolute that I was almost swept off Raymond's back by a low-hanging branch, ducking beneath the obstruction by a mere inch. I could now hear the Frenchman viciously shouting and swearing at his tired horse, trying to extract every last ounce of energy from its faltering legs.

Growling in frustration, des Barres realised that the endeavour was hopeless, suddenly pulling on his reins and turning to face me directly. Furious that he had been unable to outrun me, he wrenched his sword from its scabbard and forced his horse forwards, intending to settle the issue with steel. I knew that to falter would be to lose momentum, and so I maintained my pace, drawing Lion-Pride with my right hand and lancing it forward as if I were in a joust. I already knew how this was going to end; in the same manner that I had unhorsed Sir Oliver, an incremental change in direction would throw des Barres off balance and allow me to knock him to the ground with the flat of Lion-Pride's blade. My eyes narrowed as my knees tightened on

Raymond's flanks. I would make this French fool regret his attempt to humiliate me.

Yet Sir Guillaume des Barres was one of the most feared fighters in all of France.

And he was done playing games.

Anticipating my change of direction, des Barres simply took a step to the left as I moved to the right. Shocked that my plan had failed, I swiftly brought up Lion-Pride to defend my body from my enemy's attack, knowing that I now had to face him in sword-to-sword combat.

But he was not targeting my body. Giving an almighty roar of rage, the giant Frenchman drew his arm back and thrust his blade deep into Raymond's chest. Overwhelmed by the sudden pain, my horse reared, and I flailed my arms hopelessly as I slid from his back for the second time that day. A brilliant white light flashed across my vision as my head connected solidly with a tree trunk. When my sight cleared, Raymond had sunk to the floor, blood pouring from the wound in his chest, as des Barres gazed down at me coldly.

"Draw a blade on me again, and it will the last mistake you ever make," he growled, his voice full of scorn and contempt. I realised then that he had never liked me or respected me. It had all been a ploy to lower my guard.

I was helpless as the knight briskly rode away into the distance. Wincing at the pain in my foot and head, I crawled over to Raymond's shaking body, and stroked the horse's ears as he died.

I had failed Raymond, and I had failed Richard. Wrapping my arms around my friend's lifeless body, I wept.

Chapter 16

A full hour passed before I limped back into Richard's encampment, clothes torn and limbs aching. It became apparent that the Prince's cavalry was yet to return from Vernon, and I was grateful that Richard would not see me in this state. However, I couldn't find a single friendly face amongst the baggage guards, who stared at me curiously. Eventually, Joanna emerged from the crowd of men and women and took me gently by the arm.

"What happened to you, Alistair?" she asked, her face full of shock and concern. Evidently, she had momentarily forgotten about the awkwardness between us, such was her worry. "Where's Sir Guillaume, and your horse? Has there been some sort of riding accident?"

I briefly considered answering in the affirmative and claiming that the Frenchman had been tragically killed. Yet I knew such a story wouldn't stand up to scrutiny, and my conscience was already drowning under a sea of lies. I didn't wish to burden it further. "No, Joanna," I said miserably. "He's gone. The treacherous bastard killed my horse and escaped. I've failed." I could feel tears threatening at the corners of my eyes again and willed them not to fall. I would not add to my shame by breaking down in front of the baggage guards.

Joanna's first thought was not to condemn des Barres, but to console me. "Oh, come now, Alistair, don't say that," she soothed. "How could you expect to stand up to a big brute like him?" I refused to acknowledge her words, so determined was I to wallow in my failure. "Let me help you back to my tent," she offered. "You're in no state to be wandering about."

I gratefully accepted, and she put an arm round my shoulder to support me as we wove through the group of murmuring guards. One of them shouted from my left. "He's let the French bugger escape! That's what you get for entrusting a man's job to a child!"

Joanna turned to face the voice's direction. "You were all ordered to protect Richard's valuables," she snapped. "So you're just as responsible as he is." That wasn't strictly true, but it was kind of her to speak in my defence.

Once I'd laid down in Joanna's tent, which she'd erected as a makeshift medical station, she began checking me over for injuries. Aside from the pain in my ankle, I had sustained nothing more serious than bumps and grazes. The emotional impacts of losing Raymond, and allowing des Barres to flee, were far more severe. Although my anger towards the French knight was bitter and intense, a tiny voice inside my head acknowledged just how cunning he had been. Not only had des Barres fooled everyone by accepting parole; he had also latched onto the most impressionable member of Richard's retinue and filled his head with praise and compliments. As I lay in the shade of Joanna's tent, I wondered whether any compliment I had received could be considered genuine. If somebody as notoriously honourable as des Barres could lie so easily, then who could truly be trusted?

My thoughts were halted by the arrival of Richard, who ducked through the tent flap with a grave expression on his face. He was accompanied by Sir Oliver, and contrary to the Prince, the knight wore his customary cheerful grin. Both men were still dressed in full armour, and both were unhurt from what had been a comprehensively successful ambush. Forty Frenchmen had been killed, and forty more taken prisoner, including three knights. Such a victory would be greatly diminished by the escape of des Barres, which is what Richard had come to discuss. I think he had heard only whispers and rumours, for he directly asked me for the full version of events without so much as a greeting.

Hesitantly, I recounted the day's events, reluctant to admit my shortcomings. Whenever I faltered, Sir Oliver would give an encouraging smile, but Richard's expression became colder and darker as my tale progressed. When I concluded, describing how des Barres galloped into the distant French countryside, Richard turned away and angrily punched his thigh with a mailed fist. I exchanged a concerned look with Sir Oliver, then tried to placate my lord. "I'm sorry, Your

Highness, I truly am," I said nervously. "If I'd had any inclination that he would try to escape..." I wrung my hands helplessly.

"Then what?" he spat, swivelling to look at me with a face contorted by fury. "You would have been a little less feeble in your attempts to stop him?"

It took all of my willpower to resist the instinct to shrink back against my bed. Since we had joined up with the King's army, I had witnessed Richard's anger several times, yet it had never been directed solely at me, and it was a truly terrifying experience. He always was one of the most passionate men I ever knew, and that passion could equally lend itself to exuberant friendliness or explosive rage.

Before I could respond, Sir Oliver stepped between us, shielding me from Richard's wrath. "Lord Prince, that isn't fair," he protested. "Save your anger for des Barres. Not only did that immoral dog break parole, but he savagely attacked one of your most brave and loyal men. How is Alistair to blame for any of this?"

Richard gave him a hostile glare. "I did not ask for your opinion, Oliver," he said icily. "Get out of my sight before you're tempted to give another one."

I could almost hear the mental struggle in Sir Oliver's head. He was determined to fight my cause, but in the end, his compulsion to obey a direct order was too strong. Shooting me an apologetic glance, he withdrew from the tent, leaving me alone with Richard.

I braced myself for an enraged tirade, but it did not come. Indeed, for a full minute Richard did not speak, but instead stared outside the tent, breathing deeply. Eventually, he came to sit beside me and ran a hand through his bright auburn hair. "I wish God would grant me one day in which everything goes as planned," he said dejectedly. "We may have routed the French in the village, but the dishonour of losing des Barres will stain my reputation for a long time. I'll never come to rule my father's Empire if I can't keep one man under guard!"

I remember thinking how strange that statement was. Of course, he would rule his father's Empire, regardless of his successes or failures; he was the King's eldest living son. From what I had seen and heard, Richard would make a very capable king, far more so than many other men who had inherited crowns throughout history. It was only later that I appreciated the tense nature of Richard's family affairs. The Prince genuinely feared that the crown would be handed to his younger brother John, for no reason other than the antagonism which existed between Richard and his father. As such, Richard was determined to prove that he would be a strong, decisive ruler, so that the nobles of England and France would support his claim upon the King's death.

For now, though, I sought only to console a man whom I respected and idolised immensely. "I don't think today's events will reflect poorly on you at all,

Lord Prince," I said, sounding more confident than I felt. "You assaulted a group of French soldiers – which is more than any of the King's troops have done. Des Barres has bought shame to himself through his actions. Only a fool would blame you for his escape."

"You would call me a fool, then?" he asked with a miserable sideways glance. "For I certainly blame myself. I blame myself for trusting an overconfident butcher's apprentice to guard the finest knight in all of France. Perhaps Sir Oliver was right, and it isn't your fault."

His next words sent a wave of ice through my soul.

"Perhaps it was my fault for admitting you into my retinue in the first place." Without looking back once, he stood and walked towards the tent flap.

"Lord Prince, I..." I began, desperate to make amends. Yet he was gone by the time the words left my lips.

***

The next few weeks were my most desolate since my exile from Little Dunmow. Although Richard's words to me had been private, the army seemingly had ears everywhere. Men who did not know me now actively avoided my company, for fear of being blemished by my reflected shame. Knights and squires who had filled my ears with compliments after Château Lavardin now battered me with criticism or fell silent when I approached. I was an outcast in a host of hypocrites, and the worst part was the feeling that it was deserved.

Predictably, Eustace de Quincy revelled in my unpopularity. Taking advantage of the fact that I now spent much of my time alone, he was able to coerce me into becoming his personal manservant. No task was too demeaning; one day I was to ride alone to a nearby village, just so I could find him a suitable whore. The next day, de Quincy's pimpled squire ordered me to wash his clothes and cook his meals, kicking me gleefully if I slacked in any way. The Scot never sharpened his own weapons, watered his own horse nor cleaned his own armour. As I write this, I am sickened by the easy compliance I showed to de Quincy's constant stream of demands, but at the time, I suppose I could not see any path of resistance. Not only was I terrified that de Quincy would reveal the secret of Joanna's infertility, but my confidence had been eroded by des Barres's escape and Richard's harsh words. I simply could not find the strength of will to stand up to the bastard.

Compounding my misery was the absence of allies to offer me support. Des Barres was gone, and I swore that if we ever met again, he would be no friend of mine. Richard did not speak with me for the remainder of the campaign, and even if he had, I doubt that any conversation with the Prince would have improved my mood. Sir Oliver and Joanna tried to be kind to me – Sir Oliver even insisted that I take his spare horse – yet spending long periods of time around either of them made me feel excruciatingly uncomfortable, as I protected a secret which could ruin their marriage. At my lowest point, I contemplated giving up on Richard's army entirely. I had a fine sword, a cleaver, and a suit of rusted mail. Surely one of the countless mercenary captains in France would be willing to take me on.

I probably would have given in to this temptation, were it not for Harold. The red-haired singer stayed stubbornly loyal to me during those weeks, oblivious to the hostility that drew from some of the knights in Richard's force. Although he was obviously confused by my subservience to de Quincy, he did his best to take my mind off my worries on the few days that the Scot was not tormenting me. One of his techniques involved providing me with a lyre, which he proudly produced at the end of a long day spent frantically chasing French cavalry across the countryside.

"Where did you get this?" I asked, taking the stringed instrument and instinctively plucking a short tune. We sat away from Richard's main campfire; I gained the impression that I was no longer welcome there.

"You really are one for unimportant details, aren't you?" Harold replied airily, which of course meant that he had stolen it. I did not particularly care; if one of the spiteful knights or squires in the army was upset over the loss of their instrument, then so be it.

I continued to play simple musical melodies on the lyre, accompanied by the chirping of a host of crickets in the long grass. "I spent many evenings making music with my mother and sister," I told Harold wistfully, letting myself be absorbed by the memories. "I was never very good at it..."

"You still aren't," Harold interjected with an impish smile.

"... but I still enjoyed myself. My sister, Alice, always says that happiness isn't based on aptitude, but rather on steady improvement. But that isn't how it works here, is it?" I gazed up at the night sky, wondering if Alice was staring at the same stars at that very moment. I would have given anything to see her again. "Failure isn't accepted in our situation, regardless of whether you're a beginner or veteran. Maybe I'm such a novice that I'm just not cut out for the responsibilities Richard gives me."

"And that's a reason to simply give up?" Harold asked. "Because you fail once? If I'd given up on women because of failure, I'd have castrated myself years ago!" I chuckled, and Harold continued in an earnest tone. "If you try your hardest at anything, then failure doesn't exist. Every stumbling block is a learning experience. Richard knows that, and he sees the potential in you. He was once young too, you know. When he was around your age, he fought a war against his father, and lost his entire army in an ambush at Saintes. If that failure of a Prince can become the brilliant military leader he is now, then who knows what heights you'll reach?" He spoke with the calm wisdom of a much older man, and I had to remind myself that Harold was barely a year older than I was.

"Thank you," I said. Listening to Harold's reasonable and measured perspective had been much more beneficial than heeding my own tumultuous self-doubt. "I suppose I'll just have to put up with the comments of the other knights. One day, I'll prove them all wrong."

"Oh, just ignore them," Harold said dismissively. "One thing I've learnt about knights and nobles is that they're sheep, and that their opinions are very rarely their own. Can you imagine a knight who thinks for himself?"

"Some of them do," I said, thinking of the manner in which des Barres had manipulated me.

"Maybe some of the older ones," Harold conceded. "But most would faint at the prospect of even dressing themselves. No, you don't need to worry about them. As soon as Richard calms down, they'll be bleating their praises of you once again."

The Prince had more pressing concerns than that of my welfare. His disappointment in me paled in comparison to the fury he directed at King Henry, whose army had now come to an absolute standstill ten miles short of Mantes. The King's tactic of ravaging the French countryside had ensured that his army would not march against King Philippe, as they were now so weighed down with plunder and livestock that their lethargic pace had slowed to immobility. In between forays against Philippe's forces, Richard rode back down the road and berated Henry's knights and mercenaries for their reluctance to prosecute the type of war the Prince desired. Yet he achieved nothing, and a mere two weeks after we had left Normandy, the majority of the Angevin forces returned there, having seen no combat and enriching themselves greatly.

Aside from the mercenaries who filled their pockets, nobody was satisfied with the outcome of that campaign. King Henry's strategy had utterly failed to lure Philippe out of Paris, whilst the French King was left with a devastated countryside and a peasantry who had lost all confidence in him. Of the three, Richard was the most frustrated of all, as he had been completely unable to prosecute the daring and bold type of warfare he favoured. Vowing to win the war alone, Richard returned to the province of Berry without consulting his father. Yet once again, without the support of the King's troops, we were limited only to insignificant skirmishes. I spent most of my time riding, performing menial tasks for de Quincy, and practising with the lyre Harold had given me. Sir Oliver tried to continue my martial training, but after my easy defeat at the hands of des Barres, I had no real enthusiasm for it.

Indeed, the military fervour across France was gradually dying down. The two Kings had no appetite for a full-on clash of armed forces, and any attempt by Richard to finish the Capetians by himself was doomed to failure. Perhaps more importantly, many of the nobles in both armies, as well as the Prince and both Kings, had taken the cross and sworn to embark on a huge Crusade against the infidels far to the east. Countless papal delegates travelled across France, begging for a cessation to the perpetual warfare so that we could all properly prepare to march in God's divine army. It became increasingly apparent for both Angevins and Capetians that the war could not be maintained under such internal pressure from its own nobility to prioritise the Crusade.

King Philippe was the first to openly acknowledge this. As we were embraced by the melancholy murkiness of a dark October, the French King called a peace conference. At Châtillon-sur-Indre, the three most powerful men in France, accompanied by haughty cardinals and arrogant nobles, would sit around a table and attempt to settle with words what could not be decided by swords.

I am still not certain why anybody thought that was a good idea.

Chapter 17

"It feels like we've been here for hours," I whispered to Harold. "When exactly is this conference going to start?" I was exaggerating slightly, but not by much. For at least forty-five minutes we had been crammed into the central room of Châtillon-sur-Indre's town hall, which was totally insufficient to accommodate the dozens of nobles and knights who wished to attend the meeting. In order to save space, Richard had asked that only a select few of his retinue join him, but the rest of us had come anyway. The meeting of two kings and a prince was simply too momentous to miss.

"It'll start whenever King Henry decides that this conference is more important than his foot massage, or whatever it is he's doing," Harold replied laconically. Indeed, the entire room was awaiting the arrival of the Angevin King, who I suspect was deliberately delaying his entrance to convey that he had authority over everyone else present. A polished wooden table had been placed in a very centre of the room, and was surrounded by the most powerful earls, counts and barons who accompanied the three armies. Richard, who sat between the Earls Derby and Chester, gazed curiously across the room at Philippe, who unwaveringly returned his stare.

Unlike his two adversaries, the King of France had an entirely unassuming appearance. Clean shaven and demure, he looked to be more of a scholar than a king or warrior; his attire was not as lavish as Henry's nor as martial as Richard's. Yet his appearance belied an immensely ambitious mind that was quite adept at turning the two Angevin leaders against each other.

Sir Oliver, who stood a head above most of the men in the room, noticed that I was studying Philippe. "So much for the elm at Gisors," he said scornfully, and a little too loudly. "I thought this war was supposed to be a fight to the death. Not quite so brazen now, is he?"

"Perhaps he genuinely believes that the Crusade is more important?" I suggested, watching the French King's facial expressions closely.

"I'm not so sure," Harold said. "I'm certain many of his nobles think that way, but the King doesn't seem the type to give in to pious impulses. No, he's probably plotting something. I wish I knew what it was, but I can barely think. We're roasting in here," he complained, mopping his brow. "Why couldn't this meeting be somewhere more spacious and airy? Scotland, perhaps?"

"Because this is the closest thing we have to neutral ground," Sir Oliver explained patiently. "It's an insignificant place, so it doesn't naturally favour one side or the other." Undoubtedly, Châtillon-sur-Indre was a tiny settlement, which lay on the Angevin-Capetian border a few miles west of Châteauroux. Despite the gathering of hundreds of men who were technically at war, it had so far been a peaceful affair. Thankfully, des Barres had not accompanied Philippe, as his presence might have provoked myself or Richard to rash and violent action.

"The field outside is neutral ground as well, and it's nice and chilly out there," Harold grumbled.

"It must be far worse for the knights who insisted on wearing their mail," I told him. Dozens of men, including several of those who sat around the table, looked more prepared for a siege than for discussion. "Why are they dressed like that, anyway? It's not like anyone's expecting a fight."

"I told you before, Alistair, knights are far too stupid to dress themselves," Harold reminded me. "Some of them have probably been stuck in that armour for months."

I expected Sir Oliver to bristle at the insult, but instead he merely raised an eyebrow. "That's what squires are for, I suppose," he said.

Murmured conversations across the room were silenced as King Henry finally entered the hall. Two weeks in the saddle had done little to improve his health; he walked with an awkward, shuffling gait and his face wore a permanent scowl. He looked distastefully at the empty chair before him – evidently, it was not ornate enough – before reluctantly sitting.

The Pope's delegate, a Cardinal from the Vatican itself, began the proceedings. "By God's grace, we are assembled today so we can more effectively carry out His most divine mandate," he intoned. "The shedding of blood between honest Christians must cease, so we can turn our attention to matters far more important. We have all sworn to recapture our holy Jerusalem from the vile creatures in the east, and that must be our priority." He then recounted a long and tiresome prayer, before inviting Philippe to speak.

The French King did not bother to stand, but rather leaned forward in his chair. "We are not enemies!" he began, smiling at all those around him. "Though we have been fighting this deplorable war for far too long, I think we must now be united by our common foe. That is why, in the name of God, I ask you all for peace." He spoke affably, and in English, to show his respect for his adversaries.

"How sweet of you," Harold murmured. Sir Oliver hissed at him to be quiet.

Several men around the table made to respond to Philippe, but King Henry overrode them. "It seems you have your priorities correct, Your Majesty," he said in an uncharacteristically measured tone. There was a collective intake of breath around the hall, caused by the form of address he had used. We had expected him to be mocking and vituperative, not cooperative. "Of course, you know that we cannot simply sheathe our swords and leave it there," Henry continued. "An exchange of territories is in order."

Philippe politely inclined his head. He was the youngest and least experienced of the three leaders, but he knew the customary process of peace agreements. He had witnessed enough of them in the eight years of his reign.

Richard had evidently given the matter some thought. "I propose that we..."

Henry brusquely cut him off. "I need Châteauroux, and the estates around it," he demanded. "We can have no peace whilst Châteauroux remains in French hands."

Richard stared at him incredulously. "Châteauroux? What business could you possibly have with Châtearoux? Since your disaster of a siege last year, you've shown no interest in Berry. Why is it so important now?"

He hadn't spoken particularly diplomatically, which Henry latched onto instantly. "I need it as a reward for a servant far less impertinent than you," he retorted. "I have promised the town to William Marshal as a reward for his service."

Frowns appeared on the faces of most of the men around the table. Few of them doubted that Marshal was a worthy knight, but he was just that – a knight. They were earls and barons, and they rarely received such mighty rewards themselves.

None of them were as perturbed as Richard, however. "I've been fighting over Berry for months –

years, even," he protested. "Châteauroux should belong to me, if anyone."

His complaints fell on deaf ears. "Châteauroux would belong to you if you hadn't lost it to the French, and then botched your siege in June," King Henry replied dismissively. "I heard you were knocked off your horse and were rescued by some peasant!" Inquisitive looks were fired my way, and I squirmed uncomfortably. Henry laughed, then grimaced as a racking fit of coughing consumed him.

Philippe, who had been watching the bickering with a shrewd expression, now intervened as Richard ground his teeth. "I can agree to the release of Châteauroux, for William Marshal is a noble man and will make a fine husband to the widowed heiress Denise," he said, addressing Henry directly. "Yet this cannot be a gift freely given, as I'm sure you understand. Perhaps some meagre southern land could be granted to my kingdom in recompense? Some land that has been taken from Count Raymond?" He indicated a bearded nobleman to his left, whose holdings had crumbled under perpetual assaults by Richard's army.

"Toulouse," King Henry said instantly. "You may have Toulouse."

A sharp intake of breath sounded from Richard's supporters. The Prince's victories against Count Raymond had been some of his finest, and he took immense pride in the land he held there. Richard gaped like a stranded fish as Philippe conferred with Count Raymond and Hugh of Lusignan, before turning back to Henry. "It is agreed," the French King stated.

"Father, you can't do this!" Richard appealed desperately. "You have no right!"

"I am your king!" Henry snarled. "I have every right. And you will address me as 'Your Majesty'."

A tense silence smothered the hall. The anger on Richard's face was so palpable that I feared he was about to strike his father. I am not certain, but I think I saw a tiny smile tug at the corners of Philippe's mouth.

"Yes... Your Majesty," Richard said through clenched teeth, and the papal delegate visibly sighed with relief. "With your joint permission, I shall retire," the Prince continued, trying to preserve his tattered dignity. "I have suddenly come over very tired."

Philippe nodded. "I look forward to our next meeting," he said, flashing a friendly smile. Henry did not even acknowledge his son's departure. I sensed that he had not desired Richard's presence at all.

As we filed out of the hall, the discussion resumed behind us, but it was obvious that Richard wanted no further part in it, or any more conferences over the next days. Along with his loyal core of knights and squires, and a few mercenaries, Richard rode away from Châtillon-sur-Indre that very night, cursing his father.

Along the length of his column, his men quietly discussed their predictions of Richard's next course of action. "Do you think he'll return to his father in an attempt to make amends?" I asked Harold, Sir Oliver and Joanna. As always when I rode with the three of them, I subconsciously ensured that Harold was between myself and the married couple.

"I doubt it," Harold answered. "He's too proud for that, and besides, his father made it clear that he's trying to erode the Prince's land as much as possible. There's no way Richard will forgive that quickly."

"But why would he do that to his own family? His own heir?" Sir Oliver asked, puzzled. "Maybe instead the King was trying to broker a quick peace deal, so we can begin the holy Crusade as swiftly as possible? Maybe it's coincidence that Richard's land was forfeit?"

"Or maybe the King is trying to erode Richard's power base so that it'll be easier for John to accede the throne," Joanna suggested quietly. She spoke rarely when myself and Sir Oliver were both present, but her words had an uncomfortable ring of truth.

"If that is the case – and I pray it is not – then what choice does Richard have but to concede to his father's wishes?" Sir Oliver questioned dejectedly. "He'll lose his conquests one way or another, either voluntarily or through war with the King."

"There must be another way," Harold said, furrowing his brow.

The answer came to me with such sudden clarity that I was amazed nobody had proposed it yet. "He should make a separate peace with Philippe, without his father's presence," I said.

Sir Oliver looked lost. "Without his father? How would that change anything?"

"It seems he's going to lose territory either way," I explained, my mind racing, "and he's more likely to keep his land if he appeals directly to Philippe. King Henry seems determined to erode all of Richard's land in Aquitaine, Berry and Toulouse, but Philippe won't want that. He'll want to keep Richard strong to act as a check on Henry's power."

Joanna nodded. "And if Richard were to make a big show of presenting them as peace talks, his father couldn't complain, not with the Crusade on the horizon."

"That's the most absurd idea I've ever heard," said a sickeningly familiar voice from behind me. Unbeknownst to us, Eustace de Quincy had been eavesdropping and now sidled up alongside me, riding his squire's horse, a disdainful expression painted on his face. "Are you suggesting our noble Prince would go behind his father's back to speak to that French swine?" he exclaimed. "He would never do something so dishonourable, because deceit is a truly terrible thing. Isn't that right, Joanna?"

I felt a dreadful falling sensation in my stomach as he addressed Joanna directly. I do not know if Joanna was aware that de Quincy knew of her infertility, but I wished to deter any communication between them. I frantically tried to think of a way to warn de Quincy away from her, but I was terrified of challenging his tetchy disposition right in front of Sir Oliver.

"What is it that you want, Eustace?" Sir Oliver asked tiredly. Joanna was staring at her horse's mane, unwilling to look de Quincy in the eye.

"Just thought I'd add some small contribution to your fascinating discussion," he said. "Oh, and I need to ask a favour. My horse has thrown a shoe and my squire appears to have gone missing. Could one of you help me get my horse moving again?" I was certain that he knew exactly where his squire was, but the boy was almost as lazy as de Quincy himself. Ever since the Scot had started blackmailing me, the snivelling little toad had barely lifted a finger.

"Why yes, of course," Harold said sarcastically. "Would you like me to empty your chamber pot at the same time, and perhaps warm your bed tonight?"

"I'll go," I said, turning my horse around.

"Alistair, what..." Harold began, confusion in his voice.

"I'll see you later, when we make camp," I called back over my shoulder.

As usual, de Quincy tried to needle me with mocking comments as we made our way towards his stranded horse, and as usual, I did my best to ignore him. It was only when I picked up a spare horseshoe that he said something which truly piqued my attention.

"So, do you think you could help me in getting to know Joanna better?" he asked languidly.

"Why would you want that?" I said. She was already a tool for de Quincy's blackmail; what other use could he have for her?

He frowned. He usually didn't appreciate my talking back to him, but he indulged me on this occasion. "She's a fine-looking woman, I'm sure you'll agree," he explained, gazing distractedly at the grey horizon, "and whether Sir Oliver discovers her infertility or not, he's certain to ditch her sooner or later. I mean, he has to, in his position. He needs an heir." He was speaking faster now, as if he was trying to justify it to himself. "She'll require someone to take care of her when that happens, and I thought I could do that. I'd be doing her a favour, and because she can't carry a child, she'd make a perfect whore!"

I instinctively raised my hand to strike him, but a tiny voice in my head somehow restrained my arm. Instead, I nodded dumbly and pretended to seriously consider his request. "I apologise, but I can't get you a private audience straight away," I told him as I fixed the shoe to his horse's hoof. "Give me a few weeks to speak with her, and I'll see what I can do."

"You'd better not fail me," he said. "If you do, I'll expose Joanna's secret; then it will not only be Richard who despises you. Your friends will as well."

I meekly accepted his words and proceeded to carry out the usual menial tasks he had for me. Yet whilst my facial expression was blank, my mind was afire with thoughts and speculations. De Quincy had crossed the line. I wasn't pleased at the prospect of being the bastard's personal slave, but I was willing to do it in order to protect Sir Oliver's marriage. However, if the Scot had designs on Joanna, that was something I simply could not abide. I resolved that de Quincy's threat had to be dealt with, and his diplomatic immunity could be damned. How I could corner him with hundreds of witnesses around was another question entirely, but I was determined to think of something.

Over the next couple of days, Harold and Sir Oliver persistently pestered me to tell Richard that he should speak to King Philippe privately. Although I still thought it was a good plan, I refused for two reasons. Firstly, all of my mental willpower was directed at my plot against de Quincy, and secondly, Richard was likely to reject any idea I had out of hand, simply because he no longer trusted me. Exasperated, Sir Oliver eventually suggested the plan to Richard himself. The Prince, who had been in a dark mood since leaving Châtillon-sur-Indre, latched onto the idea like a starving mongrel does to a scrap of meat. If nothing else, Richard said, parleying with Philippe would frustrate his father immensely, and paying back the insults King Henry had offered was one of the Prince's main priorities.

Thus, Prince Richard rode to meet his sworn enemy at Bourges, in defiance of the wishes of his King.

And I planned the death of Eustace de Quincy.

Chapter 18

The journey east to the city of Bourges took me deeper into France than I had ever been before. Now that a shaky ceasefire was in place, Richard rode with only his retinue, so that Philippe would not view our journey as an invasion. Of course, travelling in small numbers held another type of risk entirely, but the Prince trusted that Philippe wouldn't take him captive. Not only would such an act anger the Pope immensely, but it would also remove a counter to King Henry's dominance.

We found the French King in the midst of an enormous military camp, disbanding his mercenary forces. This could only be a good sign; evidently, Philippe had a genuine desire to forge a peace treaty if he was so willing to dissolve his army. However, we soon learnt that the conference at Châtillon-sur-Indre had quickly turned into a farce after Richard departed. Bereft of his ability to turn father and son against each other, Philippe had been unable to negotiate effectively with the surly Angevin King. Henry had stormed out of the meeting a few hours after his son, when Philippe persistently demanded possession of the insignificant village of Pacy-en-Sure, which Henry stubbornly refused to yield.

Upon hearing of Richard's arrival, Philippe immediately interrupted his planned schedule and effusively greeted us all with handshakes and kind words. His smile when he welcomed me seemed genuine, but since my experience with des Barres, I had learnt not to trust the pleasantries of a Frenchman. As for des Barres himself, I was certain that he was somewhere in the vicinity of Bourges, but he wisely chose not to show his face.

Richard insisted on being alone for his talks with the French King, and only two guards protected the tent's entrance, William L'Etang for Richard, and a burly French knight for Philippe. Leaving our women under the guard of Sir Baldwin, the rest of us ventured into the city to explore a place that had not been touched once by Angevin occupation. Unlike Châteauroux, Bourges was not dominated by a cathedral, although one was clearly planned; we walked past vast foundations in the city's north-east corner. In a time of such heavy taxes to fund both the wars at home and the upcoming Crusade, it astonished me that funds were still available to begin construction on these grand places of worship, but they were appearing all over England and France. Yet it has always been the case, and probably always will be, that the crown funds itself and the church above all else, in order to ensure its own political and moral dominance.

We were not visibly armed as we walked through the city, so we wouldn't attract hostility from the citizens or garrison, although I am certain that most of Richard's retinue carried knives or short-swords as insurance. I myself had hidden my cleaver under my tunic, on the advice of Harold. Nevertheless, we drew suspicious stares from the people of Bourges, who had evidently heard of the ravaging of the countryside near Mantes and probably blamed all Angevin soldiers for it. Keen to escape their scrutiny, Sir Oliver ducked through the door of the first tavern he found, accompanied by Harold and myself. A few of Richard's retinue followed, and I was relieved to see that Eustace de Quincy was not among them. I was still yet to come up with a concrete plan for his demise, but I knew that his absence would allow me to think more clearly.

Having taken our drinks from a polite but sullen bartender, I gently probed Harold and Sir Oliver for information on the Scot, so I could properly plan my attack.

"So, do you think there'll be any more fighting between us and the French before the Crusade begins?" I asked, pretending genuine curiosity.

Harold rolled his eyes. "That's like asking whether it'll rain again before next summer. There's a tiny chance it won't happen, but only if God intervenes. To be honest, even if God turned up at a peace conference, they'd all still be squabbling at the end. Half of them would probably declare war on the Almighty himself."

"For once, I unfortunately have to agree with this impious lout," Sir Oliver said. "I sincerely do wish we could put aside our differences and focus on our noble Crusade..."

"Only because you gave your sword such a daft name," Harold teased.

"... but I fear this war will continue until the bitter end, regardless of how much the Pope protests; I doubt either King will be satisfied until the other is defeated," Sir Oliver finished.

I had hoped they would answer as such. "If that's the case, do you think everybody in the Prince's retinue will be happy about a prolonged war?" I asked, frowning as if the thought had just occurred to me. "I feel as if some of them may not be enthusiastic about continuing the fight."

Harold laughed. "Gossiping about your comrades already, Alistair? I knew I liked you for a reason."

"Who exactly are you talking about?" Sir Oliver enquired, concern in his voice.

"A certain Scottish friend of ours," I said quietly, not wanting to be overheard by Richard's soldiers at nearby tables. "Last night, he told me that he was fed up with the Prince's constant campaigning, and that he wished to return home to see his family." De Quincy had said no such thing, but I needed to turn the conversation in his direction, in order to discover his vulnerabilities from my friends.

As I predicted, Sir Oliver took my comments at face value. "We all miss our families sometimes," he declared. "I was lucky enough to see my kin in Normandy, but obviously Eustace wasn't so fortunate. Perhaps I should speak with him, to try and assuage his fears?"

Harold was staring straight into my eyes, a calculating expression on his face. I resolutely refused to meet his gaze. "I wouldn't do that," I said to Sir Oliver, injecting alarm into my voice. "He's awfully touchy about it." I sighed dramatically. "I just wonder why he's acting this way."

"I'll tell you my opinions on Eustace de Quincy when you tell me why you've been such a willing personal servant to him," Harold said directly. "You're answering to his every whim, and he acts like a flatulent arse around you. So why? Does he have something you want? Is he blackmailing you?"

I shifted uncomfortably in my seat; this conversation was rapidly backfiring. "He's just a friend," I protested weakly. "That's all there is to it!"

"It doesn't seem that way from the outside, Alistair," Sir Oliver said in a surprisingly gentle voice. "Harold and I have noticed it for weeks now." He placed a giant hand on my shoulder. "Whatever reasons you have, whatever he's forcing you to do, just tell us if something's wrong. If he is blackmailing you, we want to help!" I genuinely felt like he meant it.

I couldn't do it. I couldn't lie any longer. "Yes, he... he is forcing me to do work for him," I told them miserably, staring at my drink. Harold leaned back, satisfied that I had confirmed his suspicions. "It doesn't need to involve either of you, though," I added hastily. "I have a plan to deal with it. I appreciate your concern, but I really don't need your help." I was frustrated that they had forced me to admit the blackmail, but I hoped that I could make them lose interest. I certainly didn't want anybody else involved in my plot to permanently remove de Quincy.

Yet Harold's sharp mind was not to be underestimated, which I was to swiftly discover.

Once again, he did not mince his words. "This blackmail has something to do with Joanna, doesn't it?" he asked. It was half a question, half a statement. "I saw your face yesterday when de Quincy spoke to her, and you've been acting oddly around her for weeks." I felt my stomach drop like a sack of oats, and I inwardly cursed Harold for working it out. Yet this exasperation was mixed with a sudden, unexpected feeling of welcome relief; I wouldn't have to deal with de Quincy by myself anymore.

But I would have to deal with Sir Oliver.

The sandy-haired knight looked from me to Harold, brows furrowed. "Joanna? What does this have to do with Joanna?" he asked, utterly perplexed. In that moment, I felt desperately sorry for him.

"Joanna has... a secret," I told him as calmly as I could. "I found out accidentally, and Eustace de Quincy found out as well. Ever since, he's been threatening to tell everyone about it. The only way I could still his tongue was to become his servant. I'm sorry."

"My wife's been keeping something from me?" Sir Oliver asked, still in a state of confusion. His eyes widened. "You've been keeping something from me? Why?"

"You'll understand when you know what it is," I said. "I know that's a feeble excuse, but... let's go and find her. We need to discuss this properly."

I began to rise from my seat, but Sir Oliver swiftly grabbed my hand, pinning it to the table. "We are not going anywhere until you tell me this secret," he said. There was no malice in his eyes, just frustration.

"Oliver, maybe we should..." Harold began.

"Tell me!" the knight insisted, ignoring him.

"But Joanna..." I said.

"Tell me!" he pleaded, tightening his grip. We were attracting stares from around the tavern.

"Just do it," Harold told me, exasperated. Judging by the look on his face, I think he had already figured it out.

I sighed, knowing that weaving around the truth would be both foolish and impossible. "There's no kind way of saying this," I said, fearing that Sir Oliver's wrath would erupt, "but she's barren."

He instantly released my hand and slumped back in his seat. "Oh," he said, in a tiny, deflated voice. "But... she's pregnant..."

"A fabrication, I should think," Harold guessed.

I nodded confirmation. "She was so desperate to be pregnant. She just wanted to make you happy and provide you with an heir. I'm so sorry, Sir Oliver."

Sir Oliver took a deep drink of his ale and gazed across the room. Harold and I waited for what seemed like an eternity for him to speak. "Poor Joanna," he said at last.

"You're not angry?" I asked tentatively.

"I'm... disappointed that neither you nor she thought to trust me with this," he said quietly. "But she must have been going through hell recently, thinking I would replace her if I found out. She must see herself as some piece of equipment, no more useful than a sword or a horse, only useful for giving me an heir. But she's so much more than that."

I smiled, relieved by his reaction. "I didn't think you'd ditch her," I assured him. "But she was certain that you would. So I promised not to reveal it."

Sir Oliver inhaled deeply, and a sad smile crept onto his face. "Let's go and tell her how wrong she is, shall we?"

He stood, and I followed suit. "I'll stay behind and drink all your ale," Harold told us unabashedly.

"Cheeky drunken lout," Sir Oliver grumbled. Yet his smile remained.

As we strode briskly through Bourges' western gate in the direction of the mercenary camp, I voiced my concerns about Joanna's future as Sir Oliver's wife. "Do you think your family will accept your decision to stick by Joanna?" I asked, trying to avoid the hostile stares of the Frenchmen guarding the portcullis.

The knight shrugged. "I hope that they will, but that's not exactly my current priority. Joanna needs my support at the moment, and my apology." I did not ask what Sir Oliver had to apologise for, as I did not want to add any further emotional strain to his tormented soul. "When I have a spare moment, I'll seek out Eustace de Quincy," he continued in a dark tone I had never before heard from him. "We need to have a few words."

"Perhaps it would be wise to approach Richard first?" I suggested. "Surely he needs to know of de Quincy's manipulative games."

"No," Sir Oliver said bluntly. "Richard is a strong and fair man, but this doesn't concern him. De Quincy has soiled my wife's name and blackmailed my friend. This is a matter of honour, Alistair."

Honour. Bloody honour. The cause of so many headstrong mistakes.

We walked in silence for a while, and I shivered as the crisp autumn chill permeated my body. "How do you think Joanna will react when I tell her I know her secret?" Sir Oliver asked nervously as we approached Richard's small cluster of tents. "Will she be embarrassed? Angry? Ashamed? I just don't want her to suffer any more than she has already."

I smiled as reassuringly as I could. "I honestly think she'll be relieved," I told him. "I know I was when you..."

I was cut off by a sudden, shrill scream which echoed from inside Sir Oliver's tent. The voice was unmistakably female.

Without pausing, Sir Oliver broke into a run towards the sound of his wife's cry. Recovering from a split second of shock, I followed, thoughts racing through my head like leaves whipped up by the wind. Had Philippe launched a surprise attack on us? Had some vicious Frenchman snuck into our camp alone?

Bursting through the tent's flap, I saw that we had arrived just in time. Joanna sat hunched in the corner, grabbing at the folds of her clothes which had been brutally ripped. Eustace de Quincy leered over her, a savage look of feral hunger in his eyes. De Quincy's squire stood beside his master, an expression of pure delight on his face which swiftly turned to a look of horror as he beheld Sir Oliver and myself. A growl of extreme fury resonated from deep within Sir Oliver's throat as he observed the scene before him. "Get away from my wife, you lecherous whoreson," he snarled. His stocky frame blotted out the sunlight of the tent's entrance.

Startled by the hulking knight's appearance, de Quincy turned to face us. He appeared surprisingly composed. "Ah, Sir Oliver! I was hoping you wouldn't be back for a good while, but now that you're here, you may as well know the truth." He gestured dramatically at the huddled form of Joanna, who stared at de Quincy with both hatred and terror. "Your lovely wife here, and your pathetic suckling babe," he levelled a finger at me, "have both been keeping a secret from you. She's barren, Oliver!" He shouted the word with unbridled glee. "She's as useless to you as a dusty old hag. So why waste time on her? You need a real woman, and I'll generously offer to take this fruitless crone off your hands!" He grinned slyly as he finished speaking. It seemed that the Scot genuinely expected that the revelation would stun Sir Oliver into indifference.

He was severely mistaken. It was then that I caught a glimpse into Sir Oliver's true character. Family and lineage mean everything to those who hold wealth and title, especially those who value honour and chivalry as much as Sir Oliver. It was easy for him to say that he would stay true to Joanna, but the news of her infertility must have hit him like a hammer-blow. It would have been so simple for him to turn his back on her, and find a new, fecund wife. Many men whom I have known, all of them brave and noble, would have done just that.

Instead, he roared like a gelded bull and charged at the stunned de Quincy, knocking him flat against the ground with crunching force. The Scot squealed in pain as he bore the full impact of Sir Oliver's immense weight and the huge blows that the knight's fists rained upon him. I knew better than most that Sir Oliver was a deadly fighter, but this was not the finely honed swordplay that the poets so love to sing of. This was an attack borne of sheer rage; de Quincy simply could not escape the overwhelming fury that he faced.

Seeing his master in peril, de Quincy's ugly squire hesitated slightly before pulling out a small, sharp knife and wielding it over his head. Knowing I would not have time to draw my cleaver, I lunged forward desperately and grabbed the squire's arm moments before the knife would have plunged into Sir Oliver's back. Growling at my interference, the squire balled his free hand into a fist and punched me in the stomach. I gasped in pain but managed to maintain my hold on his knife arm. We grappled for a moment, grunting with effort as we tried to wrestle the blade from each other. Hatred in his eyes, the squire spat full in my face; evidently, de Quincy had not taught him to fight as a gentleman. Inspired by his example, I leaned forward and clamped my teeth onto his arm with as much force as I could muster, and he cried out in sudden pain, dropping the knife. Now with both hands free, the squire gripped my throat, and I savagely kicked him in the groin. Unable to control the pain coursing through his body, he moaned and sank to the floor.

Still leaning over de Quincy's bruised and bloodied form, Sir Oliver snatched the discarded knife from the floor, a wild expression on his face. De Quincy weakly protested from a mouth of broken teeth, but the knight was consumed by the madness of battle and paid him no heed. Scrambling across the tent, I attempted to restrain my friend. As much as I hated de Quincy, and had plotted his death myself, I knew this his murder right in the middle of a military encampment would spell political disaster for both Sir Oliver and Richard. Ignorant in his overwhelming desire for vengeance, Sir Oliver shrugged me off like a dog would a flea and raised the knife above De Quincy's throat.

"What on earth is the meaning of this?" a voice thundered from behind us, so loud that even Sir Oliver looked around. Sir Baldwin stood in the tent's entrance, sword drawn and face taut with anger. Two French guardsmen stood behind him, and a curious crowd was gathering beyond them. Apparently, Joanna's scream and the ensuing tussle had drawn significant attention.

Breathing heavily, with hands bloodied, Sir Oliver rose and jabbed a finger into Sir Baldwin's chest. "You were supposed to be protecting the women!" he shouted, not caring who heard his outburst. "How could you allow this to happen?"

"Allow what to happen?" Sir Baldwin asked in bewilderment. "All I see is a member of Richard's guard trying to murder another! And in the midst of a French encampment! What in God's name has possessed you, sir?"

Sir Oliver was clearly in no state to give a coherent answer, so I spoke up. "We heard Joanna's scream, arrived to see that Eustace de Quincy was about to... soil her honour."

Sir Baldwin frowned. "Soil her honour? You mean..."

"Rape her," Sir Oliver spat. "And his wretched squire was a willing participant."

Sir Baldwin's eyes widened. "No, I... that's quite a serious accusation," he said gravely.

"He lies," de Quincy whispered. Sir Oliver swung round, but I managed to restrain him this time. I could sense the animalistic rage flowing from him by the second.

"You see to your wife, Sir Oliver," Sir Baldwin said quietly. "We'll get to the bottom of this, don't worry." With that, he dragged de Quincy from the tent. It was unsurprising that the Scot couldn't walk – one of his eyes was completely crushed, and his ribs were bruised and broken. De Quincy's squire, still groaning on the floor, was likewise hauled from our sight.

As soon as they were gone, Sir Oliver seemed to forget they existed, and devoted all of his attention to Joanna, who was still huddled, shaking on the floor. He held her, and apologised over and over, tears in the corners of his eyes. Without a word, I left them, upset over Joanna's ordeal, but glad in the knowledge that their devotion to each other could see them through this hardship.

Chapter 19

Our days spent in Bourges stretched into weeks as the dialogue between Richard and Philippe continued. The King and the Prince were closeted together for hours on end, discussing their goals and aspirations, and above all, discussing King Henry. Ever keen to turn the two Angevins against each other, Philippe focused all his energy into persuading Richard that his father intended to place John upon the throne. In truth, I do not think Richard needed much convincing. Philippe did not create the rift between father and son, he merely capitalised on it. Henry's demands at Châtillon-sur-Indre, coupled with his past slights against his son and his incessant refusal to release Queen Eleanor from prison, convinced Richard that his only hope was to cooperate with the Capetians. I cannot say I blamed him; the Angevin King had done nothing to earn Richard's respect, and the Prince's hunger for land drove him to parley with Philippe. Such was his focus on these talks that we saw very little of him during our habitation of the French city.

He did, however, find time to banish Eustace de Quincy from his service. Determined to resolve the matter swiftly, Richard rapidly interviewed everybody involved to try and find some truth amongst the barrage of accusations. I felt a small flutter of nervousness as I was summoned in front of him. He had not spoken a word to me since I was rebuked over the escape of des Barres. If I expected more warmth from him now, I was to be disappointed. The Prince asked me questions in a cold, distant voice, and I answered them as truthfully and concisely as I could. Afterwards, I allowed myself a few moments of pathetic self-pity, bemoaning the possibility that Richard would never look upon me with a friendly face again. It apparently hadn't occurred to my young, foolish mind that the Prince had more pressing issues than the self-confidence of an insignificant adolescent.

One such issue was the outrage of Sir Oliver, who mightily protested Richard's decision to banish de Quincy instead of executing him. Yet Richard was understandably wary of risking his relations with the Scottish court at a time when he already had so many potential enemies. De Quincy's exile alone would cause problems.

"I just don't feel as though she's safe whilst that filthy rat lives," Sir Oliver explained to me one night, as we sat alone outside his tent, staring at the luminescent scattering of stars. The ordeal with de Quincy was fresh in both of our minds, and, unable to sleep, we had sought each other's company.

"If he has one ounce of sense in that twisted mind of his, he'll return to Scotland, so Joanna should be quite safe," I assured him. "Though he'll no doubt start whining to his father and the Scottish King, so I don't doubt he'll continue to cause problems." I sighed. "I'm just glad it's all over."

He smiled. "All over? We're probably about to fight a war that'll decide the fate of France, and then set out for a bloody campaign to restore God's Holy City. I think it'll be a while before anything's 'all over'," he said.

"You know what I mean," I replied.

"I do, I do," he said. "But there's one thing that still puzzles me. What was your plan for dealing with Eustace? I certainly hope you weren't going to allow him to treat you like a slave indefinitely."

"Actually... I was planning to kill him," I told him sheepishly.

"Alistair! I'm shocked... when you intend to murder someone, I fully expect to be invited!" he exclaimed, letting out a rumbling laugh. I couldn't help but join in, and our guffawing must have woken half of the camp. It certainly woke Harold, who shrieked at us to be quiet in such a shrill voice that it probably woke the other half of the camp.

As the negotiations continued, we heard only whispered rumours of King Henry's activity. Some said that he was touring western France to gather mercenaries, whilst others asserted that he had returned to England to levy fresh troops from his barons. Yet I was to find out later that the King was simply sitting on his makeshift throne in Le Mans, shouting at his servants and growing increasingly surly by the day. It seemed he could not understand why Richard had deserted him. I have ever been told that Henry was a fearsome soldier for his entire career, but it seemed that his diplomatic instincts had deserted him. Compounding the King's frustration was the fact that Prince John would not come to him when summoned. It seemed that Richard's younger brother was wisely avoiding choosing a side.

Now that the awkwardness between Sir Oliver and myself had passed, I spent my days rigorously practising my swordsmanship. Sir Oliver's comments regarding the war to come, and the Holy Crusade, had alerted me to the fact that I had only taken part in one battle, where I had survived through sheer instinct and luck. Certainly, both of these are commendable attributes for a soldier, but toughening my sword arm was also a necessity. Throughout weeks of intense combat training, I gradually began to feel more confident. Undoubtedly, I was still no match for the towering strength of Sir Oliver or the lithe speed of Harold, but both assured me that any mistakes I made would simply make me a more proficient fighter. Every so often, I was treated to the spectacle of my two friends clashing swords with each other, and on one such occasion, Joanna came to sit alongside me as I watched.

"It's difficult to remember they're friends sometimes, isn't it?" she asked ruefully as Harold delivered a ringing blow to Sir Oliver's great-helm.

"They trust each other, I suppose," I said, knowing that the two of them would never actually hurt each other, as fierce as their struggle was.

"That's why I haven't been a particularly good friend to you," she sighed. "I wouldn't be surprised if you mistrusted me, after everything I've put you through."

I was taken aback by her words, and her demeanour of guilt. "If anything, I should be apologising to you!" I protested. "I revealed your secret to Sir Oliver, without your permission. I…"

"You did something I should have done myself, a long time ago," she interrupted. "It was never your secret to keep, it was mine. I thought that by avoiding my fears, I could escape them. Yet my cowardice only left me in a perpetual state of terror."

"Fear isn't anything to be ashamed of," I said. "At least I hope not; I've felt enough of it over the past few months."

She ignored me. "I'm not going to be like that anymore. I'm not going to be the whimpering wife of a knight. I'm going to stand up for myself." There was steel in her voice. "And if I ever see Eustace de Quincy again, I will geld him myself. I'll hold him screaming on the edge of death, tormenting him, until he begs for the sweet release of the fires of hell."

From Joanna, I learnt the third rule of chivalry.

Never underestimate a woman. They hold power that can be subtle or overt, and some would just as soon cut your throat as greet you with a warm smile.

Eventually, five weeks after our arrival in Bourges, Richard and Philippe announced their desire for a new conference between the leaders of the Angevin and Capetian factions. This, they claimed, was because the talks at Châtillon-sur-Indre had not forged a peace which would last the duration of the Crusade. To those of us in Richard's retinue, however, it was obvious that agreements had already been made between the Prince and King Philippe. This new conference was merely designed to force Henry to accept unfavourable terms. What those terms were to be, we did not know, as the discussions had been extremely secretive.

In a show of unity that was quite unprecedented between Angevin and Capetian royalty, Richard and Philippe set out from Bourges together. Both men dispatched messengers to countless nobles, major and insignificant, ordering them to converge on Bonsmoulins, where the peace would be decided. The atmosphere throughout our column was tense and quiet, particularly amongst Richard's retinue. Despite my relative inexperience, I had witnessed enough of King Henry's temper to know that he would react poorly to his son's new acquaintanceship with Philippe. Many men, nervous of the outcome of such a momentous conference, were uncharacteristically silent as they rode. In an attempt to lift spirits, Harold chattered happily to anyone who would listen; that was, until Richard asked him to sing for us on the second night of the journey. Afterwards, he fell into the usual dark mood that his own angelic voice seemed to mysteriously summon.

Upon our arrival at Bonsmoulins, it quickly became apparent that we were not the first to converge on the village. Indeed, it seemed that half of the Angevin and Capetian nobility were already present, and the arrival of Richard and Philippe turned Bonsmoulins into a colossal, sprawling city of tents, ten times the size of my home town, Little Dunmow. Evidently, this conference would be on a far larger scale than that of Châtillon-sur-Indre. Numerous landowners who had never even seen battle attended in order to share their opinions; even King William of Scotland had sent a delegation. Although I was fairly certain Eustace de Quincy wasn't part of it, I still did my best to avoid his countrymen.

King Henry was already present, as evidenced by his monstrous red pavilion situated in the midst of the Angevin encampment. He did not ride out to greet his son, furious that Richard was arriving alongside the French King. Instead, we were met by one of the ugliest and most fearsome men I have ever seen. He addressed Richard with surprising informality, roughly embraced Sir Oliver, shared a filthy joke with Harold, and patted me patronisingly on the head without saying a word.

"Erm… have we been introduced?" I asked uncomfortably. It was difficult to look him in the eye because of the wretched condition of his face. Ghastly burn marks plastered one side of his head, which was balding despite his relatively young age. His eyes were both blue, but unnervingly mismatched; one was pale as the summer sky, the other dark and foreboding as midnight. Compounding his ugliness was a deep scar latticed across his mouth. I could not imagine meeting such a nightmare on the battlefield. For many unfortunate Frenchmen, that nightmare had been their last.

"I don't believe so," he replied. The scar on his lips twisted grotesquely whenever he spoke. "I can already guess who you are, though. The feared Alistair Fitzwalter! The butcher's boy who probably thinks we're all terrible savages. As for me, I'm an idiot, a drunkard, a liar, and a charming French fellow recently told me I have the foulest breath in all France. He was probably right, although at least I'm still breathing. He isn't."

I was equally intimidated and bemused by his demonic features and forward demeanour. Harold chuckled at my baffled expression.

"For some reason, I'm also in charge of seventeen castles that Richard captured from that uptight ponce, the Count of Toulouse," he continued. "I'm sure some of my men were supposed to accompany me here, but they probably died along the way because I didn't bring their mothers to nurse them." He extended a gnarled hand. "Name's Mercadier. Most feared and handsome mercenary in Richard's employ."

Despite my earlier misgivings, I now shook his hand energetically. I had not recognised his face, but I certainly knew his reputation. Mercadier was Richard's most renowned mercenary captain, utterly fearsome in battle and uncompromising in all aspects of life. Unlike most mercenary captains, he was a close personal friend of Richard's, and his ability had granted him immense power and respect throughout western Europe, despite his low birth in the Occitan valleys. "It's a pleasure to meet you, Mercadier," I said enthusiastically. "I've heard all about you. It's a relief I won't have to face you in battle!"

"Oh, I wouldn't put too much faith in that," he replied offhandedly. "I'm a mercenary, remember? I'm almost guaranteed to switch sides at some point." I assumed he was joking.

"We can only hope so. Most of us have been waiting to gut you for a long time now," Harold replied cheerfully.

"I'm sure I'll die laughing if a suckling babe like you waves a sword at me," Mercadier shot back.

Sir Oliver sighed in dramatic exasperation. "Stay away from this brute, Alistair," he warned. "His sense of humour is almost as bad as Harold's. Oh, and he's an unstable, murderous barbarian who usually ignores orders."

"Duly noted," I said as the mercenary flashed me a grotesque grin.

Whilst Richard and Philippe parted ways to tour their respective encampments and greet acquaintances, Mercadier led myself and a few others to his pavilion, a filthy, tattered grey tent which looked a hundred years old. He then introduced us to his men, who evidently hadn't died on their journey from Toulouse, and looked almost as brutal as their captain. Although rowdy and coarse, they were generally friendly, and treated our women with a courtesy which was almost overbearing. When I questioned Harold about this, he gave a rueful smile. "Mercadier is obsessively respectful towards ladies, for some reason," he told me. "You don't want to know what he does to his soldiers who assault women, whether in friendly or enemy territory."

"I probably don't," I said uneasily. "I suppose his heart's in the right place."

"If anyone upsets Mercadier, their heart certainly doesn't end up in the right place. Usually outside their bodies," Harold added with indecent relish.

"All right, all right. I get it," I said wearily.

The mercenaries spent much of the evening trying to persuade Harold to sing, and his stubborn refusals only increased their insistence. I offered to play the lyre in his stead, and Sir Oliver decided that his voice would make a fine accompaniment. After only a few seconds, most of the mercenaries, battle-seasoned warriors all, fled in terror at the sound of Sir Oliver's hoarse bellowing. Mercadier remained, laughing inconsolably and covering his ears. As the knight's song ended, only Joanna offered half-hearted praise, which Sir Oliver accepted ebulliently. Harold scolded her for encouraging him.

The first morning of the conference dawned grey and miserable, with a persistent drizzle which dampened the spirits of everybody present. After a short debate, it had been decided that the talks would take place in Henry's pavilion, simply because it was large enough to accommodate the horde of nobles who wished to attend. Myself, Harold, Sir Oliver and Joanna had departed early from Mercadier's encampment, in order to ensure that we would have a place in the King's tent which would undoubtedly become unbearably crowded. Mercadier himself had stayed behind, claiming that he had no place in the peace talks, because he would probably accidentally kill an earl or cardinal.

The pavilion was already bustling when we arrived, with busy stewards and clerks ushering attendees into position based on their social standing. Naturally, that meant we were positioned right back against the wall, despite being members of Richard's retinue. If Sir Oliver hadn't been a knight, we probably would have been banished altogether.

"This is going to be absolute chaos!" I exclaimed. "How is anybody going to make themselves heard?"

"Fortunately, we've gathered together some of the most humble and reasonable men in England and France here," Joanna said sarcastically. "I'm sure they'll all wait their turn."

"I understand your doubts, dear, but I don't think it'll all be shouting and arguing," Sir Oliver asserted. Harold snorted to show his opinion on that statement. "Most of the nobles are here just to witness the momentous decisions we'll reach today," the knight continued.

"Momentous bickering and tantrums, from what I saw at Châtillon-sur-Indre," I put in.

Sir Oliver wrung his hands in despair. "Does nobody have faith in God's anointed kings and nobles anymore?" he protested.

"I have faith in you, you big silly fool," Joanna said fondly. "Isn't that enough?"

"Of course it is, of course it is," he replied with a huge smile on his face. I couldn't help but share their joy at their newfound fondness for each other.

Then a horribly familiar voice bellowed from across the room. A voice I prayed I'd never hear again.

"I told you that the next time I saw you, I'd have you killed!" it roared. "I intend to follow through on that promise!"

Shouldering aside his fellow barons, he glared at me with eyes narrowed by rage.

My father had come to Bonsmoulins.

Chapter 20

I had thought nobody would be able to make themselves heard in that room packed with boisterous, bickering nobles.

My father's fury silenced them all in an instant.

Burly and towering in an enormous fur cloak, Baron Walter Fitzrobert stormed towards me, uncaring of whom he shoved out of the way. He was followed by two hulking knights, both of whom I recognised. They were not bad men, but they were utterly loyal to my father's command.

"You commit the most heinous sacrilege, and you dare show yourself here?" he spat venomously. "After I raised you, cared for you, promised you my title despite how feeble you were? This is how you repay me?" Every eye in the room was turned towards us. Richard and the kings were not yet present, so nobody was willing to question my father's outburst.

I simply gaped at him. Damned fool that I was, I had never anticipated that my father would be here. Yet why wouldn't he be? King Henry had summoned his barons to Bonsmoulins, and Walter Fitzrobert was his ardent supporter. Now, there was no hiding. Everybody would know my true identity, and of the falsehood I had spread. I remained speechless and motionless as my father approached our corner of the pavilion. It was as if I were ten years old again, and he was berating me for breaking a vase in his hall. I was but a weakling, a child, and I could not fight back.

Sir Oliver stepped forward towards my father, confusion evident on his face. "What exactly is the problem here, sir?" he asked politely. "What is Alistair to you?"

"I bear the great shame of being this wretch's sire," the Baron said, his icy eyes still piercing my soul. "Though he forsook his family name months ago, and this godly earth will soon be rid of his foul presence."

"His father?" Sir Oliver said, swinging round in bewilderment. "But I thought…"

"I imagine he told you some filthy lie," my father guessed. "Son of a poor farmer, is he? Or perhaps an orphan? No. He is – he was – the son of the Baron of Little Dunmow, until I found him guilty of the murder of our most holy priest, Father Geoffrey. When confronted with the accusation, he fled. And now I shall exact justice, as is my right as his lord."

"It isn't true!" I protested desperately, finally finding my voice. "The crime is my brother's. You believed his tale because it finally gave you an excuse to grant him your title, as you've always wanted."

My father curled his upper lip at that. "Falsehood typical of a servant of the Devil," he snarled. "You lied to everyone here about your parentage. Why should they believe you now?"

Sir Oliver looked at me with horror. "You stand accused of murdering a priest?" he gasped. "And you didn't tell us?" He took a step away from me, torturous conflict obvious on his face. "Alistair, I... I don't know..." he stammered. I completely understood his reluctance to defend me. His loyalty to me was far inferior to his devotion to God, and he would not risk that under any circumstance. Joanna looked similarly troubled.

"Take him!" my father barked at one of his knights. "We take him outside and string him up, like I should have done long ago. We put an end to this now!"

Gasps echoed throughout the pavilion at the sound of steel scraping from a scabbard.

"Take one more step, and I'll cut your heart out and feed it to Richard's hounds," Harold hissed, holding his sword towards the knight my father had indicated. As the Prince's royal guards, we were amongst the few men in the room allowed to carry weapons, yet the thought of actually drawing a sword on a baron and two knights was unfathomable.

Not for Harold. God bless him.

"Stand aside!" my father growled. "Or would you be condemned to eternal fire as well? He killed a priest!"

"I don't care if he killed ten priests and diddled twenty nuns whilst singing hallelujah," Harold replied, his anger matching the Baron's. "All I know is that he's a friend who's fought at my side and saved my lord's life, and now some old man who stinks of sheep turds has marched in and demanded his head." He took a step forward and hefted Wife-Tongue. "So I suggest you turn around and leave this tent, or you'll be leaving in pieces."

"Harold, just calm…" Sir Oliver began.

"The impertinence!" my father exploded, his face mottled red with rage. "Do you have any idea who you speak to?" To my horror, he pulled a hidden knife from beneath his cloak, and his knights produced short-swords. "You have five seconds to move, or you will be moved, you ignorant worm."

Harold unflinchingly held his position. "Try me," he said calmly.

"Five," my father said. Sir Oliver implored everyone to back down but was ignored.

"Four." My right hand dropped to Lion-Pride's hilt.

"Three." Onlookers backed away, fearing bloodshed. Some fled the pavilion entirely.

"Two." A tiny smile curled onto Harold's lips.

"Lower your weapons, in the name of the King!" Richard thundered from the pavilion's entrance. Harold, who had been poised on the balls of his feet, immediately recognised the voice and slammed his blade back into its scabbard. My father turned to berate the intruder but faltered upon seeing the finely trimmed red velvet and gold circlet.

"By God's legs, this is a peace conference!" the Prince exclaimed, his accented voice thick with disgust.

"How are we supposed to prosecute God's holy war if we can't stop brandishing swords at each other for ten minutes? Who are you, and why are you assaulting members of my retinue?"

My father reluctantly sheathed his weapon and drew himself up to his full height. "I am Baron Walter Fitzrobert, a loyal servant of the King," he said proudly. "I am here to apprehend this depraved young man, who was previously my son, and who despoiled the sanctity of my church and killed my priest in cold blood."

"Your son?" Richard said, his eyes widening for a moment. He quickly regained his composure. "On what authority do you dispense this justice?" he asked, staring at my father with a flinty expression.

My father frowned, as if the answer were obvious. "I am his lord, and he committed the crime on my land," he said.

"Well, I am also his lord, and he has sworn fealty to me," Richard replied in an acerbic tone. "I would think the authority of a prince outranks that of a baron, wouldn't you say? So, surely I, if anyone, should mete out punishment?"

The Baron ground his teeth. He was determined not to lose his quarry. "I would remind you, Your Highness, that I am also his father, and that is an authority outranked by none."

Richard's clerk, Master Philip of Poitou, spoke up. "Pardon me, my lord, but did you not say that Alistair had forsaken the family name? That he was no longer your son?"

I could have kissed the small, scholarly man. "He told me that I had forfeited the name Fitzwalter," I added.

"There you go, Baron," Richard said, stroking his auburn beard. "If Alistair forfeits the family name, then you forfeit the power of jurisdiction over him. I shall take it from here."

My father growled and took a step towards the Prince and was instantly faced down by the intimidating trio of Sir Baldwin, William L'Etang and Sir Oliver. "Careful, Baron," Richard said lightly. "I assure you that you don't wish to make an enemy of me."

"You haven't heard the last of this, Your Highness. I shall appeal to the King," my father threatened.

"The King currently has greater concerns," the Prince informed him. "And even if he didn't, he probably wouldn't care about your troubles." He turned to his clerk. "Philip, would you escort Alistair to my pavilion? I shall be along to speak with him later."

I flashed a grateful smile at Harold and received a grave nod from Richard as I left the tent, with uneasy conversation resuming behind me.

"Thank you for your help," I said to Master Philip as we walked away from the conference. "I didn't kill that priest, though part of me wishes I had. He was a rapist, a liar and a crook."

"As a former man of the cloth myself, I can quite readily believe that, unfortunately," the clerk replied. "His Holiness the Pope is extremely eager for this Crusade to take place, which is a noble and just cause, but I wish he would divert some attention to the corruption within his own flock." He sighed at the apparent futility of the situation. "Regarding your innocence or guilt, that is not for me to say," he continued. "Overall, I'm happy to give you the benefit of the doubt. Cold-blooded murder just doesn't seem to be in your character."

"Seeing as I'm a soldier now, I'm not sure whether to take that as a compliment or not," I told him wryly. My offhand tone belied the immense trepidation boiling within me. The Prince was still bitter over my role in the escape of des Barres. Would this latest revelation eradicate the remaining trust he had in me?

Having been left alone in Richard's deserted pavilion, I sat and waited for over three hours for him to return. Chewing absently on a piece of bread left over from the royal breakfast, I listened intently to the raucous shouts and raised voices emanating from the conference a few hundred yards away. I learnt later that Richard and Philippe were arguing fiercely over an exchange of territories, much to Henry's amusement. In fact, this animosity had been prearranged between the French King and Angevin Prince, in order to convince Henry that they were not working together, so that their later demands would be received more affably. Whether this deception fooled the ageing King, I do not know. However, I believe everyone knew that any proposal offered by Richard would immediately be met with his father's scorn.

The Prince's face was unreadable as he strode into his pavilion shortly before midday. He came alone, ordering his guards to stay outside, and sat heavily on the ground beside me. I waited for him to speak.

"If anyone asks, I started shouting and berating you the moment I came in," he said eventually. "God forgive me, but it's such a pleasure to have a few minutes' respite from all this madness."

"Yes, Your Highness," I said nervously.

He sighed. "Was that your father?" he asked directly.

"Yes, but..."

He held up a weary hand to cut me off. "Did he accuse you of the murder of a priest and banish you from Little Dunmow?"

"Yes, Your Highness," I said, miserable that I would not be given a chance to defend myself.

To my astonishment, he smiled. "If only you'd told me that you were feuding with a father who favoured your younger brother, I would have loved you even more for it."

I blinked, utterly taken aback by his amicable tone. "Do you believe me innocent of the murder of my father's priest?" I asked. Richard's piety was legendary;

if he genuinely believed me guilty of such an act of heinous sacrilege, he would have had my head off its shoulders before speaking a word.

Instead of such a violent response, he merely shrugged. "It's your word against your father's. The Baron is not only a notoriously unpleasant fellow, but he's also a close follower of the King, so annoying your father might also annoy mine, to some small degree. Anything that irritates that indolent old slug I call a father is fine by me, so I'm certainly not going to punish you. I owe you that much." Although it was widely known that Richard harboured a strong dislike for his sire, hearing the King described in such terms was shocking indeed. It was also endearing that the Prince was speaking in such an intimate manner.

"Lord Prince, I should apol..." I began.

"And that's not all I owe you," he cut me off. "I owe you an apology for the way I've treated you. You've offered me nothing but your best efforts in my service, and my attitude has been remiss. You must promise me one thing, though."

"Anything. Anything at all," I said instantly. Only a few hours ago, I had resented him for his negligence. Now, after only a few words, I was ready to die for him. Such was Richard's way with his men.

"If we ever meet Guillaume des Barres again, promise me that you'll fight at my side to knock him senseless," he said, looking me directly in the eye.

I nodded vigorously. Alone, the giant French knight would tear me to pieces, but alongside Richard I felt that no fight was impossible.

The Prince was quiet for a moment, then removed his golden circlet and offered it to me. "Why don't you wear this and pretend to be me in the conference this afternoon?" he asked in such a sincere tone I almost thought he was serious. "I could do with a break."

"I don't think I'd be very good at peace negotiations," I said. "I'd probably get angry and draw my sword on someone pompous and important."

He laughed, and I felt a warm glow of satisfaction that we were on good terms again. "I sometimes wish we had that option. I've always been much better at solving problems with my sword than with my tongue. I do wish I was a better negotiator. If I was, I could have persuaded the King to release the Queen from prison long ago." I was to learn that Richard was extremely fond of Queen Eleanor, and every day of the last fifteen years of her imprisonment had tortured him immensely. It was one thing he never forgave his father for.

"I worry about my mother as well," I confided in him. "She was always kind to me, and I hope my father doesn't punish her for that."

Richard gave me an encouraging clap on the shoulder. "My mother's a strong woman, and I'm sure yours is as well." He stood and gave an almighty stretch.

"We just have to do our best out here, and stay alive, for their sakes. Now, it's back to the joys of discussing annual revenues with uptight noblemen. You're welcome to accompany me back, if you'd like."

Unsurprisingly, the Prince's open support for me was not taken well by my father, who refused to attend the discussions whilst I was present. I do not think he was particularly missed. Indeed, the royalty and their advisors continued haranguing each other until the morning of the third day, when the negotiations took a dramatic turn.

The first two days of discussion had achieved very little, although I admit that I was not paying full attention to the conference. Instead, I was scanning the crowd of barons and noblewomen for any sign of my sister, Alice, and her husband, Gilbert Peche. The two would be married by now, and Alice was the one remaining member of my family that I could rely on. Yet there was no sign of them. Baron Gilbert had decided to stay out of the conflict. Although I understood how sensible that decision was, I was desperately disappointed by my sister's absence. I needed her reassurance after my father's barrage of hostility.

The lack of decisiveness on the first and second days at Bonsmoulins was not entirely down to the disagreeable nature of the participants. Richard and Philippe had formulated a plan at Bourges and were simply trying to wear down King Henry with inane talk of taxes and land exchanges before they activated their strategy.

It was King Philippe who finally showed their hand. After another bout of meaningless squabbling about estates in the Quercy region, he stood and addressed King Henry directly. "Your Majesty, we are no closer to peace than we were three days ago," he lamented, "and the Holy City cries out to be freed from the savage infidels who desecrate its streets. Indeed, only last night I had a dream, a dream in which a flock of angels implored me to march east, even if it meant giving up my entire kingdom." It was a mesmerising speech, and I think only I saw the smile tug on the corners of Richard's mouth.

"To which end," Philippe continued, "I will gladly return every conquest I have made in the last year, including Châteauroux, which I know is precious to the mighty King Henry." Shocked, angry murmurs sounded from the French nobility; they had lost so much to the Angevin Empire over the years, and now they were to cede even more. Philippe silenced them with a brusque wave of his hand. "In return, I have only two small demands."

Henry's rheumy eyes narrowed, but he invited Philippe to proceed. He wanted an end to these negotiations more than anyone, so that he could return to his warm bed in Le Mans.

The Capetian King inclined his head. "Firstly, I demand that my sister, Alys, be given in marriage to Prince Richard, which will secure our alliance throughout the Crusade and beyond. Secondly, King Henry must order his earls and barons, both in France and England, to swear fealty to Prince Richard as heir to the throne, so that a smooth transmission of power can take place should the King fall in battle during our Holy War."

Another murmur rippled through the tent. On the face of it, the terms were extremely generous for Henry. All he had to do was agree to a marriage, and confirm his eldest son as his heir, and he would receive copious amounts of land as well as the peace he desired.

Yet there was far more to it than that. Richard had told me that he was no negotiator, yet this was a political masterstroke. Not only would he retain all of his conquests, which Henry had been threatening, but he was also forcing Henry to openly acknowledge him as heir. Furthermore, with Alys as his wife, he would be confirming a powerful alliance with King Philippe. As for the Capetian King himself, he ensured the survival of his kingdom, and a friendship with the heir to the Angevin throne.

Without saying a word, Richard had delivered his father an ultimatum. Confirm me as heir, or risk all-out war against myself and Philippe combined.

And King Henry hesitated.

"What is your answer, Your Majesty?" King Philippe prompted.

Fidgeting in his seat, Henry frowned deeply. For years, he had tried to limit Richard's power, and agreeing to Philippe's demands would make the Prince the second most powerful man in Europe. "The logistics would be simply impossible," he said at last.

"Logistics, your Majesty?" Philippe asked, frowning.

"You said it yourself, we need to set out on this Crusade as soon as possible, and it would take months to gather all my barons to swear fealty to my son," he explained weakly. "Perhaps when we have more time, we can arrange something, but now? Impossible, unfortunately."

"So you do not agree to King Philippe's offer?" Richard asked coldly. I could tell that their relationship hung on Henry's answer.

"I am saying it's a possibility, in the future, perhaps, but right now, it would be difficult to confirm you as heir," his father replied, refusing to look him in the eye. "It's land rights, you see, and logistics."

"I see, Father," Richard said softly. "I see what I should have seen long ago. You have tried to avoid the question, but in doing so, you have made yourself perfectly clear. Now at last, I must believe what I had always thought was impossible."

What he did next stunned everybody in the pavilion, perhaps even himself.

Turning away from his father, he knelt in front of King Philippe. "I swear my allegiance to you above all men, above everything except my allegiance to the Kingdom of England, and do homage for Normandy, Aquitaine, Anjou, Maine, Berry, and Toulouse." He gestured at us to kneel in front of the Capetian monarch alongside him. A few knights, including Sir Oliver, obeyed only with great reluctance. "I beg that you allow me to keep stewardship of these lands, and accept my homage," Richard finished.

King Henry was spluttering incoherently, and Philippe seemed to be the only man in the tent who was not dumbfounded by the announcement. This eventuality had probably been a part of their talks in Bourges. "I do, on both counts," he answered. He was making a visible effort to keep a triumphant smile off his face.

Richard rose. "There is nothing more to be discussed here. And so, I take my leave. God be with you, Father." Without so much as a backwards glance, he left the pavilion, tailed by his retinue. A few minutes later, Philippe followed, his face a picture of deliberate resignation and sorrow.

That afternoon, the Prince and all his followers, some five thousand men, departed Bonsmoulins.

Thus myself and Richard permanently turned our backs on our fathers, vowing that they would pay for the wrongs they had done us.

Chapter 21

"Such a damn shame," Sir Oliver said for the third time. "This is the time when the Almighty needs us the most, and we can't see past petty family squabbles. I wouldn't be surprised if a host of angels descended to punish us." I had seen these morose moods before and hoped it would soon pass.

"I'm just a runty little Welshman, not one of God's holy knights, so hopefully this vicious horde of cherubs won't hold me responsible," Harold replied with a cheerfulness that he knew would annoy Sir Oliver.

"We're all doomed," the knight grieved. "The Holy City will never be retaken!"

"Oh, do stop being so bloody dramatic," Mercadier said scornfully. "I don't care whether we're fighting infidels in the east, Englishmen here, or babes still in their beds, so long as I get paid." The disfigured mercenary was accompanying us on our journey south, which was currently taking us through the bustling market town of Amboise, where Richard was intending to spend the night. The Prince's other mercenary captains, and many of his landowning nobles, were splitting off from the main column to marshal their full forces. Although Philippe and Henry had agreed a last-minute truce until January, nobody knew whether Richard would respect this truce, and so France once again made itself ready for war. King Philippe had departed east into his territory, apparently disappointed at the lack of a long-lasting peace. However, I imagine he was secretly thrilled by the irreparable breach which now existed within the Angevin royal family.

"Still, I can't believe the Prince would betray his father in such a manner," Sir Oliver said.

Joanna, riding close alongside her husband, took his hand reassuringly. "Richard has never let us down before," she reminded him gently. "And some would say that his father's been betraying him for years."

"Just because you're tied to someone by blood, they don't automatically earn your respect, or loyalty. I think I would know that more than most," I said. Harold enthusiastically nodded his agreement.

"So, if Richard swore allegiance to Philippe, does that make us French soldiers now?" Mercadier mused. Sir Oliver groaned at the thought.

"I certainly hope so," Harold said brightly. "At the very least, being French will improve my luck with the ladies!"

Such speculative conversations were taking place all along the column. I'm sure that many of the Prince's followers believed that the split between father and son was merely a temporary disagreement. Yet the hardness on Richard's face told another story. He had suffered years of repression and indignity at the hands of his jealous father, and even though he was now sworn to Philippe instead, I could tell this was his first step to establishing a base of independent power, and allowing his leadership instincts to shine.

As we departed the local church, where Richard had paid his respects, I pondered the future of the Angevin royal family. "Do you think the Prince will ever reconcile with his father?" I asked Harold. However, he wasn't listening. Instead, he was staring intently at a small alley we had just passed.

"Harold? What's wrong?" I asked, concerned. His face was completely vacant, eerily identical to his haunted expression whenever he sang.

Without warning, Harold turned and sprinted towards the alley. Utterly perplexed, I followed, calling his name. Turning into the dilapidated side-street, I saw that he was pursuing a frail, bent-backed priest whom I didn't recognise. Upon catching the old man, Harold grabbed him roughly by the arm and spun him round, confronting him with a savage snarl. Sensing my friend's immense anger, I increased my pace, desperate to prevent this seemingly unprovoked attack.

Yet there was no need. As soon as Harold saw the priest's terrified face, his berserk demeanour vanished. Breathing heavily, he stared at the man he had chased, before stumbling backwards, muttering stammered apologies. Before I could ask him anything, he fled the scene, heading back in the direction of Richard's retinue. Having calmed the poor priest, I pressed a shilling into his hand to keep him quiet. Determined to question Harold over this uncharacteristic outburst, I sought him out in the inn where the princely retinue was residing for the evening.

"What in God's name was that all about?" I asked as I caught sight of him sitting beside Sir Oliver and Joanna. He responded with a tiny shake of the head, to indicate that he wouldn't speak about it in front of the others. Sir Oliver was so enraptured by the tale he was telling – which involved himself unhorsing dozens of French knights, as usual – that he hadn't noticed my question. I observed as the evening wore on that Harold barely touched his food, which was most unusual for a man of his generous proportions. He also seemed generally despondent and didn't even tease Sir Oliver about his exaggerated stories of chivalric prowess.

Eventually, Sir Oliver tottered off to bed, fuddled by wine and supported by Joanna, who rolled her eyes at us as her husband stumbled and almost fell. Once he was quite certain they were gone, Harold turned to me intently.

"You may think me an infidel for asking, Alistair, but could you ever question your faith in God?" he asked in an almost sinister tone.

I frowned at such a peculiar question. Naturally I did not question the power and authority of God; such a thought was simply ludicrous. Yet my piety was certainly not on the levels of Richard or Sir Oliver. "I suppose my faith is not as strong as it should be," I admitted. "Perhaps it is not my faith in God Himself that troubles me, though. Perhaps my doubt lies in the instruments He chooses to be His priests. Father Geoffrey – the man I supposedly killed – was an abhorrent man, and I dare say that the quick death he received was a mercy." I shrugged. "Of course, I have faith in God. I just don't understand why He allows such unholy bastards to spread his message."

"I'd hoped you'd say that," he replied. "Of all the men in this army, you may be the only one who won't ridicule me for what I'm about to tell you."

"Don't tell me, you're becoming a clean-mouthed celibate priest," I joked, trying to lift his mood.

Harold half smiled. "I'd rather be Eustace de Quincy's wife than a priest," he said, with a touch of his usual humour. Taking a long swig of cider, he sighed. "Do you remember what I told you about my parents?" he asked.

I frowned, trying to recall. "I don't remember you saying much. Your father is a landlord, I think. What does this have to do with the priest you chased?"

"My father is dead, as is my mother," he said bluntly. The matter-of-fact way in which he spoke was unnerving. Before I could interrupt, Harold ploughed on. "They died when I was very young. I have no memory of them."

"Why did you tell me otherwise?" I questioned. "I know I'm not one to be giving lectures about being dishonest, but I wouldn't have thought any less of you if you'd told the truth."

"I was taken in by the church, as no one else would have me," he continued as if I had not spoken. He looked through me with a glassy stare. "A young priest named Father Erwin raised me. He was responsible for all the orphans and urchins that the church took in. To outsiders, it must have seemed that I led a carefree life. I was fed, clothed and barely had to perform any manual labour. Compared to many of the children in the rural areas of our county, I was remarkably healthy." The light from the inn's interior torches illuminated his bright blue eyes in such a way that I felt I was staring into his very soul. I did not speak. I sensed that Harold had to finish his tale to its completion, more for his sake than for mine.

"In fact, I was Father Erwin's favourite," he went on. "He even taught me to sing, which I was told was a great honour. I was the star of his choir. Yet there was a side to him that the people of my village never saw. He exacted payment for his guardianship and tutelage. Every time I sang, he took me aside, and... and..."

"You don't have to say it," I said gently, feeling equal amounts of helpless pity and unbridled horror. Harold was teaching me the fourth rule of chivalry.

Never place moral value on piety, and never trust a man who proclaims to spread the word of God.

"He violated me," Harold said in a toneless voice that belied the long-repressed turmoil behind his eyes. "It became routine, for years and years. I sang for him, and he took his reward. The other priests knew about it but ignored it. What did I matter? I was but some child, some plaything. Perhaps Father Erwin planned to kill me when I grew older."

"Oh, Harold, I…"

"But then Richard appeared, six years ago. I never found out why he came to my village, but as soon as he heard the choir sing, he demanded that I enter his service. Richard paid Father Erwin for my release." A grimace appeared on Harold's features, the first emotion he had shown since he had started speaking. "He bought me like I was cattle!" he snarled. "He paid for my voice, nothing more. That's all he saw me as. Perhaps he still does." He stared sullenly into his drink.

"Now I know that's not true," I asserted. "He couldn't have known what that… beast was doing to you. Richard values your wit, your character, your loyalty and your sword far more than he values your voice." In all honesty, I wasn't sure that I spoke the truth, but what else could I say? "I know that I do as well," I added. That, at least, was entirely sincere.

"I suppose you're right," he sighed, still looking down. "Richard freed me from that living hell, which I will forever be grateful for. It's why I'll refuse to sing for anyone but him. I suppose I feel he's earnt it." Looking up at me, he exhaled deeply. "I thought that telling someone about this would clear my mind, and ease my pain, but I feel exactly the same. Isn't that strange?"

Although I felt uncomfortable discussing such a dreadful subject, I was also touched that Harold had chosen to discuss it with me, of all people. "So, that priest we saw earlier, you thought that he was this Father Erwin?"

Harold nodded. "It's why I've spent so much time teaching myself to fight, so that if I ever encounter that slug-ridden whoreson, I'll be able to cut him to pieces in a manner so painful that he may know some measure of the suffering he caused me."

"And I'll be right by your side," I said. "You've been nothing but a friend to me since we met, even when everyone else turned against me. I don't know how I can ever repay that, but the least I can do is promise you my sword whenever you need it." I offered him my hand, and he grasped it, smiling gratefully.

In the last few months, I had made so many enemies. My father, my brother, Guillaume des Barres, Eustace de Quincy, and now Father Erwin. Yet men with reputations to build need enemies, and I had cemented a lifelong friendship to help me build that reputation.

Not knowing how else to deal with Harold's revelations, we drank ourselves insensible that night, and then staggered round Amboise until we collapsed behind a blacksmith's workshop.

***

"Richard and his men have gone. We're too late."

The gruff voice startled me awake. I groaned involuntarily; my head felt as though a thousand drummers were clattering on the inside of my skull.

"The King will be mightily disappointed that we've failed to catch him up," said a second voice, more delicate than the first. I couldn't see who was speaking, as the two strangers were in the street, whilst we were shielded from view behind the blacksmith's shed. However, if the two men kept walking down the curved road, they would no doubt see us.

"That's no reason to give up, Bertrand," the first voice replied. "We'll conduct a thorough search of Amboise. Somebody must have seen the direction he rode in. The chase isn't over yet."

Trying to keep Harold quiet, I nudged him awake, surprised to see that he had somehow fallen asleep with his head on an anvil.

"When will Richard learn how foolish it is to disobey his father?" the second man, evidently named Bertrand, asked. "I suppose the King must punish him, when we return with our prize."

Two things were apparent from their conversation. Firstly, we were the last of Richard's men left in Amboise. I wasn't surprised by that, as he had likely left at dawn, assuming we would catch up. Secondly, Henry had dispatched these soldiers – likely his most fearsome men – to kidnap the Prince and return him to his father.

Anybody who threatened Richard threatened us, and if the King's men captured us, then we would no doubt be interrogated for information regarding the Prince's location. Our position as royal guards forbade us from allowing that to happen. Therefore, these two strangers would have to be silenced before we could leave Amboise.

Motioning Harold to follow me, I crept alongside the back wall of the blacksmith's and drew Lion-Pride. Harold's Wife-Tongue likewise slithered silently from its scabbard. Neither of us wore any armour, so we would have to be especially careful.

"We subdue both of them, and then find out what the King is planning," I whispered to Harold. "We don't kill them unless we have to." He nodded his agreement.

I listened intently to the footsteps of our enemies and tensed my muscles. I had endured enough peace conferences, and my blade thirsted for the release of tension that combat brought.

Springing our ambush, I leapt out in front of one of the men, screaming a shrill cry of battle. A look of animal panic on his face, he snatched his blade's handle and deflected two of my strikes before Harold shot past and thumped the King's man with his hilt. I barely had time to register our foe's elegant attire and well-groomed moustache before he slid into the ditch at the side of the street.

Knowing there was no time to celebrate our victory, we turned towards the second soldier. I almost felt sorry for him. Although he had his sword drawn and was crouched in a combat stance, he simply stood no chance. Not only was he outnumbered, but he looked to be elderly, forty at least. He was also dressed much more plainly than his companion and walked with a profound limp to his left leg. Nevertheless, we advanced cautiously, determined to ensure an easy victory. Harold struck first, leaping forwards with a low strike that was destined to impale our enemy's leg, were it not swatted away at the last second. I followed up with a scything cut to his other leg, which, to my astonishment, was repelled just as easily. Stepping away to avoid another lunge from Harold, he pivoted back with an overhead strike that I barely countered. The connecting swords clanged with the deafening clarity of a pealing bell, and I knew I had only survived through the strength and fine craftsmanship in Lion-Pride's blade.

Despite the old man's limp, his situational awareness was like no other I have encountered on a battlefield before or since. Every time I hacked my sword at a seemingly exposed part of his body, my weapon was swept aside with a humiliating nonchalance, even as he somehow defended against Harold's blows on the other side. As time wore on, my frustration increased, and my earlier desire to refrain from killing was eroded.

In the end, my impatience was my undoing. Putting all my energy into a huge overhead strike, I hammered my sword downwards, only to be met by nothingness as my opponent stepped aside. Suddenly on the offensive, he charged forwards like an enraged bull, tripping me as he feinted with his blade. Losing my balance, I slammed heavily into the ground as Lion-Pride clattered to the cobblestones and our enemy swivelled back towards Harold. Growling in frustration, I scrabbled for my weapon's hilt, but was instantly frozen by the ice-cold touch of a sword point against my neck.

"Don't you move an inch," said the first soldier we had attacked, in his elegant, distinctive tone. Evidently, he had regained his feet and retrieved his sword. He now pinned me to the ground, ensuring that I would play no further part in the fight.

Out of the corner of my eye, I could still see where Harold and the old man strove against each other. Gritting his teeth, Harold swept forward with a blinding flurry of attacks, forcing a retreat on his opponent, who was limping more and more severely with every step. Despite myself, I smiled inwardly. Aside from his duel with the Count of Vendôme, where his sword had become stuck in his enemy's flesh, I had never seen Harold lose a one-on-one fight. Although his grogginess was slowing him slightly, his speed was evidently overwhelming for his foe, who was struggling to keep up with the feints, dodges and lunges of my red-headed friend.

The end was inevitable, and it came quicker than I thought. Stepping back into a dip in the cobblestones, the old man cried out in pain as his left knee crumpled and his back arched in agony. Triumphant, Harold raked his sword towards his opponent's arm, intent on disarming him. Yet his jubilant expression was to turn to horror in an instant. Suddenly full of vigour, the old man swept round, his limp miraculously vanished, and struck Wife-Tongue so hard that it was wrenched from Harold's grasp and buried itself in a nearby bucket of nightsoil. Victorious, the old man held his sword up to Harold's chest menacingly, his grey eyes alive with battle-fury.

"Who... who are you?" Harold stammered, his face white with shock.

"My name is Sir William Marshal," the old man replied. "And you'd better explain bloody quickly why you just tried to kill me."

Chapter 22

Sir William Marshal. The greatest tournament fighter to have ever lived. The most accomplished soldier on God's Earth. A man revered by lords, ladies and royalty alike, whose exploits had filled so many of my childhood stories.

And we had just attempted to murder him.

Harold was evidently not as cowed as myself. "You may have bested us, but you'll never kidnap the Prince," he said defiantly. "Our friends won't let that happen!"

"Kidnap the Prince?" Marshal exclaimed indignantly. "Just what sort of common criminal do you think I am? Are you always so impertinent when your life is in danger?" He held his sword menacingly close to Harold's breast. This was a foe who had been killing for over twenty years and would slaughter us both in a heartbeat if he felt it necessary.

"Forgive us, Sir William," I said placatingly, still pinned uncomfortably to the ground. "If you bear no malice towards Richard, then we bear none towards you."

"And what concern of yours is it?" he asked, eyes still fixed on Harold. "Who are you exactly?"

Harold hesitated, but I was not going to lie to King Henry's most famous knight. My instinct told me that he was not our enemy. Not now, at least. "I am Alistair

Fitzwalter, and this is Harold. We are both royal guards to Prince Richard."

An eyebrow on Marshal's weathered face rose. "Royal guards? By the saints, he's recruiting children these days. But I suppose that explains your swords. Had you not possessed such fine blades, I would have taken you for brigands and cut you to pieces." His expression grim, he sheathed his weapon, much to my relief. "I am not going to kill you, Alistair, or your impetuous friend here, but only because my lord has not ordered me to, and because we are not at war, not yet." He gestured at his companion. "Bertrand, fetch their swords."

The refined-looking nobleman released me from the ground and retrieved our blades, wrinkling his nose as he pulled Harold's weapon from the foul-smelling nightsoil bucket. As I stood, I realised that a small crowd of townspeople had been watching our struggle and was melting away now that the excitement was over.

"So you bear no ill-will towards Prince Richard?" I asked warily as Harold frantically wiped Wife-Tongue on the grass.

Marshal sighed. "No, I do not. I don't expect you to understand. I have known Prince Richard since you were a babe, and I have been able to reconcile him with his father more than once. I have been sent to speak with him, and persuade him, nothing more." So he simply wished to negotiate. The thought of such a notoriously frightening warrior sitting down to talk seemed absurd. But William Marshal was much, much more than a simple fighter, as I was to learn.

He gazed at me, deep in thought. "Alistair Fitzwalter... I recognise the name, but not the face. Why is that?"

"He caused quite a stir at Bonsmoulins, whilst you were still in England," Bertrand provided. "Family dispute, if I understand correctly."

"Ah yes!" Marshal exclaimed. "The young man detested by his father. You and Richard are a good match, I think." He gave a tiny hint of a smile. "I wish I could have been at Bonsmoulins, but alas, I was visiting with Queen Eleanor."

That intrigued me. "You know the Queen? I thought she was imprisoned?"

"She is, and though I must not criticise the King for his decision, she is a remarkable woman. I believe the Prince inherited his best traits from her." Despite what he had just said, his criticism of Henry was implicit. Marshal was exceptionally cunning, not only in how he fought, but also in the words he spoke.

Although I wanted to hear more about Queen Eleanor, I knew we could not stay in Amboise any longer. "It has been an honour to meet you, Sir William, but we must catch up with Richard. Every second we spend away from him is a dereliction of our duty. If you wish to speak with him, you could accompany us?" It was an offer made more out of politeness than genuine enthusiasm; Marshal's intimidating presence was beginning to unnerve me.

"No, I think not," Marshal said gravely. "I fear this has been a wasted journey, and that the breach between father and son is now too severe. Yet I shall return to the King's side, nonetheless. Tell Richard that his father regrets his actions, though I doubt he will listen." Marshal turned and strode away from us, before hesitating and turning back. "The two of you fought well today, and your loyalty is commendable. I know that young men seem to have a terrible enthusiasm for getting themselves killed, but if you keep yourself alive, I think you have potential. But know this; if we ever meet on the field of battle, I will slay you without a second thought." His threat delivered, he strode back up the path, towards the north edge of the village, with Bertrand in pursuit. There was still no sign of the limp he had displayed earlier.

"The greatest knight in Christendom," I said in wonder at his retreating back.

"He knocked my sword into a shit-bucket!" Harold wailed despairingly.

"But he..."

"A shit-bucket! I thought bloody knights were supposed to have honour!"

I chuckled and pulled him to his feet. "I'll have to tell Richard. If we ever have to execute an ambush, the enemy will smell you long before they reach us!"

"Don't you dare tell anyone," Harold pleaded.

"We'll see," I replied mischievously. "Come on. We have a long ride ahead of us."

"Wonderful," he grumbled. "You always know how to lift my mood, Alistair."

Having fetched our horses from the inn, we bolted south in pursuit of our lord, to join him for the climactic conflict to come.

***

Then, for the next six months, nothing happened.

At least, that was how it seemed. Judging by Richard's mood, I had expected an instant declaration of war against King Henry, which would pit both Angevin factions against each other in a bloody brawl to the death. Instead, France became drowned under a sea of envoys, sent by a Pope desperate to delay the conflict, whereas King Philippe sought to constantly confuse the situation. I sometimes feel that the King of France did not know his own intentions; he seemed determined to pit Richard and Henry against each other, but at the same time, he did not want France obliterated by the ravages of war. As such, he arranged peace conference after peace conference, whilst whispering in Richard's ear that his inheritance would be denied.

Though fierce and ambitious, the Prince's military mind was not without good sense. He would not commit to an all-out war against his father without the full support of the Capetian King, which was not forthcoming. In truth, I think that King Philippe was waiting for Henry to die. The feeble Angevin monarch grew weaker by the day, and if he perished by natural causes, Philippe would achieve his ultimate goal. He would gain an unblemished France, and the King of England would either be an unpopular John or a subservient Richard.

If King Henry's health was failing, his support was as well. Determined to show that he still held the strongest authority in France, he forced himself to tour Aquitaine in the frozen midst of winter. Yet he achieved nothing. The stubborn Aquitanian nobles refused to accompany his armies or even declare their open allegiance. Not only did they see the strength of his enemies growing, but they also held ancient grudges for the imprisonment of their duchess, Queen Eleanor. At last, King Henry's mistreatment of his family was returning to punish him.

It was not only Richard and Aquitaine that had deserted the King. The ailing monarch, who spent a lonely Christmas at Saumur, summoned his barons to his side. A year before, a wave of nobles would have rushed to join him, but now, only a trickle stayed loyal. Yet it seemed there was one baron who would never desert him, as I discovered when I received a letter on the very first day of the year of our Lord 1189.

It was delivered to me by a wool merchant who had travelled south to trade his winter fleeces with the wealthier members of Richard's army. It was obvious he had no clue who I was; the letter had changed hands several times since it was dispatched. He approached Richard's retinue, shouting my name, which interrupted my sword practice.

"I didn't think you were one for receiving correspondence," Sir Oliver said curiously as the merchant handed me the folded yellow parchment.

My head streaked with sweat, I pulled off my mail coif and removed the unfamiliar seal. "I've never been sent a letter before," I confessed. "I wonder who it could be from."

"Your father, wishing to make amends?" Sir Oliver offered hopefully.

I shook my head. "I would recognise his seal," I said. Moreover, I had accepted by then that we would never be reconciled; my father was as stubborn as he was cold, and my pride was too severely damaged.

Upon seeing the handwriting within, my heart soared. Barely able to contain my excitement, I excused myself from Sir Oliver and ran to the outskirts of Agen, where Richard's army was encamped, so I could find a secluded tree by which to sit and read.

The letter was from Alice, and it was the first I had heard from her since I had left Little Dunmow. It must have cost her a substantial amount of money to send, and so I knew it must contain something more significant than mere pleasantries. I kept the letter, and still have it with me now, so I shall record some of what she wrote.

Dear Alistair, she began, *I would have tried to write earlier, but I did not know where to send the letter. I now know you are a close confidant of Prince Richard, which is terribly rude of you. I had thought for once that I was more important than you, being the wife of a baron.* Alice's wit was always able to make me smile, as it did then. *My wedding was actually rather tedious. I don't think most of the men there even acknowledged my existence, but Gilbert certainly did. He's a wonderful husband, and I'm sure you'd be firm friends if you met.* I was glad to hear that Alice had found happiness; many marriages within nobility did not end as such. She wrote a little more about Gilbert, about Bourn, and about Robert who was apparently more smug than ever. Yet the crux of her letter was to come, and I frowned in alarm as I read it. *I believe you will recognise the name Eustace de Quincy, a most sour creature who has begun following Father like a tame dog. He claims that you lied to have him removed from Richard's service. I do not think Father believes him, but he does not care. Any enemy of yours is a friend of his. So be careful, Alistair. If it comes to war between the King and the Prince, you and Father will no doubt be on opposite sides. Watch out for Father's vengeance and watch out for Eustace de Quincy. He seems utterly rabid in his devotion to hunt you down. I pray for you, Alistair, and I pray that God allows us to see each other soon. I have faith that God will provide that opportunity, and I have faith in you.*

I allowed myself a second of self-pity, mourning the fact that Alice and I could not have a proper conversation. Yet I only allowed myself a second. Leaping to my feet, I sprinted back into the town, seeking out Sir Oliver and Joanna. Once I had sat them down, I told them exactly what Alice had related to me. A low growl emanated from Sir Oliver as he heard de Quincy's name, yet Joanna seemed calmer. "Good," she said in a flat, steely voice. "If he's joined King Henry, then we'll have an excuse to kill him when the war begins."

It seemed she would not have long to wait. Claiming ill health, King Henry failed to appear at Philippe's January peace talks. Although we were in doubt that Richard had intended to participate in these negotiations at all, he accused his father of falsehood and made an immediate declaration of war.

The whole of Christendom held its breath, but still nothing happened. We travelled, we trained, we visited all of Richard's supporters, but still we did not march, because the French army was not ready to support us. Weeks turned into months, and we soldiers were left to entertain ourselves. The Prince's mood, initially bright at the prospect of a campaign, darkened as Philippe hesitated. Much to my dismay, Richard asked Harold to sing for him increasingly frequently in order to cheer him. Although I could not remove Harold's pain, I think I was able to help. Every time he sang, I would try to distract him afterwards, with some silly story or bawdy joke. One evening, we even stole all of Sir Baldwin's horseshoes, just to see his furious and haughty reaction. We were almost caught, but Harold's laughter was worth the risk. We did not talk further about the cause of his sorrow, for what was there to say?

I may have made it sound like those months were wasted, yet that was certainly not the case. I practised with Lion-Pride every day, resolute that I would never again be humiliated as I had been by Sir William Marshal. Sir Oliver and Richard alike chided me for my shame, asserting that any soldier should be proud to stand against Marshal for more than a few seconds. Yet in my stubborn youth, I would have none of it. I worked with Lion-Pride relentlessly, and thus my strength grew. I had still never killed a real warrior in battle, but at least I was now more physically capable.

Eventually, the pressure on King Philippe became too much. We discovered this one quiet, serene spring evening just before Easter. I had spent the previous half-hour sitting opposite Richard at a chess table, much to the amusement of his retinue; I am certain they were taking bets as to how badly I would lose. I did not mind, as I was simply content to spend whatever little leisure time I had together with my lord. Indeed, I was somewhat perturbed when William L'Etang burst through the pavilion entrance, interrupting our game.

"Your Highness, His Majesty King Philippe sends a message," L'Etang announced without preamble. "He requests your presence at a conference in Whitsun, near La Ferté-Bernard, where your father will also be present."

Richard was on his feet in an instant, his eyes full of fire. "By God's legs, another infernal conference? I thought I'd made myself explicitly clear last year. I've said all I have to say to that dishonest swine. What on earth has possessed Philippe?"

L'Etang shrugged. "Papal legates, Your Highness. They've been wearing him down for months now."

"Anything's got to be better than meandering around, waiting for the French to organise themselves," Sir Oliver put in.

Richard rolled his eyes. "I suppose I have no choice, if I'm to maintain amenable relations with the Capetians," he said, his voice full of resignation. He turned away to begin his preparations, abandoning our game of chess.

I expect most of those who write accounts of Richard's life to make a great deal of the conference of Whitsun. However, I do not think it was especially important, certainly not as crucial as Bonsmoulins. It is true that figures of enormous authority were present. As well as the royalty, the archbishops of Rheims, Bourges, Rouen and Canterbury were in attendance, ostensibly to cast jurisdiction. In the event, I believe everyone ignored them. Indeed, nothing was resolved at Whitsun, and nothing changed. What mattered were the events after the talks were over, but for posterity's sake, I will give a brief account.

It almost seemed as though none of the involved parties expected a peaceful resolution. Armed men glowered at each other, and my father glared at me with flinty eyes from across the room, although we did not speak. Eustace de Quincy, if he was with Henry, had sensibly hidden himself, though that did not prevent scuffles from breaking out. When two knights charged at each other with fists flying, William Marshal forcibly dragged them apart and bellowed that any man who wanted to fight would have to face him in single combat. After that, no more open brawls occurred, but the simmering resentment remained.

Richard's demands were simple, and I think he knew that Henry would not agree to them. The first two were reminiscent of the discussions at Bonsmoulins: Richard would marry Philippe's sister, and would be confirmed heir. It was the final demand that was crafted to deliberately insult Henry; Richard insisted that John take the cross. It was a bare-faced accusation of favouritism, and naturally, Henry refused, speaking through teeth gritted by pain. The assembled clergy protested mightily, with the papal legate John of Anagni threatening to lay an interdict across all of France if an agreement was not met. Yet without Richard's approval, Philippe could not make any further offers, and so the conference simply dissolved.

Many people observed that Whitsun was the cause of the short and brutal war which occurred afterwards. In truth, it was the split between Henry and Richard at Bonsmoulins which resulted in the inevitable conflict. It was only delayed for so long because of Philippe's indecisiveness and the Pope's interference.

Regardless of the cause, Richard's patience was exhausted. So many words had been spoken, and the Prince now resolved to settle the matter by the methods for which he had the most talent. He was not going to wait for his father to die and hope that his inheritance fell to him.

As he always had before when he desired land, he was going to take it with the sword, until his blade was so soaked with blood that nobody could deny his birthright.

He was such an inspiration to me.

The very next morning, we finally marched to war.

Chapter 23

"Dashing knights performing heroic deeds on horseback, that's what I thought soldiering was," I grumbled as our cog slid down the inky river. "The Prince should have told me that boats would be involved. I'd have stayed as a butcher's apprentice if I'd known. Maybe it's not too late to go back."

"Well, aren't you going to be a joy during the month-long voyage to the Holy Land?" Harold asked airily. The gentle rocking of the ship clearly hadn't brought him any discomfort; in fact, his voice was more full of life than ever.

Sir Oliver chuckled. "Strange, isn't it, Harold? Someone's complaining and it isn't you." Even if it hadn't been the depth of night, I would only have recognised him if I'd heard him speak. The knight's great-helm transformed him into a terrifying being of iron which belied the gentle soul beneath. "Don't you worry, Alistair. God will have the ground beneath our feet again soon."

My complaints were partly genuine, but partly an internal distraction from the battle to come. In truth, I hadn't had much time to contemplate the upcoming bloodbath. Following the abortive conference at Whitsun, King Henry had retreated to the frontier with his army, expecting Richard and Philippe to do the same. However, the Prince had been marshalling his full forces for months and knew that a rapid strike after a conference would surprise and unsettle his father. Thus, we found ourselves floating along this narrow, black river that led into the town of La Ferté-Bernard which was Richard's first target of his vengeful war against the King.

Deception and surprise were crucial elements to our attack, which was why the Prince had decided on a water-borne assault. Of course, the entire army would not be able to fit onto the four cogs that had undertaken the long journey south from the sea. Instead, two hundred of his finest men would sail into the heart of La Ferté-Bernard, where half of them would rush to open the town's northern gate, and the other half would fight off reinforcements from the town centre.

It was with great reluctance that Richard conceded he could not lead the landing party himself. Instead, he had charged two of his most reliable men to command; Sir Baldwin would attack the gates, whereas Sir Oliver would stand his ground and buy time for the rest of the army. The remainder of Richard's troops would hide silently in the fields west of the town, and Philippe's men were winding their way round the southern perimeter, to assist if necessary.

The Prince's plan was in place. Now, everything depended on us reaching the town undetected.

"I never had a chance to thank you for choosing me to accompany you," I said to Sir Oliver, trying to ignore the nausea summoned by the current's swell. "I couldn't bear the thought of staying behind to guard the baggage again."

He smiled. "I'm sure you would have found your way to the front line regardless. I was just cutting out the part where you're chastised for disobeying orders. It's terribly tiresome."

"And what about me?" Harold asked. "What use could a sacrilegious little Welsh runt be in your band of merry warriors?"

"Oh, someone has to be the arrow fodder," Sir Oliver said disdainfully. "I'm going to check on the men. Keep your eyes open for the city walls. Just one watchful defender could seal our doom." Clapping me on the shoulder, he began traversing the ship, his mail clinking quietly as he moved.

I shivered, despite the mild spring temperature. "They're Englishmen. We'll be killing Englishmen," I said with a note of trepidation.

Harold looked at me quizzically. "And it wouldn't be a problem if they were French? The French aren't inherently bad people, Alistair. Enemies are enemies, no matter where they rolled out of their mothers. We can't afford to humanise them." He was right. Reputation didn't care about the nationality of the foes you killed. Chivalry didn't care. I hardened my heart and sharpened Lion-Pride one last time. We had killing to do.

As Richard's scouts had told us, the river entrance through La Ferté-Bernard's city walls was mostly unguarded. The one guard overlooking the edge of the parapet, illuminated by his torch, was silently eliminated by the handful of crossbowmen we had on board. All conversation on the four cogs had ceased entirely.

The garrison slept, and we entered the town's perimeter, intent on slaughtering them.

Our goal was a bridge in the north-western sector of the town, which was where we would disembark and resist any reinforcing garrison troops, so that Sir Baldwin and his men could open the gate. It was obvious that our enemy was not expecting us, as there were only a few sentries on the walls and no visible military presence amongst the town's buildings.

Quite suddenly, our plan, which had been executed flawlessly up until that point, went quite horribly wrong. Without warning, I was thrown off my feet as an enormous vibration swept through the ship, and our vessel juddered to a stop as several of the oars snapped against the riverbank. Unseen to the helmsman, we had drifted towards the edge of the river, and to my horror, we had run aground.

Sir Oliver was swift to react. "Ship oars! Grab spares, off the side and lever us back into the water. Quickly now!"

"Why not just abandon the ship?" I asked urgently. "We can't be far from the bridge now. We could run along the riverbank and keep pace with the other ships!" A couple of other men murmured agreement.

Sir Oliver shook his head. "We can't leave the ship. When the fighting starts, some of the garrison might use it to escape. Richard's orders were clear. No enemies are to be allowed to flee. Now, go and stand guard fifty yards away. Let us know if any soldiers approach."

Patting the cleaver at my belt for luck, I vaulted over the ship's edge and walked away, exhaling deeply. I knew how crucial my role was; I would have to either turn back any curious enemies or tell Sir Oliver that an attack was incoming. It would undoubtedly take a little while for the ship to be dislodged, and I heard Harold hissing at our men to be quiet as they worked. Scanning the buildings for movement, I observed how peaceful the town was. It was not unlike Châteauroux, in fact. I wondered whether Henry the butcher was prospering. I hoped he'd found somebody else to assist him. Despite his gruff bravado, I knew he couldn't cope on his own.

"You all right, mate? You look a bit lost," an unfamiliar voice suddenly said from my right.

I spun around, trying to ignore the dread boiling in my stomach. I had been so fixated on the town that I hadn't considered somebody might spot me from the walls. The man who had approached me did not look particularly threatening; he wore only wool and tattered leather, with his head unhelmeted. Clearly, he was not expecting a fight, but he posed an immense danger nonetheless, as there was no way I would be able to warn Sir Oliver without arousing his suspicion. I briefly considered rushing him with Lion-Pride, but the risk was too high. I would have to talk my way out of this predicament.

"Just enjoying the night air," I replied, trying to sound casual. "My mercenary company is a rowdy bunch, so it's nice to have a moment to myself."

"A mercenary, eh? Where..." He stopped abruptly and stared past me towards the river, his bleary eyes straining into the night. "What's that noise?" he asked, more out of curiosity than distrust. I inwardly cursed our men by the ship, who were faintly grunting and groaning as they tried to haul it off the bank.

After a moment's panic, I somehow knew what to say. "All right, you've figured me out," I said with a smile. "I'm not just out here for a stroll. I'm standing guard."

A bushy eyebrow on the soldier's face rose. "Standing guard for what? It's not like we're at war here."

I lowered my voice to a murmur. "You see, my brother's taken a fancy to a local girl. Daughter of the tanner or cobbler or something like that. Anyhow, her father's a right fierce git, so he's had to bring her out here for some... private time. I'm to make sure they're not interrupted."

He laughed, baring a mouth almost absent of teeth. "You ought to ditch him. It'll teach him for not taking her somewhere decent." He itched a louse in his hair. "You're obviously a proper Englishman like me. Whereabouts are you from?"

I knew my answer had to be instantaneous, so I named the first town which came into my head. "Little Dunmow," I replied.

"Ah, I see," he said, as if my response had made perfect sense. "Well, good luck standing vigil." He turned, still chuckling to himself, before returning to his post. Letting out a sigh of relief, I watched his retreating back, knowing that he would probably be dead in a few hours. Such was the misfortune of fighting for a liege who opposed Prince Richard.

Only a few moments passed before Harold's voice whispered out of the darkness. "We're floating again, so we need you back at the ship. Unless you'd rather stay with your handsome new friend, of course." I nodded and joined him. "You handled that well," he continued. "I'd probably have panicked and sat on him as soon as he appeared."

"It wasn't difficult," I told him. "He wasn't expecting trouble. Harold, they're completely clueless."

He grinned. "Best news I've had all day."

Thankfully, the rest of the short voyage was uneventful, and a few minutes later, we moored the boats by the bridge, looping rope around balustrades and tree branches to keep them steady. Picking up a shield, I joined the men disembarking from the ship, marvelling at the fact that we were still unnoticed. Sir Baldwin clasped Sir Oliver's hand, gathered his troops behind him, and set off at a trot to the western gate. If all went to plan, he wouldn't be disturbed by reinforcements from the town centre. To ensure this, Sir Oliver began lining us up across the bridge's width, blocking the path with a wall of shields and iron. As we were being manoeuvred into position, a fox burst out of a bush next to me, causing me to leap aside in shock. As I watched the creature scampering away, I observed the thickets of trees and bushes surrounding the bridgehead, and a wild idea began to form in my head.

"Sir Oliver! Sir Oliver!" I exclaimed as quietly as I could, shouldering my way through the throng of men.

"What is it, Alistair?" replied the dark, hulking figure. "Do you see the enemy?"

"No, no," I said hurriedly. "I have a proposal. Our foes will come this way in response to the alarm at the west gate, correct?" The men around me nodded.

"Well, even though they'll be at arms, they still won't know we're here, only that there's an attack at the gate. When they come this way, we needn't show ourselves at first. We have all these trees, bushes and foliage…"

"An ambush," Harold breathed. I knew he would catch on first.

"When the first group comes past, we wipe them out before they even know we're here, then we form up on the bridge," I said, speaking faster and faster. "Not only will we kill a significant number, but we'll demoralise the rest."

Frantic whispering broke out amongst the soldiers, but Sir Oliver silenced them instantly and gazed intently into my eyes as he thought. It was undoubtedly a big risk. By arranging ourselves for an ambush, we would sacrifice the security of the bridge and risk being outflanked. But if we were quick enough, we would be able to regain the bridgehead whilst the enemy were reeling.

Sir Oliver nodded abruptly. "We do it," he said, and an itch of excitement wriggled up my spine.

Thus, we made ourselves shadows. I crouched beside Harold in a tangle of bushes, and one by one, our men vanished as they melted into the darkness. All was silent aside from the churning of the river and the ragged breathing of the concealed soldiers around me.

Not a minute later, a frantic alarm bell shattered the night's calm serenity, and a grim smile crept onto my face. The fall of La Ferté-Bernard was now underway.

The wait was excruciating, as we could faintly hear Sir Baldwin's men battling their way towards the gates, but eventually our patience was rewarded. A troop of sixty men, the first to respond to the alarm, came sprinting towards the bridge in a ragged formation, intent only on reinforcing their comrades as swiftly as possible. As they began to cross, I clasped Gilbert's locket, still round my neck, and prayed for God's wrath to bless my blade. I heard the first men run past me, and tensed my muscles, like a wolf poised to spring at its prey.

"For Richard!" Sir Oliver roared, and finally, our hungry swords were released to the kill.

It must have seemed that a wave of demons erupted from beneath the earth, and most of our foes were so stunned that they didn't even have time to react. I charged, snarling, at a young man who simply gaped at me, and was still gaping as Lion-Pride took him in the mouth. He collapsed, gurgling and choking on his own blood, but I had already turned away, to strike at a bearded mercenary. Managing to keep his wits, my enemy raised his shield, but I simply feinted, knocked him off-balance with my own shield, and then took him in the throat with Lion-Pride's needle-sharp point. Battle fever roared through my body as I desperately sought my next target, and I was faced by a grizzled man-at-arms who swung an axe at me, then shrieked in pain as Harold's Wife-Tongue stabbed him in the spine. King Henry's startled men were being cut down all around me, one of whom was nervously backing away from Sir Oliver's terrifying presence. I simply kicked him in the back, and the knight's enormous blade impaled him through the abdomen. The soldier gasped, and Sir Oliver twisted his sword, before retrieving it in a fountain of blood.

A small cluster of men had gathered round a moustached mercenary captain, back-to-back, and I savagely threw myself at them, splitting their formation in two. Ignoring the blades which brushed off my mail hauberk, I ducked under the captain's wild swing, sliced at his shins with Lion-Pride, before brutally hitting him with the hilt and stabbing him through the heart when he fell. Blood gushed out of his mouth for a few seconds, and then he was still. Enraged by the death of their captain, the mercenaries bravely charged at me, but were cut down by Harold and my other allies before they could even lift their weapons.

Quite suddenly, there were no more enemies to fight. Most of our foes were dead or wounded, and we had only lost one killed and three with light injuries. A few of Henry's men had fled towards the gate or the town. They would not find refuge in either direction.

The ambush had been a comprehensive success, yet there was no time to celebrate. The group we had massacred was only an advance party, and a much larger force was undoubtedly on its way. Sir Oliver, his blood-spattered surcoat complementing his fearsome appearance, ordered us onto the bridge. I shouldered my way into the front rank, between Sir Oliver and his squire. Ninety-nine of us braced ourselves as we spotted a fresh wave of enemies spilling onto the street opposite us. The small army of men-at-arms and mercenaries hesitated as they saw the sprawl of corpses behind us, and our tightly packed formation on the bridge, bristling with bloodied steel. Yet their knights and captains urged them on, knowing that they had to smash through our defence to rescue the western gate, and prevent the breach of La Ferté-Bernard.

"Shields!" one of our men shouted as crossbow bolts spat at us, plucking two from the front line. Our crossbows returned fire, but the feeble exchange could not last long, given the urgency of our opponents. Without any discernible order given, the mass of foes, at least five hundred in number, rushed our position, determined to brush us aside. There was no order to their attack, but they simply came as a screaming horde, emulating the barbarians of old.

Tightening the grip on my shield, I locked eyes with a leather-clad mercenary wielding a spear, who evidently saw my youth and targeted me with a devilish grin. Pretending fright, I shuffled backwards slightly, and his expression became one of gleeful victory as he reached our line and lanced his spear towards my eyes. Pivoting back towards him, I glanced his spear aside with my shield, kicked him in the groin, and almost beheaded him with an almighty sweep of Lion-Pride. His head flopping to the side, he crumpled to the ground, and his place was almost immediately taken by a heavily muscled man-at-arms who pinned me back with his shield, spitting curses into my face.

Across the bridge, the lines had clashed together. Although outnumbered five to one, our position was well entrenched, and we were the finest of Richard's army. We were knights and squires, armed and armoured with the finest equipment in Christendom, and we reckoned ourselves immortal. I felt untouchable as my blood sang in my veins and Lion-Pride snatched soul after soul.

As I kicked another corpse off my blade, a mountainous enemy barrelled his way into the front rank and struck a colossal blow which cleaved my shield almost in two. His furious attack had left him open to a counter-strike, but he seemed not to notice Lion-Pride sinking into his thigh. Instead, he drew back his axe to split my skull, but suddenly stopped, surprise registering in his eyes, as Sir Oliver's squire stabbed him through the neck. Not a moment later, I was fountained by warm blood as a sword beheaded the squire, and his killer was silenced in turn by Harold's blade which pierced his eye and punctured his brain. Such is the chaos of battle. I have mentioned before the importance of luck to a warrior, and I cannot recount the number of times I was inches from death in that fight.

Despite the pile of corpses mounting in front of us, it soon seemed as though we must be overwhelmed. Reluctant to charge into the front of our formation, our enemies began swimming across the river, discarding their heavy armour on the bank. Instead of running to reinforce the gates, these men circled around behind us, intent on avenging their dozens of fallen comrades. Quite suddenly, we were fighting for our lives from the front and the back. Of course, these thoughts weren't occurring to me during the fight, as I was simply concerned with the foe in front of me and planning how they were going to die.

My shield damaged beyond usefulness, I dropped it and drew my cleaver in my shield hand, instantly using it to decapitate the forearm of a burly mercenary who had over-extended himself. He reeled away, screaming in an eerily high-pitched voice, and I used my second's respite to glance at my surroundings.

We were losing. It was inevitable, given the fact we were surrounded. To my right, Sir Oliver was particularly hard pressed, as he was the tallest and most resplendent warrior in our group, and so became a target for every foe who sought glory and reputation. He wasn't helped by the fact that he now had to defend me with his shield, and he grunted as a spear thrust took him in the left shoulder, piercing his shining mail. Shouting his incoherent rage, he took a step forward and eviscerated two mercenaries with one almighty sweep of his sword, causing the others to back away in fear. Yet they soon came forward again, inexorably pressed forward by the weight of the men behind.

The lithe soldier who had struck Sir Oliver with the spear now advanced on me, and without a shield I felt terribly exposed. Clearly my foe was an experienced soldier, for he approached me with caution. Trying to catch him off balance, I leapt forward, inside the range of his spear, but he simply swept the shaft under my legs, causing me to stumble to the ground. I winced, waiting for his weapon's cold point to enter my flesh, but instead the spearman was looking behind me, panic on his face.

"The Prince! The Prince comes!" a squire shouted, and never have so few words brought me so much joy.

Having ridden through the gates that Sir Baldwin had captured, Richard now led an armoured cavalry wedge which smashed into the soldiers attacking our rear, killing many and scattering the rest. Their screams were muffled by the dirt as hooves trampled them into the ground. Seeing that their fight was lost, the men in front of us began to melt away, retreating to either hide or seek refuge in the town centre for one final stand.

"After them! Hunt the wretches down!" Richard called, magnificent atop his stallion, with his golden circlet reflecting the virgin dawn sunlight. Though battered and exhausted, we obeyed instantly, and I followed a group of Sir Oliver's men into the town itself. I could not see the knight himself, or Harold, but that didn't matter. The urge to kill was driving my tired limbs forward. This was chivalry, and it was exhilarating. A year ago, I had been a mere timid child, but now I was a warrior. Horrendously rash and reckless, but a warrior, nonetheless.

Rounding a street corner next to a pristine new chapel, which was hiding a throng of cowering women and children, we encountered a group of defenders rushing the other way. Unsighted, I ran headlong into a tall man with heavy, polished mail and an elegant sword, who wore a bright steel spangen-helm with a full faceguard. I began to lift my weapons, but then I felt a sudden drowning sensation as I realised that I had seen that helmet before.

I had collided with the garrison leader of La Ferté-Bernard. Baron Walter Fitzrobert. My father.

Who recognised me, snarled in pure hatred, and lunged his sword forward for the kill.

Chapter 24

That moment of hesitation should have been my death. For a few seconds after I recognised my father, a cacophony of thoughts echoed in my head. Shock at his appearance, fear of his displeasure, and uncertainty over whether I could actually raise my blade against him. Despite the abhorrent manner in which he had treated me, he was still my sire, and I did not know whether I could kill him. An image of my mother's tear-stained face flashed before my eyes, which compounded my confusion further.

Baron Walter had taught me very little during my childhood, as he preferred to shower praise and advice on my brother, Robert. Yet, on that day, he taught me the fifth rule of chivalry.

Never, ever hesitate, even if you think you are facing one that you love.

My father did not hesitate, and lanced his sword towards my breast, seeking to avenge the grief I had caused. Even though my conscious mind was paralysed, some instinct miraculously prevailed. To my own amazement, my cleaver rose and parried my father's sword to the side.

"Die, you insolent runt," he hissed with a malice that was truly terrifying, given that he was speaking to his own son. Raising his blade once again, he brought it crashing down onto Lion-Pride with such force that I staggered backwards. Once again, swords were clashing all around me as Baron Walter's retinue honoured their vow to their lord. I recognised most of them and was dimly aware that men I had known all my life were bleeding to death on the nearby cobblestones. I surprised myself by feeling no pity. If they fought by my father's side, they were complicit in his misdemeanours.

Shouting my defiance, I rose and swung Lion-Pride high and my cleaver low, attempting to unbalance the Baron, yet he simply stepped back, evading my cleaver's short reach, and thrust away Lion-Pride with his own weapon. Not only was my father a more experienced swordsman; his equipment was superior to mine, and he was not fatigued from battle, as I was. Yet I would not have men say that Alistair Fitzwalter conceded without putting up an almighty struggle, and so I came forward again in a flurry of steel.

I did not see the sword coming towards my head until it had penetrated my flesh.

The blade gouged into my face and carved a path down my left cheekbone, leaving a trail of white-hot pain as it was withdrawn. Yet it was not my father who had struck. I rapidly turned my head to identify my aggressor and found myself staring into the one remaining eye of Eustace de Quincy.

Alice had been right, and the two men who had caused me the most grief over the past year now stood before me. I growled and raised my weapons to fight them both. Yet de Quincy, shabby in his borrowed mail and eyepatch, was not looking at me. Instead, he was staring past me, and on his face was a look of unbridled terror.

I heard, rather than saw, Sir Oliver approaching. Unhelmeted, and with one arm sheeted in blood, he roared in anger at the sight of de Quincy's face and thundered towards us like an avenging horror from hell itself. Rather than stay and fight this demonic adversary, de Quincy stumbled backwards, all thoughts of revenge gone, and fled towards the city walls. Brushing my father's men aside as if they were not there, Sir Oliver pounded down the street after him, determined to finish what he had started months before.

Yet I did not have time to observe the chase. I had a family quarrel to settle.

My father furiously pressed the attack, knowing that he had to kill me before any more allies appeared. "Your name is detested in Little Dunmow," he spat as our swords rang against each other. "The villagers pray daily for news of your death." He easily dodged a laboured swing from my cleaver, then attacked with three quick strikes which Lion-Pride only just turned aside. The blood from my wound was running copiously down my face. "Your brother always knew you would betray us. I always had more faith in him." My hauberk barely withstood a powerful blow to my shoulder, and my return strike bounced off his spangen-helm, our family's hereditary piece of armour. "Your mother never speaks of you. She wishes you had never been born." He feinted left, then switched his sword's direction so that it was cutting towards my right arm. I intercepted with Lion-Pride, but the force of his blow knocked the sword from my grasp, so that it clattered onto the blood-soaked street. "As for your precious sister, I know she's been contacting you. Maybe I'll keep you alive just long enough to watch her being beaten for her impertinence."

My father's first mistake was to underestimate me.

His second was to mention Alice.

Suddenly filled with renewed vigour, I screamed a shrill cry of rage and hammered at the Baron with my cleaver. He had thought me exhausted and defeated, and this new energy took him aback. Anger now allowed my tired limbs to move with deadly speed, and my father could only desperately defend and dodge. All the Baron's men had been killed or routed, yet Richard's troops did not interfere; they sensed the personal nature of our fight.

Eventually, my father made a mistake. Worn down both mentally and physically, he tried to block one of my strikes far too early, and now, I did not hesitate. Gleefully knowing that this was the end, I altered the direction of my cleaver and hammered it onto the hilt of the Baron's sword, severing two fingers of his left hand. Crying out in anguish, he dropped his weapon and sank to his knees, clutching his wound. He glanced up, and for the first time in my life, I saw something in his eyes other than cold disdain. I saw fear.

I remembered the first rule of chivalry and brought the cleaver down in a crushing arc towards my father's skull.

Yet the blow never landed. From behind, a strong arm suddenly restrained me, a second before the Baron's head would have been cracked open like an egg. Completely infected with the fervour of battle, I swung round to cleave at my assailant, but the blow faltered as I realised that I was staring into the eyes of Prince Richard.

I struggled against him for a moment. "Let me go!" I cried. "Let me finish this! You don't understand what he's done to me!"

"Really? Don't I?" he shot back angrily. Like me, he was covered in blood, and his eyes were alive with the fury of battle. "Do you have any idea how many times I've been close to my father with a blade in my hand, and wished to spill his sorry guts across the floor?" His grip on me tightened as he spoke. "For half of my life, the King has plotted against me. For half my life, I've wished I could strike him down. But I can't kill my father, and you can't kill yours."

"But why not?" I asked, bewildered. "We're warriors! We kill our enemies! And if anyone deserves death, our fathers do!"

The Prince sighed, and I sensed the anger seeping from him. He gave a small, sad smile, and released me. Although still desperate to finish off the Baron, my desire to hear Richard speak held my attention.

"Because I have a brain as well as a sword, my dear Alistair," he said in a gentler tone. "Yes, I want to be feared as a great warrior, and a great commander, but I want to fulfil my destiny as King of the Angevins even more. If I kill the King, I will be condemned across Christendom as a murderer of my kin, and my brother John will be granted the crown. Likewise, you will never be accepted in Little Dunmow if you are seen to butcher your father. I know it is difficult to accept, but we have no choice. One does not gain great power through the strength of one's sword arm, but by proving to his people that he is worthy of their trust and loyalty. Otherwise, what are titles but vain self-affections?"

I truly heard the empathy in his voice, and to my surprise, I pitied him. He had never felt loved within his family, aside from his mother's affection, which had been severed by prison bars for the last seventeen years. Only a character of enormous personality could combat the pressure and antagonism that Richard faced, and still emerge with his pride and geniality. Of course, I do not claim to have completely understood him. All I knew was that I would follow him until my death. I still cared about Little Dunmow and knew that I would take it back one day. But for now, service to Richard would be my only priority.

My lord took a step back. "If you still want to kill the Baron, then that is your business. But please, consider what I have said. Consider why I have restrained myself all these years."

I do not think anyone else could have persuaded me to spare my father's life. As it was, I turned back to the Baron, and wrenched the spangen-helm off his head. "This is mine now," I sneered. "If you want it back, feel free to try and take it." He did not move or speak, but remained kneeling with his head bowed, nursing the stumps of his fingers, and shuddering as pain wracked him. I wondered why I had ever feared him.

Stony-faced, Richard now addressed him. "Baron Fitzrobert, you have been bested and your garrison routed." Indeed, the cacophony of battle had died out all over the town. Men who put up an armed resistance tend to do so noisily, and an eerie quietness had descended on La Ferté-Bernard. "Do you accept your defeat and surrender yourself to my authority?"

"I do," my father replied sullenly.

"Good," the Prince said carelessly, refusing to grace the Baron with any more of his attention. "Alistair, take thirty of these men and return to the bridge. We have injured men there, and I need them taken back to our camp for treatment. Get your own wounds seen to as well." I had almost forgotten about the state of my face, but I felt a sharp, stinging pain now that the adrenaline had subsided.

"Of course, Your Highness. You men, with me, if you please," I said, gesturing at the group of soldiers who had fought with my father's retinue. I was uncomfortably aware that this was the first time I had ever given orders, but the men obeyed without question. I imagine Richard's presence had something to do with their obedience.

"Oh, and Alistair," the Prince called to my retreating back. I turned around instantly. "Well done today. I'm sure that your reputation will soon surpass even mine!" I was unable to contain a broad smile. I no longer cared that my father would never speak to me as such. Richard's praise was enough.

Upon arriving back at the bridge, I realised that we were not needed, as Joanna and a group of women had already entered the town to treat the wounded. Harold was with them, and to my relief, he was uninjured. Remarkably, he did not appear to have a scratch on him. This was despite the fact he had been in the thick of the most brutal fighting, and he had been the most lightly armoured man in our group.

"What happened to you? Cut yourself shaving?" he asked as I approached.

"I would have defended myself, but some old man had knocked my sword into a nightsoil bucket," I responded.

"You're never going to let that go, are you?" he said with a pained expression.

"Not until you do something even more embarrassing," I assured him.

"Alistair! Thank the Lord you're safe!" Joanna exclaimed, running towards us. She was covered in even more blood than I was, though none of it was her own. "Your face! You must have been cut to the bone! Let me see to it." She pulled off my mail coif and began to clean the wound with a damp rag, although I insisted it wasn't necessary.

"At least you were ugly to start with," Harold chimed in. "If I'd received a wound like that, the girls of France would be weeping for weeks."

"Who did this to you?" Joanna asked. "And where's Oliver? I'd hoped he'd come back with you."

"The answer to both questions is the same," I said grimly. "Eustace de Quincy made an appearance."

Her head shot up at the name. "He's here? What happened?"

"He tried to take my eye out whilst I was preoccupied," I told her, gesturing at my face, "and then he scampered off when Sir Oliver caught sight of him. The way things were going, it looked like he was about to be gelded by your husband. I didn't see anything after that."

"May God bless Sir Oliver's blade," Harold said piously.

We prepared to set out and find the knight, but Sir Oliver found us first, trapesing back through the town not a few minutes later. Having been embraced and scolded by Joanna with equal ferocity, he sourly recounted the chase.

"I was right behind him," he said wearily, wincing as his wife bandaged his shoulder wound. "The filthy rat knew that as much as I did. So, he dived into an empty house, and I followed. I thought him cornered." He shifted uncomfortably, and Joanna unsympathetically told him to stop squirming. "But he managed to wriggle out of a window, which was too small to allow my pursuit."

"I've been telling you to lay off the gingerbread," Harold said.

Sir Oliver shot him a withering look, then continued. "When I returned to the street, he'd simply vanished. I like to think that the devil swallowed him up for his crimes, but I suppose he's still scuttling about somewhere."

"He has no way out of the city," I asserted. "Richard has control of all the gates, and even if he does make it over the walls, then the French army occupies the plains outside. We'll catch him."

"I hope so," Sir Oliver said grimly. "And this time, I don't want Richard involved. I'll deal with that snivelling vermin myself."

Despite my confidence, the Scot failed to appear over the next few hours, and we were forced to confront the frustrating truth that he had somehow eluded us. It was, as Sir Oliver had said, as if the ground had simply consumed him. I was certain we would see him again some day, as both sides still had grievances unsettled.

That night, as Richard's army loudly celebrated their victory throughout the streets of La Ferté-Bernard, I sat for a while, staring at my father's spangen-helm. Its basic design was that of a conical helmet, but the craftsmanship of the full-face guard was anything but simple, with riveted plates for added protection, and ventilation slits which were as intimidating as they were practical. As I stroked the helmet's iron aventail, I thought about the times I had seen this helmet on its pedestal in Little Dunmow. Then, it had frightened me immensely, as it represented all the expectations of my father, expectations which I had always failed to meet. Now, it meant something entirely different to me.

"Fancy entertaining us with one of your... unique tunes on the lyre?" Harold asked as he approached me. Seeing me cradling the spangen-helm, he frowned. "What's that? Where did it come from?"

"This? This is a helmet, Harold. A helmet which proves that no one in this world can intimidate me anymore," I replied quietly.

Harold laughed at my cryptic response but didn't push me for any further answers. Once again, he invited me to show off my questionable lyre skills, and I gladly accepted.

We did not have long to celebrate, as we were soon busy requisitioning supplies from the town, fixing armour and sharpening weapons.

I had my revenge against my father, and now it was Richard's turn. Three days after the assault, we marched from La Ferté-Bernard, ready to crush the remainder of King Henry's crumbling empire.

Chapter 25

I have probably made it sound as if Richard's tactical genius was the driving factor behind our success at La Ferté-Bernard, but that was not the case. If there is one weakness in my recounting of this tale, it is that I am given to overbearing and extravagant compliments about Richard. I hope it gives some reflection of just how completely I idolised him in those early days.

In fact, his plan to take the town had been straightforward and entirely predictable. Any respectable commander would have placed sentries by the river during a siege, and as much as I detested my father, he was no fool. The simple truth is that King Henry's army was totally unprepared for a war. They had become accustomed to a cycle of conferences, posturing and deliberation. Despite the Prince's threats, and his actions at Bonsmoulins, nobody expected him to actually raise a sword against his own father. If anyone should have seen it coming, it was the King himself, as he had been fighting his family since before I was born.

I have no doubt that this sudden outbreak of war disheartened the King's garrisons immensely, and this low morale was exacerbated by the easy nature of our victory in La Ferté-Bernard. As such, many of Henry's remaining men had no stomach for a fight, and castle after castle yielded to us rather than face a siege. The

King needed these castles to resist our advance whilst he gathered more forces, but instead they simply surrendered. Although Philippe's army tailed ours closely, I do not think that a single French sword was bloodied during that campaign, as the Capetian King had always intended. Yet I suspect that he hoped Richard's army would take significant losses, and place him in a weakened position, so that the Capetians could take advantage.

Montfort, Maletable, Beaumont and Ballon all opened their gates as we approached and submitted without drawing a sword. Although Richard relished a fight, he was relieved by their quick capitulation, as the acquisition of land was always his driving prerogative, and the estates of these castles were prosperous and wealthy. If Philippe was disappointed that Henry and Richard had not engaged in an enormous, blood-soaked war, he managed not to show it. Instead, he was polite and diplomatic, allowing Richard to keep and garrison every castle we took. Although I and many others were suspicious of the French King's motives, Richard treated him like a brother, and took every chance to loudly proclaim that they were allies.

Of all those days spent traversing the area northeast of Le Mans, I remember one afternoon in particular. We sat on the lush green grass outside the walls of Ballon, bathing in the early sunlight of what promised to be a magnificent summer. Richard was arranging the castle's new garrison, so we had several hours to simply enjoy each other's company. Sir Oliver pranced about on his stallion, showing off and enjoying himself mightily. Joanna demanded an attempt at wielding a crossbow, and happily fired away at makeshift targets. When Harold snickered at her inaccuracy, she demanded that he show her how it was done, and I laughed myself insensible when he couldn't even load the bow properly. In the evening, the castle's French cooks timidly offered us some of their cooking, including *Minces*, which were peculiar tiny cabbages that I loved but Harold instantly spat out.

I don't know why I recall that day in such vivid detail. It may seem that it was a completely normal afternoon, yet in fact, it was fairly remarkable, simply because nothing remarkable happened. In the frantic and deadly life that Prince Richard led, anybody caught up with him rarely had a chance for peace and contemplation. I do not think that Richard himself had any relaxation time at all. Of course, such tranquillity could not endure, and the next day we were riding hard once again.

Even the Prince had been taken aback by the ease with which the King's fortresses had surrendered, and so he decided on a bold strategy to end the war as swiftly as possible, as the Crusade had been delayed for far too long already. Henry was still quartered in Le Mans, floundering at the news that his castles were capitulating, and desperately sending message after message to his barons. Knowing that capturing the King would put a decisive end to the conflict, Richard decided on a feint south towards Tours, before suddenly swinging back around north and heading directly for Le Mans itself. Henry still had about two thousand loyal soldiers defending the town, and so he could have put up a fierce resistance, but his resolve had crumbled along with his health. Abandoning the civilians, who had thought themselves in the safest place in France, he fled northwards, frantically trying to reach Normandy, where he believed he might find some military support.

Yet Richard had no interest in Le Mans. Against the advice of Philippe, he ignored the town entirely and set off in pursuit of his father. Never before had he been so determined to confront the King, and he ruthlessly drove us onwards. In fact, we rode so rapidly that we left both the Capetian army and our own infantry behind, so that only the knights, squires and mounted mercenaries remained. A few wives managed to keep up with the harsh pace. Naturally, Joanna was one of them.

"What will the Prince do with the King once we capture him?" I asked as we rode briskly through a wooded valley. I mopped my brow as I spoke; although I was only wearing riding leathers, the afternoon heat was relentless. In addition to this, I was exhausted, as we had only snatched a few hours' sleep since we'd left

Le Mans two days prior. I pitied the poor horses tremendously.

"Richard's a godly man, as you know, so there's no chance he'll ever harm his father," Sir Oliver replied. I do not think that was meant as a barbed comment towards me; he was simply being his blithely chipper self. "I expect they'll have a long conversation, to see if their relationship can be mended."

"I'd like to think that were possible," Joanna said, though she did not sound particularly confident in her husband's opinion.

"Oh yes, I'm sure they'll be skipping through the meadows of England together in no time," Harold sneered. The dappled sunlight penetrated the trees to give his hair a fiery glow, but his mood was dark as night. Like me, the lack of sleep had shortened his temper considerably. "There'll be no reconciliation for them, and you know it. The King's made that clear. If Richard has any sense, he'll gut that old fool the second he lays eyes on him."

"He would never do that," Joanna asserted. "Killing his father would risk the damnation of his barons and his God, regardless of how Henry has offended him."

I nodded agreement. Richard, who rode at the front of his retinue, had a demeanour which was impossible to read. Yet I knew he would not kill the King, not after his words to me at La Ferté-Bernard. Hypocrisy was not in his character. "He should hold Henry at sword-point until he is recognised as heir," I said. That was exactly how I intended to resolve the issue of Little Dunmow, once I was finished in Richard's service.

"You're all acting like the King is in chains in front of us," Harold grumbled. "We're still fighting a war here."

Sir Oliver chuckled. "Barely!" he said. "A group of kittens could put up more of a struggle! I wouldn't be surprised if..."

He was interrupted by the deep blast of a horn which echoed through the trees. I looked around, bewildered, but the men surrounding me looked just as confused. The noise had not emanated from our column.

Harold's eyes widened. "Oh, shit."

Answering the horn's call, a rumble of hooves announced a wave of horsemen who burst from the treeline like a pack of feral wolves. Levelling swords, spears and lances, they thundered towards our startled men, none of whom even had weapons drawn. "To arms!" I heard Richard cry, and then they were upon us.

Somebody was trying to turn the tide of the war. Somebody was fighting back.

Eager for the honour of killing a member of Richard's bodyguard, one mailed enemy was several paces ahead of the others, aiming his sword directly at my throat. Still reeling from the shock of the ambush, I clawed at Lion-Pride's hilt, but was rescued by Sir Oliver who slammed his stallion into my assailant's horse. Grabbing my attacker's arm, the knight thrust him to the ground with brute strength. Meanwhile, a second enemy had closed in and swung his sword in a haymaking sweep at Joanna, who shrunk away from the blow. The blade was intercepted by Harold's Wife-Tongue, which then impaled the man through the abdomen. I had finally drawn Lion-Pride but was too bewildered to use it. Everything around me was a chaotic scene of horse flesh, screaming men, and an abattoir of blood.

"Joanna! Get to safety!" Sir Oliver cried, using his huge sword to desperately defend his unarmoured body against the blows of two enemies. She hesitated, unwilling to leave her husband in such an ominous situation, before realising that her presence was only a hindrance to him. Digging her knees into her horse's flanks, she swerved out of the fight and into the forest, ducking underneath a spear-thrust as she went. Other women were likewise fleeing. Those that stayed were either killed or dragged off their horses. I saw one brute of a woman swinging an axe and screaming like a creature from hell, wounding any who came close to her.

Pandemonium raged throughout the column. The surprise attack had been a comprehensive success, and we were paying a dear price in lives for our lack of scouting and our blind urgency. However, Richard's knights were holding together. They were the most ambitious and fierce fighters in all of Europe, blessed by

God and their Prince, and they fought like lions. Yet the mounted mercenaries behind us were beginning to slip away into the trees, as mercenaries are prone to do in a dire situation. Their crumbling resistance left our baggage vulnerable, and many pack-horses were either captured or driven away. Our enemy – presumably King Henry's men – now scented victory and circled behind our tired knights.

Caught in the middle of the frantic brawl which had erupted around the retinue, I desperately hacked my way towards Richard. An attack of this magnitude could have only one purpose: to capture or kill the Prince. I had seen him fight in two sieges and innumerable skirmishes, but rarely before had he been under such immediate threat. Parrying spear thrusts and sword swipes, I forced my way through the crowd until I was only a few paces from my lord. He was protected by only a thin screen of his fiercest bodyguards, and his sword was already reddened. Richard was livid with himself at being caught unawares and was unleashing his fury on anybody who came close. Such was his battle-prowess that I thought he might be able to win this conflict alone, and my spirits lifted.

But then I saw the knight.

He was yet unengaged, and riding towards us. He was clad in shining, scarred steel from coif to chausses, mounted on a magnificent horse of beauty and muscle. He held a lance as long as I was tall, tipped with a wickedly sharp point. I noticed all of this, and I noticed something else.

He was galloping directly towards Richard.

I glanced around at my companions, praying that somebody would intervene. Harold, now dismounted, was stabbing a rider in the leg. Sir Oliver was nowhere to be seen. Sir Baldwin and William L'Etang were grimly thrusting their blades into the mass of horsemen in front of them. Nobody had seen the knight except me.

Knowing that I could not hesitate, I pulled on my reins and placed myself between the knight and my Prince. He looked to be a formidable foe, and I had only padded leather protecting my flesh. Yet Richard was in danger, and that was all I needed to know.

Ignoring the flicker of panic in my breast, I spurred my horse into a trot, but my heart sank as I gained a clearer view of the rider's face. I now knew who was responsible for this masterful ambush, and I knew that I stood no chance.

I shouted a defiant battle-cry, though a heavy trepidation lay within me. I charged directly at Sir William Marshal, the greatest knight in all of Christendom, who had sworn to kill me if we ever met in battle.

Chapter 26

The difference between a soldier and a warrior is instinct. A man can have perfect preparation, the best equipment, and the most practice, but if his instincts are not sharp in the madness of battle, then he is nothing more than a lump of meat to be thrown at the enemy. When young men ask me how to become an accomplished warrior, I do not tell them how important instinct is. It would be fruitless, as it cannot be learnt, and you only discover whether you have it when you are seconds from death.

It was on that bloody summer's day, when Richard's ambitions almost ended in catastrophe, that I discovered my warrior's instinct.

In one moment, I was spurring my horse towards Marshal, hoping that my sacrifice would slow him down enough for Richard to escape, and hoping that somebody would tell Alice I died bravely. In the next moment, I experienced a sudden clarity. I saw that Marshal's lance was pointed upwards at an angle towards my neck, intent on skewering my exposed flesh. I remembered that he was a proficient tournament fighter and had won hundreds of jousts through perfecting his technique. In those tournaments, he had triumphed by unhorsing his opponents, not by killing them. All of this information coursed through my head in a second, and I knew how to react.

I held my course until I was only a few paces from Marshal, and then dropped flat against my horse's back. It had occurred to me that it was a tactic the knight would never have fought against, as ducking would be useless in a tournament situation. However, now that Marshal's lance was pointed high instead of low, it was the perfect reaction, and I was rewarded by the sight of his weapon's point sailing past my head. Triumphant in my victory, I raised Lion-Pride to strike at the knight as I passed him.

Yet Marshal was an old man who had been fighting all his adult life. One does not survive that long unless he has a finely-honed instinct of his own, or he is a coward. I had no doubt, even then, that Marshal was no coward. Our previous encounter had taught me that much.

He had not been able to adjust his lance-point to skewer me, but he still reacted faster than I would have thought possible. Even as I was flattening myself in the saddle, he brought his heavy kite shield around to his right side and used it to both block my sword strike and thrust me away. Having thought he was defenceless, I was caught off balance by the collision. Had I been fully armoured, I might have withstood the blow, but instead I was lifted clean out the saddle, freeing my left foot from its stirrup at the last moment. The world spun as I sailed through the air, and my impact with the dirt sent hot streaks of pain up my back and Lion-Pride flying into the trees.

Gritting my teeth, I struggled to my knees and looked up, but Marshal's attention had moved on. I was nothing to the knight: as important to him as a louse is to a wild boar. Instead, he had couched his lance once again and was accelerating towards the Prince.

I had failed. My instincts had saved my life, but they could not save Richard's. I pulled out my cleaver and crawled towards Marshal, but I was far too late. My Prince was completely defenceless. Hearing the thundering hooves behind him, he turned and saw the knight, but there was no escape. I saw him shout something, but the sound of battle drowned him out. Whatever he said, it did not halt Marshal, who closed in for the kill. I almost looked away, but morbid fascination held my gaze.

At that moment, Sir William Marshal made a decision which determined the fate of the Angevin Empire.

Thrusting forward with all his strength, he lunged his lance into Richard's horse, which screamed and reared, toppling the Prince from his saddle. Leaving the lance trapped in the horse's flesh, he then pulled a horn from his saddle and blew one long, deep note. Unsurprisingly, it was the same horn we had heard which commenced the attack. To my astonishment, the attackers began to retreat. One moment, they had been swarming around our survivors, surrounding us, and the next they simply stepped back and rode northwards up the path, following King Henry. I was to learn later that these men had formed the rear-guard of the Angevin monarch's army, and they now returned to him triumphant.

This victory, however, was not the King's, but Marshal's. He was amongst the last of his men to withdraw, and he gave me a sideways glance as he trotted past. There was no jubilation in his eyes, no smugness. In fact, he seemed more resigned than anything. I simply stared at him. I could not fathom why he hadn't killed Richard, though I was to find out later.

Our once-proud column of famous knights and vicious mercenaries was now a scene of confusion and devastation. Men looked around with baffled expressions, bleary-eyed, as if they still couldn't comprehend that we had been attacked. An eerie silence pervaded the forest, punctuated by an occasional scream from the wounded. Bodies littered the ground, particularly to the rear of our formation, where the mercenaries had routed and our baggage horses had scattered. I saw Sir Oliver, who was miraculously unharmed, ride into the treeline, shouting Joanna's name, and crying with relief when he found her. Seeing that Richard was safe amongst his knights, I stumbled into the undergrowth to find my sword. I was joined by Harold, who was limping slightly from a cut to the thigh.

"It's a scratch, just a scratch," he said, waving away my concerns. "I do hate fighting from bloody horseback."

I said nothing. Much like the rest of Richard's men, I was in shock. Marshal's band of warriors, half the size of La Ferté-Bernard's garrison, had done ten times the damage.

"I saw what their commander did to Richard's horse," Harold said. "It was Sir William Marshal, wasn't it?"

I nodded gloomily. "That's twice he's beaten us."

"And if we fought again, he would make it thrice," Harold asserted. "I knew it was him, even though I didn't see his face. Aside from Richard, he's the only man I know capable of such a daring attack."

I saw a glint of shining metal amongst the leaves and picked up Lion-Pride. "You sound as though you admire him."

Harold frowned. "Of course, I do."

To my surprise, I realised that I did as well. "We've all been taught a lesson today, I suppose. At least now that he's humiliated all of us, nobody will remind you of the time he knocked your sword into a shit-bucket."

"Except you, of course," he said, managing a smile. "Some of the more block-headed knights – by which I mean all of them – will want to give chase to Marshal, but we're in no condition for that. We'll have no choice but to wait for reinforcements."

He was right. Our casualties had been surprisingly light, but many men were injured or missing. Even if we didn't have wounded to care for, the disruption of our baggage had severely reduced our supplies. Besides, Richard was not about to repeat his mistake and hare after his father without proper preparation and scouting. Our only option was to allow King Henry to escape northwards, which completed Marshal's victory.

Thus, the Lionheart suffered his first defeat for over a year. Yet that did not diminish my opinion of him. A warrior should not be judged only by his victories, but by how he reacts to defeat. After a few hours of brooding anger, Richard responded with remarkable charisma.

Later that evening, we did not all gather round a communal fire, as was our custom. Instead, we huddled in small groups, seeking solace in the company of intimate friends. Instead of sulking alone, as I probably would have done, Richard walked from group to group, speaking to as many men as possible.

"I am so glad to see you all unharmed," he said earnestly as he approached us. A fall from a horse is a bruising experience – as I well knew – and he walked a little stiffly. "Especially you, Joanna. I cannot imagine how frightening it must be for a woman caught in the violence of battle." Sir Oliver had found her just a few feet into the treeline, or rather, she had found him. She had rushed back towards us as soon as the sound of fighting had subsided.

"I should have stayed, Lord Prince," she said quietly.

"The King's men should be grateful that you didn't!" Sir Oliver said, trying to lift our spirits. "When you're angry, you're more fearsome than a Norse berserker!" He alone seemed to be speaking at his usual booming volume.

"Your Highness, I do not know if anyone has told you this, but I faced Marshal before he reached you," I said, staring into Richard's steady gaze. "He swatted me off my horse as if I were a child. I'm sorry."

"I don't believe it," the Prince said softly, and I recoiled slightly, expecting a tirade. "You've drawn a sword against him twice now, and yet you still live. I doubt anyone else in the world can claim that. You continue to surprise me, Alistair." Only Richard could have turned my shame into pride so quickly. "The fault is mine, and mine alone. That's all there is to it." He turned to Harold. "What should I have done differently, my budding strategist?"

This was the first I had heard of Harold's interest in strategy, but it didn't come as a surprise, given his sharp mind and aptitude for warfare. "We should have scouted, we shouldn't have outrun our infantry, and we shouldn't have fought Sir William Marshal," he said.

"True, especially on the last count," Richard agreed.

"We also should have been better rested, as our lack of stamina was a hindrance," Harold finished.

"You're just fishing for a lie-in tomorrow morning," Sir Oliver accused.

"I think we're all due a lie-in. It's certainly deserved," Richard said.

"Agreed," Harold said, a little too quickly.

We had our lie-in, and remained encamped for the next two days, so we could re-gather our baggage and allow our infantry to catch up. Some of the mercenaries returned, full of excuses, but Richard coldly ordered them to leave. Though he took responsibility for the ambush, he had no tolerance for unreliable men in his army. When King Philippe arrived on the infantry's heels, he expressed concern and anger over the fate which had befallen us. However, Richard knew as well as anyone that the Capetian King could have sent his knights ahead to accompany us, but he chose not to. Philippe was satisfied to watch and wait, and no doubt exploit the situation if he so desired.

Sir William Marshal had provided King Henry with a golden opportunity to recover his strength and mount a serious opposition to our alliance. Although many barons had been forced to abandon him – such as my father, who was still captive in La Ferté Bernard – Henry still commanded the loyalty of powerful lords in Normandy. Resigned to the fact that the King would have gathered a new army, Richard hired new mercenaries, established a huge supply train and marched north to confront his father in battle.

Yet everything changed when we received a remarkable message from our scouts just south of Alençon. Riding fully armoured as a precaution, I was a few paces behind Richard when he heard the news. I did not hear what the haggard-looking scout told him, but I certainly heard his response. "Chinon!" Richard exclaimed, astonished. "By God's legs, what on earth is he doing in Chinon?" His words sparked a crescendo of murmurs amongst the retinue.

"Chinon?" I said with a frown. "Isn't that south of Le Mans? What's going on?"

"King Henry's circled around us," Joanna guessed correctly. "He's doubled back south, and now he's in Chinon."

"But how is that possible?" I asked. "We'd know if the King's army had changed direction. The movement of hundreds of men can't be kept secret."

"The only explanation is that he's left his army behind, and gone to Chinon with only a few followers," Harold ventured. We later found out from the scout that this was indeed true.

"But why? What possible tactical advantage can be gained from returning south?" pondered Master Philip of Poitou, who was riding alongside us that morning. He had been busily writing letters to the Norman nobility, attempting to ensure they wouldn't join Henry. As such, his hands were spattered with ink stains. "All the lords in that region are loyal to Richard, and besides, the land is too scarred by war for the King to raise an army there."

"Sounds like more trickery by Marshal," Harold commented, brow creased in thought. He was determined that the King's most loyal knight would not outwit us again.

"Sounds like a blunder," Sir Oliver said confidently. "You can overthink the situation as much as you like, but the simple truth is that our enemy is now without an army. And without an army, you can't hold land."

Therefore, we took the remainder of King Henry's land. He had spent his entire life forging the largest empire for a century, and we snuffed it out in just a few days. I remember thinking it peculiar. Every chivalric tale I had ever heard ended with a climactic, bloody battle which decided the fate of kingdoms and the future of the land. In reality, Henry's empire died with a whimper, and that is how so many empires die.

We swept through Maine and Touraine with no resistance offered. In fact, Richard's coming was celebrated rather than opposed. I recall our entry into Tours in particular. Men, women and children lined the streets to welcome us through the imposing gates of the city walls. Standing in the shadow of the enormous basilica of St Martin, they cheered us wildly as we passed. I was amazed, and initially cynical. I imagined that they would cheer whichever army had entered their city, so as not to incur the wrath of soldiers. However, I was to learn that I was wrong. These civilians held a grudge against Henry for the destruction of their cathedral twenty years before, but Richard's triumph meant far more than that. We were ragged, we were dirty, but our arrival signalled the end of the war, which would allow the townsfolk to finally return to their lives. I have never tilled a field, so I do not fully understand the turmoil caused by the conflict, but the prospect of a future absent of marauding warriors truly filled them with delight.

Their peace was not permanent, of course, but we could not deny them the joy of the moment.

For the rest of that day, and most of the evening, they showered us with affection. My comrades laughed uproariously at my embarrassment when two French girls fought for the honour of kissing me, and the matter was happily resolved when Harold humbly offered to kiss one of them in my place. People held out young children for our priests to bless, and the inns refused to charge for our food and ale. They seemed to view us all as glorious knights who had freed them from the shackles of war.

If only they had known the rules of chivalry, they would not have worshipped us as such.

I managed to slip out of the celebrations for a few moments as dusk dimmed the horizon. Seeking some peace, I made my way outside the basilica's walls and over to the ancient amphitheatre which loomed immensely against the dying sunlight. The interior was huge, filled with tiers of seats and massive pillars, and I wondered about the amphitheatre's creators. I know little about the Romans, except that they were soldiers, and they had giants to help them build such colossal structures. Did they ever desire peace as the people of Tours did, given that their every success was built on war? I had just begun to discover my talents as a warrior, so did I desire peace, knowing how wonderful it was for civilians? As I sat on the ground, dwarfed by the colossal stone encircling me, I was struck by a strange feeling that this fight wasn't quite finished, as everybody thought it was. Something still itched inside me, one final battle to wage, one final grudge to settle, yet I couldn't quite identify it. I stared into the star-sprinkled sky and I asked God why I felt this way, and why I had these questions, but He didn't reply.

Or perhaps He did, for the next day, I received answers.

Chapter 27

Richard had intended to take us north, to quell any remaining resistance in Normandy, but just after dawn he received a message that changed his plans instantly. I struggled to identify the messenger for a moment but recognised him as soon as I heard him speak. He was Bertrand de Verdon, the man who had accompanied Marshal in Amboise, and his elegant voice was now strained by exhaustion.

King Henry wished to meet his son once more. Bertrand would speak only to Richard, and he would say only: "Come to Ballon. Come today. Bring no more than a hundred men. We now know truly that peace is the only option." Yet everybody knew that this would be no peace conference. It would be a surrender. We would have no doubt descended on Chinon to capture Henry eventually, and if we accepted the offer of a conversation at Ballon, nobody could accuse Richard of taking his father's kingdom at sword-point.

King Philippe was not invited, though he informed us that he was returning to Paris anyway to begin preparations for the Crusade. "I do not wish to interfere in this strictly family matter," he told Richard demurely. "Join me in Paris when you can. We have a much more important war to fight." As usual, Philippe had an ulterior motive for his actions. He desired the defeat of King Henry above everything, and he knew that the

Angevin lords of France would be much more likely to accept Henry's surrender if it were taken by Richard alone.

The ride to Ballon was a sombre affair, and the atmosphere was in stark contrast to the celebrations of the night before. Every man and woman was in a contemplative mood. The members of Richard's retinue had spent most of their lives waging war in France, and the thought that the conflict might cease was unfathomable. I am sure that we were all consumed by thoughts of how the war had changed us. I reflected that I had been a frightened boy in Châteauroux, but now I had faced down my father, and drawn my sword against the most famous warriors in the world. Harold, who had sung for us the night before, was no doubt dreaming of his revenge on Father Erwin, as he so often did. Sir Oliver and Joanna grasped each other's hands as they rode. The war had so nearly torn them apart, but they were now stronger than ever. Richard was entirely unreadable. He had worked so hard for his victory, but it was not the victory he had planned.

When we arrived at the castle, we saw that the King was already present with barely fifty men. I recognised most of them as William Marshal's troops, and Marshal himself rode tall and dominating beside the King's litter. He was unarmoured, which was a remarkable sign of passivity for a man with so violent a reputation. As the Angevin monarch was lowered onto his horse, I

353

understood everything. I understood why Marshal had not killed Richard. I understood why Henry had not raised an army and had instead returned to Chinon.

King Henry was dying. He had been in poor health when I had last met him, but he was now little more than a breathing corpse. His skin was repulsively blotchy and pale, his eyes wild and haggard, and his flesh bulging. He was swathed in heavy fur despite the summer's heat, and he shivered uncontrollably as if he were naked in a snowstorm. I admit I felt a moment's pity for him, despite the abhorrent way he had treated his family. I hope that when I die, it is to a swift sword thrust, and not to some dreadful affliction that slowly drains your strength. Every tiny movement of his horse caused him to wince in terrible agony, but he would not cry out, and he would not be carried in his litter. When King Henry had nothing else, he still had his pride; a deadly sin to some, but an asset to a warrior.

The two parties rode towards each other in silence, with none of the usual fanfare or heraldry. I briefly locked eyes with Sir William Marshal, who stared at me haughtily, showing no sign of recognition. It was now obvious why he had spared Richard's life. The King would not survive long, and with Richard dead, the crown would have passed to John, who was no warrior. The thought of such a monarch would have disgusted Marshal, to the extent that he would show mercy to an enemy of his lord just to prevent John from inheriting the throne.

The King's body had failed him, and so had his spirit, it seemed. His retreat to Chinon had not been a tactical manoeuvre; he had simply desired to die in the town of his birth. When I had seen him before, he had boasted a vile tongue and vicious temper. Now, he was but a shell, and he sat drooped in the saddle, waiting for his son to speak. None of the King's men, not even Marshal, spoke in his defence, such was their wariness of displeasing him who would soon be their new lord. In contrast to the King, Richard was a beacon of physical prowess on that day. He sat straight-backed and proud, with his strong face and bright hair glowing in the sunlight.

If Richard was concerned about his father's health, he did not show it. He certainly did not enquire about it.

"Was it all worth it?" the Prince asked stonily.

Henry looked at his son through half-closed eyes and said nothing.

"You denied me my birthright, you halted my marriage, you imprisoned my mother, and for what? For John? For John, who has deserted you. I was willing to fight and win your war for you, Father. It need not have come to this, and it's all down to your damned stubbornness." I think I heard a note of regret in Richard's voice, though I know it would have angered him if I'd told him that.

Henry shuddered slightly, though whether the agony came from his physical ailment or from Richard's words I do not know. I learnt later that the King had attempted to summon John to his side; perhaps the Angevin King would have believed the war was worth fighting if he could pass his kingdom onto his youngest son. Yet John had not come, and I think abandonment by the last loyal member of the King's family destroyed his will to keep fighting.

Once again, the Prince paused, but a reply was not forthcoming. He had come to expect nothing but disapproval and conflict during these meetings. Yet instead of verbal sparring, the silence from Henry and his followers persisted.

Resigned to the fact that this would be a monologue, Richard turned his attention to the formalities of his victory. "You will return to Chinon until Lent next year, when we shall assemble in Vezélay for the Crusade," he began. Though we all found it highly unlikely that the King would live that long, Richard had to make provisions to restrict his movement in case of a miraculous recovery. "You will pay King Philippe a sum of 20,000 marks," he continued. Of all Richard's demands, I think that I expected Henry to react scathingly to this one more than any other, yet the King was as unmoved as ever. In truth, I think that this particular request was rather a token gesture from Richard to Philippe: in fact, Richard probably hoped that

Henry would die before he could pay the sum out of the Angevin Empire's coffers.

"King Philippe's sister, Alys, will be handed over to a guardian of my choosing and then restored to me after the Crusade," Richard ploughed on. I understand that this had been a point of some contention between Philippe and Richard. The Prince had fully expected to be granted Alys's hand in marriage immediately, but the Capetian King had insisted that a decision wait until after the Crusade. Richard had been disgruntled, but he was unwilling to disrupt the hard-won goodwill between them, and so had accepted Philippe's decision. Clearly, Henry didn't have an opinion on the matter, and if he did, he kept it to himself.

Richard then delivered the most important demand, and the one we had been anticipating most keenly. "By your order, every single man who pays you homage will now swear allegiance to me and acknowledge me as the next King of England and of all your wordly possessions." Months before, Richard had almost begged his father to accept him as heir and was rewarded with evasions and hesitance. Now, he was not asking. Richard was always better at the direct approach. "God will be my witness that you have accepted these terms, and he will ensure that you uphold them." He savoured every word.

For a moment, silence hung in the air, only to be disrupted by a single cricket chirping in the long grass beside us. "What happens if he doesn't reply?" Harold whispered to me. I had no answer. I supposed we would have to take the King's silence as acceptance.

Sir William Marshal stirred slightly by Henry's side, though I do not know whether he intended to speak for his lord, for the King's cracked lips parted at that moment. "I agree," he whispered.

Just like that, King Henry lost his empire. But Richard was not finished. Now he sought to take what was left of his father's dignity.

"As a show of good faith, you will now give me the kiss of peace," he said, unable to keep a trace of smugness from his voice. The kiss of peace was traditionally given by him who was subservient; a father granting it to a son was unheard of.

A barely discernible growl came from Henry's throat, and he edged his horse forward. I was now glad that Richard had persuaded me to spare my own father's life. I wished to see him humiliated like this before he died.

Walking his horse alongside Richard's, Henry tentatively placed his arms around his son. I wondered when they had last embraced. Leaning over towards Richard, Henry suddenly grasped the Prince's arms with an immense strength. His eyes wide open, he spoke directly into Richard's ear. "You are the greatest disgrace a father could possibly sire," he hissed. To my astonishment, the fierce old King had emerged one last time. "You whore yourself to the enemy, and you will lose my empire. You will never be the warrior I am. God grant that I may not die until I have had my revenge on you." His tirade over, he slumped back into his saddle, utterly exhausted. His men led him away and guided him back down the path.

Since I had met him, Richard had tried to give the impression that he didn't care how his father viewed him. Just for a second, after the King's moment of defiance, the façade slipped, and I saw the horror behind his eyes. Yet the Prince was well versed in the art of shielding his emotions, and he regained his stony expression almost instantly.

The King was hauled back into his elaborate litter. Surrounded by his thin screen of followers, he began the journey back to Chinon.

It was the last time I ever saw him alive.

Chapter 28

I shall never forget the sound of Harold's voice on that fateful day, at the climax of high summer in the year 1189, when it seemed the world was finally at peace.

We sat on the grassy bank of the Vienne river, underneath a crystal sky utterly devoid of clouds. Inspired by the tranquil setting, I had taken up my lute and strummed a few notes. To my amazement, Harold's quiet voice joined in after a few minutes, singing softly at first, and then with more confidence. I had never heard him sing before unless Richard specifically requested it. I hoped this change suggested that the pain inside him was lessening.

Gradually, a small group of townspeople formed around us, drawn by Harold's angelic melody. The civilians of Chinon had initially been wary of us when we had entered their town the day before, as they had thought themselves far from Richard's wrath in the town of King Henry's birth. Yet we had been under strict orders to show compassion and not aggression, for soon this town would be a part of Richard's domain. The Prince did not tell us why we had followed Henry here, but we assumed it was so we could await the King's death.

As Harold's voice eventually faded away, his face assumed a solemn expression, as it always did when he concluded his songs. I placed a reassuring hand on his shoulder, knowing that there were no words to comfort him. A young French girl timidly approached and handed him a delicate flower, and he managed a small smile of gratitude, before waving away the applause of the watching townsfolk.

Their praise was interrupted by the arrival of Sir Baldwin, who looked imposing even when not dressed for battle. I had come to know him as a decent, if uncompromising man who would give his life for Richard in a heartbeat. "His Highness Prince Richard summons you both to Fontevraud Abbey," he said. We knew the abbey; it lay a short ride west of Chinon.

"For what purpose?" I asked.

"You'll know when you arrive there," he said tersely. "Could you also inform Sir Oliver? I must track down the rest of the retinue, to give them the same instruction. Who knows what sorts of sordid brothels they'll have quartered themselves in?"

We gave our assent, then crossed the street to the small church where Sir Oliver was at prayer. We found Joanna waiting outside; she had also been seeking her husband. Although she was unwilling to interrupt his worship, she conceded that a direct summons from Richard was too important to ignore. To our bemusement, however, we found no sign of the knight inside, and we approached the priest to discover his location.

"The English giant? He was summoned to the chapel of St. George, inside Chinon castle, to meet with Prince Richard," the priest informed us. He was a small, bookish man with a nervous demeanour.

I frowned. "But Richard's retinue has been ordered to Fontevraud Abbey, not St George's chapel," I said.

Harold was likewise puzzled. "The orders were carried by Sir Baldwin himself. There's no doubt they were genuine." He spoke to myself and Joanna rather than the priest. He knew how poor he was at controlling his temperament around men of God.

"So if it wasn't Richard, who ordered Oliver to this chapel?" Joanna asked, alarm in her voice. "And for what purpose?"

"The English giant was still at prayer when the messenger arrived, so I conveyed the order in the messenger's stead," the priest said, trying to be helpful.

"Who was the messenger?" I demanded, a tingle of dread crawling down my spine.

"He never gave his name," the priest said, wringing his hands.

"What did he look like?" I insisted.

The priest paused, obviously flustered by our intense questioning. "He had dark hair... he was not French, I am certain of that, but his accent was not English either. He wore a sword..."

"Anything more? Anything defining?" I was almost shouting now.

"He had only one eye," the priest finished with a whisper.

"No," Joanna mouthed, her face white. Harold was speechless. I was already turning to run for the door, trying to ignore the horror clawing at the inside of my stomach.

I knew only one man with a single eye.

And I knew only one man with a death-wish against Sir Oliver de Burgh.

Without waiting to see whether Harold and Joanna were following, I raced out of the church and sprinted down the riverbank, which led to the Château de Chinon. I had never been to the fortress before, much less the chapel of St George inside, but it was impossible to miss. It was a marvel of modern architecture, designed by King Henry as his personal fortress, but that wasn't on my mind. All I knew was that Sir Oliver was in mortal peril.

Ignoring the screams of protest from my legs, I ran as swiftly as I could up the steep slope which led to the château's central portcullis, thanking God that I had chosen to wear Lion-Pride today. As I struggled towards the gate, I registered footsteps behind me. I briefly considered telling Joanna to stop and wait, that we were running into terrible danger, but she would have ignored me. Besides, there was no time. We were probably already too late.

Wary of our approach, a mailed guard stepped in front of us and held up a hand. Yet desperation had lent me a furious strength, and I collided with the appalled guard, pinning him against the gate's interior wall.

"Where is St George's chapel?" I shouted without preamble. He hesitated, probably considering whether he should offer defiance. "Tell me or I'll cut your damned throat!" I roared.

The poor man's resolve broke. "In... in the easternmost enclosure," he stammered, pointing.

Without another word, I released him and set off running again, with Harold and Joanna in hot pursuit. Several other guards had been watching the confrontation but hadn't intervened. Their King had already lost the war, and my demonic appearance convinced them not to lose their lives as well.

The path to the chapel was straightforward enough, and we took the most direct route, leaping off ledges and vaulting over rocks. The chapel itself looked as peaceful and innocent as any I have ever seen, and I dreaded to think what had happened inside. Ignoring the protest of two clerics, we smashed our way through the oaken doors.

A huddled mass lay unmoving on the chapel's floor, in the middle of the aisle. It was surrounded by five men, who struck it repeatedly with blunt objects, using brutal force to deliver as much pain as possible. Some were grunting with the effort, and one of the men was laughing almost hysterically. Joanna screamed as she recognised the bloodied man as Sir Oliver. His handsome features had been battered almost beyond recognition.

Joanna's outburst caused the men to cease the beating and look sharply towards us, and my suspicions were confirmed as I locked eyes with the hateful glare of Eustace de Quincy. He had been cast out by Richard, he had fled at La Ferté Bernard, and now he was finally relishing his revenge. His men looked appalled at our appearance, but one-eyed de Quincy smiled. The bastard smiled.

Unable to control my anger, I tore Lion-Pride free from her sheath and began pacing forward. "Step away from him, the lot of you, before I tear out your entrails and strangle you with them," I snarled. I was willing to take them all on, and what's more, I was confident that I would win. But I wouldn't fight alone – Harold, his face taut with fury, stood alongside me, his sword poised, eager for blood.

De Quincy's hired thugs obviously hadn't expected any interruption, and they backed away from the motionless Sir Oliver, uncertain how to react. One of them unbuckled his sword belt and cast it onto the floor, unwilling to draw a weapon against us. Seeing his advantage slip away, de Quincy spun towards his men. They looked unshaven and merciless – outlaws, then. Probably as desperate as they were fierce.

"Don't you see what an opportunity this is?" de Quincy cried shrilly to his three remaining men. "They're all rich, and that incredible wealth will be ours when we kill them!" That was a lie, of course, but de Quincy would have said anything to get his revenge. "That's not all, though!" he continued. "When they're dead, we can take turns on that pretty wench!" He pointed at Joanna, who was on her knees next to Sir Oliver, sobbing inconsolably. There was no sign of life from the knight.

Another of the outlaws threw his weapons to the ground, but the others pulled out grimy swords and turned to face us. De Quincy likewise drew his sword, his expression feral.

"You take those two rotten turds. De Quincy's mine," I growled to Harold as we stepped in front of Joanna.

"They're dead men," he said.

My tale had begun with death in a church. Now, de Quincy's would end in the same fashion.

Shouting incoherently, the Scot charged directly towards me, lancing his blade towards my eyes, trying to end our fight quickly. Standing my ground until the last moment, I knocked his weapon to my right with a swift flick of Lion-Pride, then pivoted around and brought my sword down towards his head. Showing surprising speed, he caught my strike with his weapon, and Lion-Pride scraped down the blade until our two hilts locked together. The scar on my cheek burned as we pushed against each other, and I remembered my forced slavery at his hands. Likewise, he was probably reliving the shame he had suffered because of me, and his anger lent him a confidence in battle that I had never witnessed before.

This was not a battle of sword craft or skill, but rather of passion and rage. Hissing with pain as his knee slammed into my groin, I spat in his one grey eye, causing him to recoil. Intent only on causing him as much pain as he had caused Sir Oliver, I followed up with haymaking sweeps of Lion-Pride which de Quincy frantically blocked. I could hear steel ringing from across the church, but I paid it no heed. Nobody in the world, not even Richard, could have torn me away from my fight.

Pinned against a low table, de Quincy ducked to the side. Swinging in a downwards trajectory, Lion-Pride clattered into a display of candles and became trapped in the metal candle-stand. As I sought to free her, de Quincy's sword razored towards me. I leaned away at the last moment, and the blade passed an inch from my neck.

Now on the back foot, I frantically parried a barrage of strikes from the crazed Scot, who poured all his energy into an overwhelming attack which sought to wear down my defences through sheer strength. I was struggling to keep up with such ferocity, but then he made a mistake. Instead of intercepting his sword with Lion-Pride, I simply stepped backwards from one lunge, and he tried to attack again without adjusting his feet. Moving forwards, I feinted high, causing him to lose his balance even further, then swept Lion-Pride downwards and slashed him across the shin. He toppled over, crying out, and I brought up my sword to finish him off, but to my astonishment, he rolled away, and regained his feet, wincing.

Eustace de Quincy's will to survive was truly remarkable, but I resolved that it would not save him. Allowing anger to fuel my limbs once more, I hammered blows onto the Scot, but he was equal to my every move. Desperate to finish him, I swung Lion-Pride in a powerful sideways cut, which he deflected, and then to my horror, he grabbed my sword's blade and held it, mauling his hand horribly but rendering me defenceless. Grinning savagely, he pulled back his sword to stab me through the abdomen.

Screeching like a banshee, Joanna flung herself in front of me and collided into de Quincy with an enormous impact, sending them both crashing to the floor. Imbued with a towering fury which topped even my own, she screamed and clawed at the stunned Scot's face. He tried to bring his blade up to stab her in the side, but I stamped on his hand, which released the weapon, and I kicked his sword away.

Having left his opponents choking on their own blood, Harold rushed over to join me, but the fight was over. Knowing he was disarmed, de Quincy whimpered, still trapped underneath Joanna, who had paused in her terrifying assault. "Please don't," de Quincy begged. "I didn't mean anything by it, I... I was trying to help you. Just let me go!" He wailed the last four words. I had almost been impressed by the way he had fought me, but now he was revealing his true nature once again.

"Give me one good reason why I shouldn't kill you slowly," Joanna hissed. "If your reason's good enough, I'll kill you quickly instead."

"I'll give you a reason, my love," said a slurred voice from behind us. "You'll deny me the pleasure."

I do not think I have ever seen a miracle in my life, though that moment may have been the closest I ever came. I turned to see a dead man walking. Several of his bones were broken, his face had been completely pulverised, most of his teeth were missing, and he limped horribly, but Sir Oliver de Burgh was alive.

Joanna's rage was instantly replaced by elation as she ran to her husband and embraced him – albeit gently to avoid hurting him further. "I thought you were gone," she whispered, trying to hold back tears. "I couldn't imagine if... if..."

"It'll take more than some mangy Scot and his ungodly henchmen to finish me off," Sir Oliver assured her through lips that were bleeding profusely. "But it seems that we have some unfinished business which needs resolving, once and for all." He picked up a discarded sword and paced towards the prone de Quincy, steel in his eyes and Joanna at his side. "Thank you, Alistair, and thank you, Harold, but I think we can take it from here."

De Quincy's eye flickered around the room. "Alistair!" he appealed to me. "I'll serve you! I'll do anything you desire! We could be friends! Allies! Just don't leave me with these beasts! They mean to torture me!"

Harold sheathed his bloodied sword and clapped me on the back. "Come on," he said. "Our lord has summoned us."

I nodded and left the church at his side. As the door closed behind us, I heard the first scream.

I kept walking.

Re-tracing our path through the fortress, I paused to gift a silver shilling to the guard at the main gate, who shrank away from me as we approached. I was still in something of a daze, but I remembered the Prince's orders to treat the people of Chinon with respect, and I reluctantly concluded that I should make amends for my death-threat.

It was only as we saddled our horses that the enormity of our actions struck me. The rage of battle had drained from my limbs, only to be replaced by trepidation. "Harold, we just killed men in a church.

Christian men." I could barely believe the words as they left my mouth. "The penalty for such a crime is awful – I should know."

Clambering onto his horse's back, Harold snorted derisively. "If de Quincy and his thugs were Christians, then I'm bloody Mary Magdalene," he said. I ignored his sacrilege; I was used to it by now. "Anyway, it was clearly self-defence. They attacked us, and I don't think that greasy Scot will be in any position to argue. He can shout as loud as he likes from Hell, but nobody will hear him."

"Regardless, I don't regret what we did," I told him. "Sir Oliver is more pious than both of us combined, and I like to think he would have done the same for us."

"He would," Harold replied instantly. "He may be a brainless lump of a knight, but I couldn't ask for a better friend."

"Present company excepted, of course," I said, pretending to be offended.

"Naturally," Harold said with a laugh. As usual, I couldn't tell whether he was being sarcastic.

Our journey took us through the outskirts of Chinon and into the short stretch of open country which lay before Fontevraud Abbey. As I gazed across the endless green carpet and to the horizon, a thought struck me. "It's all over now, isn't it?" I asked quietly. "De Quincy's gone, King Henry's dying. Everything's going to change."

"Still naïve, I see," Harold chuckled. "Our battles are far from over, Alistair, and they never will be over in Richard's service. He's too hungry for land. He values the thrill of war too much. Assuming we ever do set out east on Crusade, we'll face enemies and conditions harsher than ever before. But I don't think you should be too concerned. Even I was a little frightened of you back in that chapel."

"Thank you for the compliment," I said dryly. "I don't know whether I'm looking forward to the Crusade. But I do know that we've done well over the past year."

"Yes, we have," Harold vehemently agreed. "We've done bloody well."

Upon arriving at the colossal Fontevraud abbey, we stabled our horses and made our way inside, curious as to why Richard had summoned us. In the central chamber, we found our answer. Our lord stood, surrounded by his bodyguards, and all of them gazed solemnly at a bier circled by candles. I did not need to see the corpse to guess its identity. King Henry was dead, only two days after we had met him at Ballon. He had sworn revenge against Richard and had not achieved it. Despite all his past triumphs, he would be remembered as a failure who had surrendered to his son's every demand.

We joined our comrades by the King's corpse, and I gazed at Richard, trying to guess his emotions. I wondered whether he felt any sense of loss. I suppose I wanted to know how I would feel when my own father died. I wanted to know whether any compassion would permeate the antagonism.

Richard looked at his father's lifeless face and smiled.

During the year I had known him, Richard had been teaching me the sixth and final rule of chivalry. It was the most important rule of all, and I was only realising it now.

Loyalty is everything. Once you find a lord who deserves your loyalty, you must dedicate yourself to him with every single ounce of your being. Whether you follow the other rules of chivalry or not, loyalty will ensure that you survive and prosper. A knight can be a murderer, a thief, and a scoundrel, but if he is loyal to his lord, the chronicles will shower him with praise, and his betters will bequeath him land and titles. Eustace de Quincy had shown loyalty to no one – not his companions-in-arms, not Richard, not even my father. His reward was his life's blood which now spilled across the floor in St George's chapel.

Having read this account, you will know more than most that I had made mistakes during the past year. Yet even when Richard refused to speak with me for weeks, I never abandoned my loyalty to him, and I had been rewarded. I was now a warrior with confidence and purpose, with a reputation which could only grow in the future. In the end, King Henry had not deserved

Richard's loyalty, but I was already certain that Richard the Lion-Heart deserved mine. He was a mighty warrior, perhaps the greatest I have ever known, but he was more than that.

He was my lord. He was my friend.

He was my King.

Author's Note

I have always desired to read a series of historical fiction focused on the military campaigns of Richard I of England, yet I have struggled to find any such novels currently on the market. Therefore, I decided to write them myself, and I hope I have done some justice to the writing style of the authors who inspired me, such as Bernard Cornwell and Simon Scarrow. I also hope I have managed to convey the complexity of Richard's passionate personality, and the bewildering nature of chivalry in the twelfth and thirteenth centuries.

Alistair Fitzwalter is fictional, and his origin derives from a myth. One contemporary account of Richard's campaigns, that of Gervase, recounts that during the Prince's attack on Châteauroux in 1188, he was thrown from his horse and saved only by the intervention of a butcher. The improbability of this situation piqued my interest, and thus Alistair came into existence.

Although the course of this novel does follow the true path of Prince Richard during 1188 and 1189, I have deviated from accepted historical fact on numerous occasions. Indeed, many of the key characters did not actually exist. Aside from Alistair, Harold, Sir Oliver de Burgh and Eustace de Quincy are fictional, though all of them except Harold belong to families which have crucial roles to play in the upcoming conflicts of the Angevin Empire. I was always determined to relate this story from the point of view of a fictional character, so that I could place him wherever was convenient to witness important or interesting historical events. Unfortunately for Alistair, these events – such as the escape of Guillaume des Barres – often had traumatic consequences, but such is the curse for a protagonist of historical fiction.

Aside from characters, I knowingly changed other elements for the sake of the story. In reality, King Philippe was present at the final meeting between Richard and Henry, but I wished to emphasise the struggle between the two Angevins, and so he is absent. Furthermore, it is unlikely that the Count of Vendôme met Richard in battle in 1188, although the Prince did take the town of Les Roches. We do not know whether the Prince even attacked the Château Lavardin, though I think it is probable, as he would be unable to resist the prospect. If the Count did fight the Prince, we do know that he did not die in the conflict; he lived until 1202. Yet he did tentatively support King Philippe, and he conveniently provides Alistair with his first taste of the horrors of battle.

Although Guillaume des Barres did defend Châteauroux from Richard in the summer of 1188, he was not captured during the siege – in fact, it is debatable as to whether he was ever captured at all, as sources differ in their accounts. For example, Howden claimed that Richard took the French knight captive during a skirmish in the autumn, and des Barres broke parole to escape. However, in William the Breton's account it is Richard who is portrayed as dishonourable, as he thrusts his sword into Guillaume's horse. I decided to combine these two accounts – des Barres breaks parole and kills Alistair's horse – yet Alistair refrains from calling him dishonourable, as he is beginning to understand the truth behind chivalry.

I am certain that Alistair's internal struggles with the tenets of chivalry were not unique to him. Though many texts survive written by churchmen about the importance of piety, honour and justice to a knight, we have remarkably scarce information regarding the views of the knights themselves. It is not until the mid-14th century that Geoffroi de Charny wrote a knight's own guide to chivalry, and it is a chivalry which focuses almost entirely on martial prowess, and very little on piety and mercy. It is my view – as well as Alistair's – that chivalry was a not a code, but a social construct which elevated knights above peasants and allowed them to conduct the type of brutal warfare favoured by successful warriors such as Sir William Marshal and King Henry II.

It may seem as if the novel has over-emphasised the lack of cordiality between King Henry and Prince Richard, but it seems as if their relationship actually was that turbulent. In fact, the line "God grant that I may not die until I have had my revenge on you," is a direct quote from Gerard de Barri's account of their final meeting. Many historians praise King Philippe for turning the two against each other – and understandably so – but Henry's bitterness over Richard's past rebellions, and Richard's suspicions about John's potential ascension to the throne, assured that the two could not work together. Simply put, they did not trust each other, and if Henry had not died when he did (probably of a festering wound) father and son likely would have annihilated each other in all-out war. As it was, Richard inherited an Angevin Empire that was, at last, reasonably coherent and united.

I would thoroughly recommend John Gillingham's *Richard I* for anybody who is interested in learning more about the life and personality of the Lion-Heart. It delivers both succinct historical fact and explanations into Richard's rationale. Without it, this novel would not exist.

Alistair has faced some cunning and fearsome enemies during his first year as a warrior, but the Third Crusade now looms on the horizon. Richard has sworn to take part, and Alistair is obliged to follow. Thus, new challenges and bigger battles await, and his tale has only just begun.

About The Author

Tim has had a passion for writing ever since his mum encouraged him to write short stories at the age of 5. He has completed both an undergraduate degree in History and a Masters' degree in Archives and Records Management, which has fostered an enthusiasm for research which almost matches his love of writing. He is a qualified archivist, and spends much of his time trying to persuade people that archives are far more exciting than they might think! He also likes tennis, swimming, video games and dogs (particularly dogs with beards).

Tim simply desires to write the sort of book he would enjoy reading, which is what he has done with his inaugural novel, The Rules of Chivalry. He looks forward to a long career writing historical fiction.

About The Publisher

L.R. Price Publications is dedicated to publishing books by unknown authors.

We use a mixture of both traditional and modern publishing options to bring our authors' words to the wider world.

We print, publish, distribute and market books in a variety of formats including paperback and hardback, e-books, digital audio books and online.

If you're an author interested in getting your book published; or a book retailer interested in selling our books, please contact us.

www.lrpricepublications.com

L.R. Price Publications Ltd.,

27 Old Gloucester Street,

London, WC1N 3AX.

020 3051 9572

publishing@lrprice.com

Printed in Great Britain
by Amazon

83503930R00220